Other SIGNET Suspense Novels

(50 cents each)

The Big Night (Dreadful Summit) *by Stanley Ellin*
A suspense novel revealing the mind of a boy who plans murder to avenge an affront his father has suffered. (#D2921)

The Blue Room *by Georges Simenon*
A psychological nightmare evolves from an adulterous affair between a man who never planned murder, and the woman he couldn't stop from accomplishing it. (#D2756)

A Murder of Quality *by John Le Carre*
England's oldest and finest public school plays host to murder, and George Smiley exercises his quiet and penetrating ability to solve the crime. By the author of *The Spy Who Came in from the Cold*. (#D2529)

Return From the Ashes *by Hubert Monteilhet*
A chilling study of depravity revealed through the diary of an avaricious woman. By the author of *The Praying Mantises*. A movie starring Maximilian Schell and Samantha Eggar. (#D2414)

To Our Readers: If your dealer does not have the Signet and Mentor books you want, you may order them by mail enclosing the list price plus 10¢ a copy to cover mailing. (New York City residents add 5% Sales Tax. Other New York State residents add 2% plus any local sales or use taxes.) If you would like our free catalog, please request it by postcard. The New American Library, Inc., P. O. Box 2310, Grand Central Station, New York, N. Y. 10017.

The Paper Dolls

L. P. DAVIES

A SIGNET BOOK

PUBLISHED BY
THE NEW AMERICAN LIBRARY

SIGNET TRADEMARK REG. U.S. PAT. OFF. AND FOREIGN COUNTRIES
REGISTERED TRADEMARK—MARCA REGISTRADA
HECHO EN CHICAGO, U.S.A.

SIGNET BOOKS are published by
The New American Library, Inc.
1301 Avenue of the Americas, New York, New York 10019

PRINTED IN THE UNITED STATES OF AMERICA

The Paper Dolls

1

The metal-framed windows had been thrown wide to catch
what little breeze there was. Sunlight, misted with a slow-
drifting chalk haze, patterned the floor between blackboards
and desks like limelight flood on a stage. Through the antiseptic, floor-polish smell I caught the sweetness tang of freshly-
cut grass, and I thought: Slater mowing the centre field ready
for Saturday. It may not be needed. If he dies they'll have to
cancel the game.

It had come to Tomkin's turn to read aloud. Standing by
his desk, ginger-red bullet head and freckle-rashed face bent
laboriously over the open book clutched tightly in both hands,
he was reading aloud, slowly and painfully, oblivious as
always to punctuation and meaning.

Suddenly irritated I cut him short with more impatience
than his effort warranted.

"All right. That'll do. Next boy."

Blake came to his feet. There was a chalk and cheese difference. I found some degree of pleasure in not having to
mentally adjust each phrase.

" 'For night's soft dragons cut the clouds full fast,
And yonder shines Aurora's harbinger,
At whose approach ghosts, wandering here and there,
Troop home to churchyard. . . .' "

He stood erect, mouthing the words carefully, giving meaning to each. The sunlight laid blue streaks across his night-
black hair and wiped the shadows away from the hollows
beneath his high, Slavonic cheek-bones. A narrow face made
sensitive by over-large, oval sloe-black eyes.

Going over to the window I rested one foot on the cold
radiator pipe. Now I could hear the distant hum of the mowing machine, but the row of tall, pale-green limes beyond the
wall cut off sight of the fields themselves. Heat mirage-shim-

7

mered on the tarmac of the playground immediately beneath
me. A black saloon whispered its way through the open double
gates, accelerated gently to swing away out of sight. I looked
at my watch. There was still half an hour to go before the
midday break.

Turning back to the class, I said, "Thank you, Blake. That
will do. You can sit down." I went to stand behind my desk.
"Put your Shakespeares away." Desk lids clattered, but not
over-loudly, and when I warned, "Quietly, now!" it was only
from force of habit. "Take out your drawing-books."

Something to keep them occupied for half an hour.

"I want you to draw a scene; any place that comes to
mind."

A hand shot up.

"Yes, Watson?"

"Some place where we've bin, sir?"

"If you like. Or you can invent a scene. And let's have no
noise while I'm away. Otherwise there'll be trouble. Right?"

I went into the corridor and along to the door of the adjoining classroom. Through the glass panels I could see the im-
maculate-suited Philby propped against his desk, one leg
rested on the corner in an attitude of studied nonchalance.
Approved posture for the use of self-assured teachers. He
was talking to his class, book in one hand, spectacles in the
other being used to point and stress some fact. He caught
the movement as I raised my hand to knock, and he came
over to open the door.

We both lodged in the same terraced, stale-cabbage-smell-
ing, Victorian house; two sets of three rooms on the first floor
with a cold bathroom to be shared. Sometimes we went for
walks together; occasionally to a show. At forty-two he was
ten years my senior. He had been eleven years at the school
to my five, and he was one of Gregg's chosen senior masters.
On the school premises, apart from encounters in the common-room, we were formal with each other. One of the rules
of the teaching game. At least so far as the Cookley Secon-
dary Modern was concerned.

"I wonder if you would be kind enough to keep an eye on
my class for a while, Mr. Philby?" I asked him.

He nodded. "Certainly, Mr. Seacombe." He edged into the
corridor, closing the door behind him, lowering his voice,
curiosity cancelling rules. "They've sent for you, then, Gordon?"

"Not yet. I saw them arrive a few minutes ago." I nodded
in the direction of my class. "They shouldn't give any trouble; I've left them plenty to do."

Frowning, he closed his glasses with a click and used them to scratch his cheek.

"This is a nasty business." He'd said the same thing a dozen times before. "There's a—an atmosphere about the place."

"Considering it's the end of term my lot are certainly subdued."

"Yes." He sighed heavily, made as if to say more, thought better of it and opened the door again to return to the interrupted lesson. Geography. I saw the glazed map hung over one of the blackboards.

Without any particular hurry I made my way along the corridor. At the corner a black-legged and gym-slipped schoolgirl collided with me and became breathlessly apologetic before recognition set her delivering her message.

"Oh! Sorry, sir. Oh! Mr. Seacombe! Mr. Gregg sent me to tell you that——"

"Message received, Janet. Thank you." That was intended as dismissal, but she trotted alongside, her face turned to mine a mixture of excitement, curiosity and awe.

"Do they know how it happened yet, sir?" she asked.

"You'd better cut back to your class," I told her.

"It's only art, sir. Miss Grey sent me out for some new rubbers an' Mr. Gregg saw me an' sent me for you."

We went down the stairs and parted at the art-room door. I had a glimpse of Miss Grey's blonde head, heard her sharp: "Janet! Where on earth have you been all this time?"

The headmaster's study was at the far end of the ground-floor corridor, near the main entrance. I tapped on the door and Gregg's unctuous voice called: "Come!"

He ruled the room from behind the massive desk, large white hands clasped and laid in the precise centre of the pristine, leather-bound blotter. Semi-baldness, large shining forehead, small eyes and rimless glasses gave something of the accepted appearance of a war-time Gestapo agent. Seated at the far corner of the desk a man with an expressionless anonymous face nursed a grey trilby in his lap. Behind him, standing against the wall, another, tweed-suited, brooded over an open notebook. Gregg didn't invite me to sit down. "Ah. This is Mr. Seacombe, Inspector."

The man with the trilby nodded, smiling faintly.

"I'm sorry to have dragged you away from your work, Mr. Seacombe. I promise I won't keep you longer than is necessary. My name is Fernley; Detective-Inspector. This is Sergeant Dodd." He crossed his legs and stared hard at the carpet. "I understand that Thorne was in your form."

I had been expecting something like that.

9

"He's in 4B," I explained. "I happen to be his form-master. All the teachers here have their own particular subjects and move from form to form. I probably don't see any more of Thorne than do any of the others."

Gregg used his censorious cough.

"I have already explained our system to the inspector. You were in charge of the form at the time of the incident."

I looked at Fernley. "Is he——?"

"He was still alive half an hour ago when I called the hospital. But he's still unconscious. I've spoken to the parents, of course, but they were in no fit state to tell me very much. Is there anything you can tell me about him, Mr. Seacombe? I want to try to get a picture of his character."

"He was a left-over," I started, and Gregg used his cough again at the expression. "He came to the school last year, in the middle of a term," I explained. "And because he didn't manage to catch up with the rest of the class he stayed down when the others moved up. That means he is about a year older than his class companions now."

"I see." Fernley regarded me closely. "I think I know what you're trying to say. An older boy than the rest. Perhaps inclined to throw his weight round as a result? Aggressive?"

"I didn't say that."

"No." He fingered his hat. "Tell me your version of what happened yesterday."

"There are only three days left until the end of term. Some subjects have completed the curriculum. That means there are certain periods when I can either give the class private study or else take them out to the fields. There was such a period yesterday. It was fine, so I took them out to the nets. But Mr. Philby's class had beaten us to it. So I decided to use the second eleven pitch. I sent three boys—no, four. . . ."

I had detailed Tomkin, Blake and Watson to cut back to the games-room and collect the gear from Slater. Thorne had taken it into his head to go trailing after them. When I had called after him, although he must have heard me, he had ignored me completely.

"Four?" Fernley asked.

I nodded. "I told them to go to the games-room, which is just across the playground from the gym. Slater, the school porter, is in charge of all the sports gear. Perhaps five minutes after they'd gone, Tomkin came racing back to tell me what had happened. That's all I know first-hand. The rest is just hearsay."

10

"I'm going to talk to the three boys," Fernley said. "I'd like to hear the version they told you first."

"They went to the games-room and knocked for Slater. He opened up and so he saw what happened. For no apparent reason Thorne suddenly turned and without saying a word, ran across the yard to the gym, climbed on the sill of one of the ground-floor windows—it's a tall building with two rows of barred windows—swung over to a drain-pipe and shinned up to the flat roof. Slater shouted at him but he took no notice. So far as I can make out he threw himself backwards off the roof. That's all I know."

Fernley sighed. "Yes. Thank you, Mr. Seacombe." He looked at the headmaster. "I would like to have a word with the three boys."

Gregg was ponderously co-operative.

"We will do everything within our power to clear up this unfortunate affair. You might detail the boys when you return to your form, Seacombe."

I went back to my classroom. A hum of conversation died away as I opened the door. Forty pairs of eyes watched me curiously as I went to my desk. There was still five minutes to go before the bell.

"Tear the drawings out of your books," I told them. "Put your names in the top left-hand corner and put them on my desk on your way out." And as they started to come to their feet: "Blake, Tomkin and Watson; report to the headmaster's study. Knock at the door and wait until you are told to enter. Right?"

There was a crowd flurry at the corner of the desk while they piled the sheets of paper. I spotted some of them trying to slip away without leaving their drawings. I told them to go back and collect them. Blake was one of them, which was unusual for him. But there was the excuse that he would be thinking about the coming interview with the police.

When they had gone I lit a cigarette in defiance of regulations. I stood by the window to smoke it. For no reason at all a boy—a stolid, unimaginative boy, not over-bright and certainly a bully—had taken it into his head to throw himself backwards off a roof.

For no apparent reason at all. I reached through the window to stub out my part-smoked cigarette on the outside wall. Philby came in, a pile of notebooks under his arm.

"They didn't make a murmur," he said. "Any news about Thorne?"

"He was still alive three-quarters of an hour ago. But he hasn't regained consciousness."

11

"Do the police have any ideas?"

"They didn't give me that impression. There seems to be no rhyme nor reason to the whole affair. It doesn't make sense."

Setting down his load Philby lowered himself to my chair. He had a theory.

"It's very obvious to me what happened. He was showing off."

"They said he went over backwards," I reminded him.

He started to leaf idly through the pile of drawings.

"Lost his footing. It could easily happen. Is this what you set to keep them busy?"

"Yes."

"Encroaching on Miss Grey's territory. We don't seem to have any budding Picassos amongst us. Hullo? I spoke too soon. This is good. Who's responsible for this effort?"

"I haven't looked at them yet," I told him, going to stand at his side. In point of fact I hadn't been going to examine them at all. They had only been a means to an end.

He was right. The drawing he held up was good. I'm no great judge of art but it was obvious that this was the work of someone who knew what he was doing. It was clearly a picture of a real place; the wealth of detail precluded imagination. A village street; white-walled cottages; a cluster of trees, a background of oddly-shaped hills. Offhand, without looking at the name in the corner—Philby's large thumb was plastered across it anyway—I could think of not one of the boys who possessed the visual memory and the talent to produce such an effort in the twenty minutes I had been away. Philby moved his thumb and the name was Rodney Blake.

He said suspiciously: "Master Blake, eh?" and turned to his notebooks, shuffling through them, finding one, opening it to make comparisons. "And this is the best he can do, so he assures me, in the way of map-drawing."

The map was a blotchy ill-formed affair of barely-recognisable outlines and blurry detail. There was no comparison at all between it and the drawing.

"You wouldn't think that the same boy was responsible for both," Philby stated. "I must have a word with him about this. Lack of natural talent I'm prepared to tolerate. But not slackness." He came to his feet, gathering up the books. "We'd better be thinking about lunch, Gordon."

I rolled up Blake's drawing and slipped a rubber band round it. Philby waited in the corridor.

"Don't be too hard on him," I said for some reason.

He blinked at me through his glasses. "Blake?"

12

"He's something of a sensitive type. And don't forget he was one of those who saw Thorne——"

"With only two days to go before the end of term," he remarked, "I'm in no mood to be harsh with anyone. But I certainly intend to have a heart-to-heart with him."

In the teachers' dining-room we faced each other across grey potatoes, cold mutton and some mess of once-green vegetable. At least the meat was edible. I filled up with biscuits and cheese and left the place while Philby was still eating.

Miss Grey was alone in the common-room, her head bent over a magazine. She would be somewhere in her mid-twenties and had a fragile, triangular-shaped face and a high forehead disguised with a sloping semi-fringe of pale blonde hair. She looked up from her reading.

"Any fresh news of Thorne, Mr. Seacombe?"

I recited a report that had become monotonous. Then I unrolled the drawing and laid it across her magazine, holding the ends down.

"I thought you might like to see this. With apologies for dabbling in your subject. I had to leave my class for a while and this seemed as good a way as any of keeping them occupied."

She smiled. "The police. I know; one of my girls told me." She studied the drawing. "But this is excellent! Did one of your boys do this?"

"Rodney Blake."

"Blake?" She frowned, pursing her lips. "A thin boy, twelve, with an unusually-shaped foreign-looking face and very black hair?"

"That's the one."

"He didn't do this," she stated simply. "I only see him for half an hour each week, but I know his capabilities. He can't draw to save his life. This has been done by an artist. And a mature artist at that. I only wish I could do half as well."

She held it at arms' length.

"The balance is at fault; otherwise the technique is perfect. You know Charidon then, Mr. Seacombe?"

"Where?"

"Charidon." She turned the sketch to face me. "This."

"I told them to choose their own subject. No; I don't know the place at all."

"It's a little village way up in the wilds of Northumberland. Not well known to tourists but something of a beauty spot.

13

Quite a lot of artists go there during the summer. There are certain"—she raised her shoulders in a gesture—"approved view-points. You know? Every so-called beauty-spot has them. But this wasn't done from one of them. That's why the balance isn't good." She pointed out details. "This line of hills; see those three humps? They're called the Three Sisters. And this second cottage, with the geraniums in pots; I stayed the night there. That vase was in the window then."

She laid the drawing down again, holding it open with delicately extended fingers while she puzzled over it.

"It's odd. I remember now that I showed Blake's class the paintings I did of Charidon. I asked if any of them knew the place. They all said they didn't. But Blake must have been there."

"Or else seen a picture of it," I suggested significantly.

She looked up at that, understanding my meaning.

"No. My paintings were all done from the approved spot at the top of a rise looking down on the village. This is obviously a view from the village street."

She removed her hands and the paper crisped into twin rolls.

"I can't believe that Blake did this. Did you show it to me for any particular reason?"

"Only because I thought it was good and I suppose I wanted my opinion endorsed by an expert."

I had never noticed her teeth before. But then it was the first time I had seen her laugh in close-up.

"An expert is one thing I don't pretend to be. But I can recognise talent when I see it."

The room had gradually filled. Philby joined us.

"Latest report," he offered. "The headmaster rang the hospital a few minutes ago. No change."

"It's a terrible thing," Miss Grey deplored. "Whatever could have possessed him?"

Philby had his explanation ready, hardened now by repetition. "He was showing off and he slipped." He was so certain that that had been the way of it. "You'll see; when he comes round he'll admit to it."

"In a way," she mused, glancing at her watch then closing her magazine, "it's not unlike that affair at the Brandbatch Primary three years back. I must fly. I haven't tidied up the art-room after the morning session."

"What affair was that?" I asked her.

She was doing things to her hair in front of the mirror over the dusty, foil-filled fireplace.

14

"At Brandbatch? Oh, a boy suddenly got up from his desk—it was during class—bolted across the room and flung himself headfirst through a window. He cut himself very badly."

"I hadn't heard about that." I looked at Philby who shook his head.

She turned from the mirror.

"It happened during my last term at the training college. We were taking it in turns trying our hands in front of a proper class. Stewpots, you know. I wasn't in the school at the time, but two of our girls were. They told me all about it."

I walked down the corridor with her. We parted at the art-room and I went upstairs alone, the drawing under my arm. There was still five minutes before the bell. Tomkin, hands in pockets, lounged against the wall facing the classroom door. Seeing me coming he took out his hands and straightened. It was obvious he had been waiting for me. But I had a question to put first.

"You sit next to Blake in class, Tomkin."

Eyes wide he nodded up at me. "Usually, sir."

I unrolled the sketch. "Did you see him actually do this?"

"Oh yes, sir. It's smashing, isn't it?"

"Did he tell you where the place was?"

"The place? Oh, in the picture. No; he didn't speak at all. Not once. I spoke to him, but——" He stopped.

"That's all right," I reassured him. "This is off the record."

"I spoke to him lots of times, sir, but he took no notice like. An' he did the drawin' with his left hand, sir."

"You mean he's right-handed as a rule?" I couldn't remember. I tried to visualise Blake seated at his desk. A teacher ought to know that sort of thing.

Tomkin was sure. And he gave away his cribbing capabilities by proving it.

"Oh, yes sir. I sit on his left an' usually I can't see what he's doin' on account of his shoulder bein' in the way. Well, this morning I could see everything what he was doin' 'cos he was leaning the other way. See, sir?"

"Everything that he was doing," I corrected automatically. I let him enjoy his triumph of reasoning without wanting to know why he liked to look over Blake's shoulder. A thought struck me. "Did you know him before you came here?"

"Oh, yes, sir. We was in the same class at the school afore this. That was at Brandbatch, sir."

I rerolled the drawing, my thoughts racing. Coincidence? It

15

had to be. There were probably dozens of ex-Brandbatch boys here at Cookley. Then I became aware that Tomkin was still waiting, his country-freckled face turned anxiously to mine.

"Well, what is it?" I demanded, and was immediately ashamed of the brusqueness. "Yes, Tomkin?"

"This mornin', when we had to go to the head——"

"Yes?" What was coming now?

"We all went in together an' they asked us to tell what happened about Thorne. Watson told them an' we just sort of added bits. Then the big geezer—I mean, the one sitting down, asked if that was the lot, an' we said yes."

"You're trying to say there was something you didn't tell him?"

He looked down at his feet and shuffled uncomfortably.

"Watson didn't say anything about it an' neither did Roddy, —I mean, Blake, sir. Well, on the way to get the bats and stuff we was all running, an' Thorne kept on barging into Blake an' trying to knock him over. An' just as we went through the playground gate he knocked Blake right against the wall. I think he must've hurt him 'cos Blake was holding his elbow an' limping."

The picture was clear enough. Every teacher knows of the devilment boys, left to their own devices, get up to. And it didn't seem all that long since I had been a twelve-year-old myself and had been barged, as Tomkin described it, painfully off my feet.

The bell rang at that moment.

"Should we've ought to have told the coppers, sir?"

"The police, you mean. Yes; I think you should have told them. Not that it could have had any bearing on what happened afterwards."

Boys came clattering noisily up the stairs and surged along the corridor. I stepped aside while they jostled, chattering, into the classroom.

"That's all right then, sir," Tomkin declared with obvious relief, and having in his own way passed on the responsibility, joined the others.

I gave the class a couple of minutes to settle down before joining them. The first afternoon period was history. For forty minutes I automatically discussed the implications of the Industrial Revolution. It was an oddly uncomfortable period. I found my thoughts wandering and my eyes seeking out the empty seat in the far corner which had once been occupied by a boy who was now lying seriously ill in hospi-

16

tal. It was a relief to leave the place and spend the remainder of the afternoon reading poetry with a class of senior girls.

At half past four the school knew that Thorne had died without regaining consciousness.

2

Standing with his back to the common-room window, his face arranged in a suitably grave mask, clearly very aware of his status as senior master present, Philby took it on himself to mouth the usual things, the platitudes to fit the occasion. His verbose pomposity settled on the room like a black velvet pall.

Thorne would be missed by all; pupils and staff alike. A most tragic affair. The headmaster was extremely upset. It was the first time anything of this nature had happened at Cookley. Nobody had been to blame. No member of the staff could find cause to reproach themselves. It had been a tragic accident.

So much for generalities. Now down to the details.

"I suppose it will mean an inquest. . . ."

He brooded on that thought for a moment.

"The Old Students' match will have to be cancelled. Advising all concerned will be Upton's responsibility." Upton was the games' master. Then: "Wreaths. One from the staff; one from the pupils. Perhaps a special one from Thorne's form-mates. . . ."

His eyes, sorrowful behind his glasses, sought me out.

"You were his form-master, Seacombe."

"I'll arrange that," I told him.

"There will have to be an expression of condolence to the parents." He was still looking at me. "Some form of permanent testimonial, I think; something they can keep and treasure."

I think that in his own way he was enjoying the moment.

"Perhaps we had better discuss that with Mr. Gregg," I told him, and went out into the passage.

It was well past six o'clock. Apart from the common-room the building seemed deserted. Briefcase under my arm, footsteps echoing emptily, I went along the passage and up the stairs to my classroom.

Thorne had sat in the far corner by the window, a place chosen because of its remoteness from authority. In class he had undeniably been a bad influence. Every disturbance had had him at its centre. Out of class, an arrant bully. Requiem for a schoolboy. One can control words but not thoughts. I felt sorry for his parents, wondering what kind of people they were. That was something else a teacher should know; something about his pupils' parents. In the States they went in for that sort of thing more than we did. Parent-Teacher organisations.

What had made Thorne climb to that damned roof?

And what had made another boy, at another school, throw himself through a window?

Blake had been a pupil at that other school. Blake had been tormented and hurt by Thorne just before the accident yesterday.

Coincidence?

That was one mystery. There was another.

Taking the drawing of Charidon from the drawer I unrolled it and held it flat on the desk.

Blake was right-handed but he had done this with his left. For Philby he could barely outline a recognisable map. According to Miss Grey he couldn't draw to save his life. But in twenty short minutes he had produced a drawing that could only have been done by a talented and experienced artist. So Miss Grey said. And with his left hand. And with a wealth of detail, of a place which he said he had never seen.

I had never caught him out in a falsehood. Not in the twelve months he had been in my form. Of the two subjects I taught he was always the inevitable bottom in history, the equally inevitable top in English. Three of his essays had appeared in the school magazine. In class he was invariably well-behaved and attentive. So far as I could recall he had never disobeyed an order. Except once. This morning.

He had been one of those who had tried to slip away without depositing their drawings on my desk. At the time I had found an excuse—his anxiety over the coming interview with the police. Now I wasn't so sure. While the other boys had jostled, crowding round, anxious to be rid of their drawings so that they could be away, Blake had made no attempt to join them. Instead, empty-handed, he had been edging towards the door when I called to him. Then he had had to return to his place to collect his drawing. There had certainly been reluctance in his adding it to the pile.

Was that how it had been? Or was my imagination embellishing the episode?

Opening my case I slipped the drawing inside. Philby would probably be waiting for me at the staff entrance so that we could walk home together as usual. The last thing I wanted this evening was his pontifical company. I went down the stairs. The door of the secretary's room stood open. The filing cabinet was alongside the window. The cards were arranged in forms, in alphabetical order, so that it only took me a moment to find Blake's. Jotting down his address on the back of an envelope I went back into the corridor, making my way now towards the main entrance.

Miss Grey came out of the art room as I turned the corner. She was ready to leave, hatless, a light blue coat hanging empty-sleeved from her sloping shoulders. Turning from locking the door she waited for me, greeting me with a smile.

"You don't usually leave the premises by the posh way."

I shook my head without replying, relieved that her opening remark hadn't been about Thorne.

Her high heels clicked briskly on the marble steps as we went down into the bright sunlight.

"Another lovely evening," she commented lightly. "Let's hope it lasts. I shall be glad when we break up."

I replied: "Yes," absently, and she glanced sideways at me, her smile fading, concern taking its place.

"It's upset you. We all feel the same way. But you mustn't let it worry you. You can't possibly blame yourself in the slightest for what happened."

Blame myself? I stared at her incredulously. Then realisation dawned. Was that what Philby had been driving at when he had said that no member of the staff had cause to reproach themselves?

"I didn't tell him to go for the gear," I told her. "He went on his own accord. I called him back but he took no notice, even though he must have heard me."

"I didn't know that." She laid her hand on my arm. "Then you're upset because he was in your form?"

It would have been the easiest thing in the world to agree with her and let it go at that. But for some reason I told her the truth.

"I'm more puzzled than upset over Thorne's accident. But I am worried about Blake."

"Blake? Why? Because of that drawing, you mean?"

"That, and other things." It was a relief to put thoughts into words. "Perhaps I'm worrying without reason. Trying to make

19

mountains out of molehills. Putting significance into coincidence."

She frowned. "There's our little mystery about the drawing, and Blake was one of the boys who were on the spot when Thorne fell off the roof. Is that your coincidence?"

"Partly," I said, and then I told her about my talk with Tomkin. I explained that Blake must have been a pupil at Brandbatch at the time when the other boy flung himself through the window. I told her how I didn't want to ask Tomkin if Blake had actually been in the same classroom at the time for fear of starting a rumour.

She stopped in her tracks, her face aghast.

"What are you trying to say? That Blake was in some way responsible for what happened to both boys?"

"I didn't say that at all!" I retorted sharply, and then was immediately ashamed and contrite of my brusqueness. "I'm sorry, Miss——" I fumbled for a name lost in the anxiety of the moment.

"Joan." She spoke absently, looking at me and through me.

"I'm sorry for snapping at you like that, Joan. It came out without thinking. I suppose I was really talking to myself. I wish I could get this damned idea out of my head. It stands to reason that Blake couldn't possibly have had anything to do with what happened to Thorne."

"No." She started walking again, slowly. "All the same, there is the coincidence. Are you going to do anything about it, Gordon? It is Gordon, isn't it? Or are you just going to keep on worrying?"

"There doesn't seem much I can do. I did have some idea of paying a visit to his parents. I mean, he's been in my form for a year and I seem to know next to nothing about him."

"Except that when the mood takes him he can turn himself into a talented artist," she rejoined with some return of her former lightness. "And produce into the bargain a detailed drawing of a place he says he's never seen." She hitched her coat back to her shoulders. "Won't you need some excuse for going to his home?"

"I think I've got one. He's brilliant at English; essay-writing in particular. He could have a future as a professional writer. I could mention the drawing at the same time."

She laid her fingers on my elbow again. "What do you think you'll be able to find out, Gordon?"

"I don't know," I told her. "I just don't know."

A listener rather than a talker and never very happy during

interviews of any kind, particularly with strangers, I had made up my mind, once the ice was broken, to say as little as possible. The few times I had had dealings with the parents of pupils—usually on Speech Day—I had found that they generally required little encouragement to enthuse about their offspring. I hoped that Rodney Blake's parents would be equally enthusiastic.

Their home was a small detached bungalow, half brick, half timber, with a fair-sized garden. It was a ten minute walk along a dusty winding lane from the bus stop on the main road.

Mr. Blake bore no shred of resemblance to the mental picture I had envisaged, based on his son's appearance. He was thick-set and slow-moving, with a dark, large-pored face, over-wide jaws and fierce brown eyebrows. His wife was a timid, indefinite creature with nondescript features and colouring—a pale wisp of a woman—with a way of nervously working her fingers in the pockets of her faded pink overall. There was no sign of the boy.

Opening the door to me—tieless, collarless, flannel shirt-sleeved—Mr. Blake was inclined to be surly and suspicious until I introduced myself. Then he relaxed, but without any easing of his solid features, inviting me inside, leading the way heavy-footed to a blatantly little-used and over-furnished parlour.

"This is the first time we've ever seen one of Roddy's teachers," he said. "I thought you was a——" He pulled himself up. "I thought at first maybe you'd come about that kid what hurt himself. They say Roddy saw it happen."

"How is he?" his wife asked anxiously from the background.

"I'm afraid he died this afternoon. Didn't Roddy tell you?"

"He never tells us nothing," Blake grunted. "We wouldn't have heard about it all only one of my work-mates told me."

"Joe," Mrs. Blake said, timorously reproachful.

"Go an' make Mr. Seacombe here a cup of tea," he ordered, without first asking if I would like a drink, and she pattered away, pausing at the kitchen door, just across the narrow passage, to peer back a little fearfully over her shoulder.

He waited until she had gone before turning to regard me intently.

"So you're Roddy's teacher. He's never mentioned you. How does he make out at school?"

"Very well, by and large. I take him for English and History. He's particularly good at English, with quite a talent for writing. That's what I wanted to discuss with you."

21

He seemed to have no interest at all in his son's abilities. "You get much trouble out of him?"

"None at all. He seems very well-behaved."

No sounds were coming from the kitchen. There should have been a clatter of crockery, water running into a kettle, the usual noises one associates with tea being made. I had the feeling that Mrs. Blake was listening from behind the partly-open door.

"That's something," Blake said doubtfully. "You never can tell with our Roddy. What's he like with the other kids, eh? Get on all right with them?"

"I don't see very much of him out of school. He does seem to prefer to keep himself to himself."

"It's the same story here at home. Nothing to do with the neighbours' kids. Always off to play on his own. Usually in the woods. It's not natural. Not at his age. . . ."

I let him talk. He spoke in short jerky sentences, coarse, work-hardened hands clamped on corduroy knees.

"He's run away half-a-dozen times and more. You don't know about that, eh?" I shook my head. "He's got a damned good home here. I never raised my hand to him from the day we had him. We told the police the first two or three times. You know how it is. Sometimes they bring him back. Mostly he gets back on his own. Never a word out of him where he's been. Longest he's been away was a whole day. When he goes off now we just let him be. It's the best way. He's old enough to take care of himself."

"We never can find out where he goes to," Mrs. Blake said from the kitchen door.

"That's not the only kink he's got," said her husband, ignoring the interruption. "He talks to himself when he thinks he's alone, an' that's a sign of a weak mind, they say. Many's the time I've had to go looking for him when he's not come in for meals, and there he'd be, chatting away twenty to the dozen. Just like there was someone else there. Talking to someone he calls 'Tony'. We mentioned it to the doctor once, but he didn't seem interested. . . ."

"All children who like to be alone invent playmates for themselves," Mrs. Blake put in. "I know I did the same when I was a child."

"Other kids grow out of it," he retorted dourly. "Roddy's twelve. He should be past that sort of thing."

He half-turned to glance at the window behind him. Opening my briefcase I brought out the drawing, unrolling it, holding it up so they both could see. Admiration drew Mrs.

Blake like a magnet. She steadied the paper with reddened hands.

"Now that's what I call real pretty. . . ." She discovered the name in the corner. "Did our Roddy do that?"

"His art teacher thinks it excellent," I told them. "Did you know he was a budding artist?"

"We don't seem to know much about him at all," Blake commented sourly, no time to spare for the picture.

"We know he can draw when he wants to, Joe." Mrs. Blake padded to an ugly, mahogany-stained sideboard. "I kept the one he did some time back." She rummaged in drawers. "Where was that one done, Mr. Seacombe?"

"In class."

"No. I mean what place is it?"

"Apparently it's of a village called Charidon." I watched Blake's face. His expression didn't alter. "Roddy drew it from memory."

"He's never seen the place that I know of," he said. "No more have I, come to that. We don't get about much. He must've seen a picture of it somewhere."

Mrs. Blake came to proudly lay a second drawing across my lap. It was a portrait done in pencil with the same delicate, detailed touch as the first. The head and shoulders of a middle-aged woman with placid eyes that slanted upwards from the bridge of an over-wide nose. Smooth, greying hair was centrally parted and drawn back in a bun, low on the nape of the neck.

"This is very good indeed," I said, because it was indeed a fine portrait, and not because she was clearly awaiting my approval. "A relation?"

She shook her head. "Roddy said he made it up out of his head."

I examined it more closely. A small white scar had been etched in high on one cheek. When you are drawing a face out of imagination you don't usually think of adding a disfigurement. I was ready to wager that the woman in the portrait was a real person.

"He makes too damned many things up out of his head," said Blake. "What about that tea, Emily?"

I called after her: "Do you mind if I borrow this, Mrs. Blake? I'd like his art teacher to see it."

She smiled then, for the first time since my arrival. I think she smiled very rarely.

"Take it, and welcome."

Blake swivelled heavily in his chair to watch her go, not

23

speaking until she had vanished into the kitchen again. Then he faced me, leaning forward, lowering his voice to a confiding whisper-growl.

"This is the first time I've had a chance to talk with someone what knows Roddy. Like I said, I asked the doctor about him and all he could say was not to worry, that all kids have their little ways. It's not that he's any trouble. Apart from his running away, and he can take care of himself there. Right from when he first started to walk he could always take care of himself. He don't need nobody. He don't need us. There don't seem anything we can do about it."

His eyes were drawn again to the lace-curtained window. He raised his voice. "Emily! Where is he now?"

Tea-pot in hand she came to the kitchen door. "Out in the woods, I suppose, Joe. He went straight off after tea as usual."

The kettle shrilling sent her scurrying. Her husband pushed himself to his feet with weary clumsiness to go to the window, raising one corner of the curtain and peering out.

"He's not our kid," he said in a steady monotone as if reciting a previously rehearsed speech. "We adopted him when he was about a year old. He came from a sort of nursing home. They told us that he was one of twins, and the other had been taken just the day before. Emily, she was upset, saying it weren't right for twins to be broke up like. So I tried to find out who'd got the other in the hope that we could take that as well. But they wouldn't tell us who'd got the other."

He turned, then, speaking with a kind of low, savage intensity.

"Having just the one's been worry enough. I reckon I haven't got much to be thankful for, but I'm thankful enough we weren't able to take two of them."

He lumbered back to his chair and eased himself down, staring at the carpet between his feet.

There was a short silence. I found myself looking at the window that seemed to hold so much attraction for him. The time for thinking, for reasoning, for adding this new knowledge to what I already knew or suspected, would have to come later, when I was alone. I said the first thing that came into my head, the sort of thing that anyone says under the circumstances.

"Does he know?"

He shook his head at the carpet.

"We aim to tell him when he gets a bit older. I'm not looking forward to it. With a kid like him there's no way of tell-ing how he'll take it."

Mrs. Blake, burdened with a loaded tray, caught his last words as she edged sideways into the room.

"You've told him then, Joe. . . ." She set the tray down carefully on the table. There was a crisp white cloth; deeply-indented creases; only brought out for special occasions. . . . She busied herself pouring tea.

She looked into my face as she brought the cup to me.

"I've tried very hard to think of him as my own child," she said quietly. "We've had him eleven years and he's still a stranger."

"You know nothing about his real parents then?" I asked them.

"They wouldn't tell us nothing at the home. They said it wasn't policy. About three years back——" He glanced at his wife and she nodded, "Three years last May, Joe."

"Three years back, when he was nine, we knew that there was something different about him. You can't live with any-one for all that time without noticing. . . . We went back to Banford, to the home, to try and get something out of them. I'd got my mind made up. I weren't going to be put off. Only the home weren't there any more. It had closed down."

"The scars on his arms," Mrs. Blake said, nursing the sugar basin. "We don't know if he was born with them or if his people. . . ." She broke off. "You've seen them, Mr. Sea-combe?"

"I've never noticed them," I replied, and tried to recall the few times when I had seen him out on the sports' fields. Usually at the nets. His sleeves, in my mental pictures, were rolled down.

"He's inclined to be a bit touchy about them." She put the basin down. "Not that they show very much. There's one on the outside of each arm, from a little way above the wrist to just under the elbow. Just like someone had run a nail up the flesh, zig-zag like, and it had come up in a white weal. They seem to fidget him at times. . . . The doctor, he said they was nothing to worry about."

"There's a deal of things the doctor tells us not to worry about," Blake put in heavily.

"Tell him about the time he had toothache, Joe. And that time when he fainted and come up with bruises all over his legs."

He told me.

It was nearly ten o'clock when I left the bungalow. The sun

25

was low behind the trees, the lane mottled with shadows. Deep in thought I made my way slowly towards the main road. Already some sort of theory was taking shape in my mind. An impossible theory but one that fitted everything I knew. I needed confirmation of a kind, and I knew who would be able to help me there.

At the first bend in the lane the trees closed in on either hand so that I was walking through a cool, green and gold cavern. The world was silent. Then the feeling came that I was being watched; that from somewhere in the under-growth invisible eyes were following each step I took. So strong did the sensation become that I stopped and looked about. There was nothing to be seen. Branches rustled softly and then were still again.

In front of me the cavern started to shimmer and dissolve, outlines becoming hazy, shifting like a scene under water. Fresh shapes appeared, mixing into a bewildering confusion of colour and perspective.

I blinked hard and then rubbed my eyes with the back of my hand, trying to clear the vision. The lane, the bushes and the trees became ghosts, fading as fantasy came to super-impose itself upon reality.

Ahead and above was empty sky. The horizon was a far-distant unbroken line. I was standing on the verge of an abyss, looking down, head whirling sickeningly, into fathomless depths. One step forward would send me plunging down into nothing.

It was hard to say how long the hallucination—for that was what it had to be—lasted. Perhaps for one second. Perhaps for five minutes. It was eternity. Then the sky and the abyss and the empty horizon vanished, wiped away, and the trees were back again. The ground at my feet became solid—the familiar rough, reassuring surface of the lane. Even so it was a while before I could bring myself to take the first step forward. Then I walked quickly, almost breaking into a run, fighting down waves of persistent vertigo.

When I reached the comfort of the main road I took out a cigarette. I found that my hands were trembling so much that I had difficulty in lighting it. And when I came to rest my weight against the pillar of the bus stop my clothes became cold with sweat.

Half an hour later, dropping from the bus at the corner of my street, I had almost recovered. But I had only to close my eyes and the terrifying abyss was back again like a night-mare that refuses to be forgotten.

Before going home to face Philby's mutely enquiring and

reproachful eyebrows I indulged in the unaccustomed luxury of a double whisky, and felt all the better for it. Then I spent a quarter of an hour in a telephone kiosk, dragging Brother Harold, protesting only mildly, from his pre-bed bathroom.

3

There were five vacant desks, apart from Thorne's, in the classroom the following morning. The last day of the summer term always produces a small flock of absentees. But I hadn't expected to see Rodney Blake's place empty. That was the first desk I had looked at when I had followed the boys into the room. I was aware of a surge of relief at his absence.

When I had marked the register I drew a red line through Thorne's name and then sat looking at it for a few minutes. The class waited quietly and expectantly. There were two envelopes on my blotter, notes from the parents of two of the absentees. I read them automatically and made the appropriate marks on the register. I wondered if Blake had taken it into his head to go off on one of his journeys.

The morning periods drifted by in a desultory, time-wasting manner. For the last half hour before the midday break I let the boys loose on the tennis courts, superintending from a perch on the sun-warmed wall.

After lunch I made my way as usual to the common-room. It was more crowded than usual, with Philby installed at a folding table, a box and a pad at his elbow, industriously gathering in contributions towards the staff wreath. I made my offering, saw Joan seated in the corner by the window and went over to join her.

Philby's voice followed me.

"Have you arranged about your form wreath, yet, Seacombe?"

I called back that it was under control, that I would collect the boys' contributions during the afternoon and that I had a feeling the best we would be able to manage would be a bunch of flowers.

"I see." He sounded disappointed. Then: "Have you seen the headmaster yet?"

"No. Why?"

"I think he wants a word with you about composing a suitable written tribute."

Then Upton, pipe in mouth, thick tweed jacket over turtlenecked pullover, came to join us.

"Your holiday all laid on, old man?" he asked breezily.

"Not that you'd notice," I retorted, having made no arrangements at all about going away.

"Time you were getting a move on. Sunny Spain for yours truly. Vino, garlic and senoritas. In that order. How about you, Miss Grey?"

"I don't usually make firm plans," she told him. "I think it's a lot more fun when you're on your own to leave everything till the last minute and then go where and when the spirit moves." Meeting my eye she smiled faintly. "Most likely I shall find time for a week in the Lakes."

Upton enlarged upon his holiday intentions for a while and then wandered away in search of more congenial company. Joan lowered her voice.

"Did you have any luck last night, Gordon?"

Philby hadn't finished with me. He called across the room before I could reply.

"Seacombe! As soon as you've collected in your money you'd better let me know the total so that I can contact the florist."

"We can't talk here," I said to Joan.

We met that evening at the wrought-iron gates of the park. I carried the rolled drawing of the woman's head under my arm. We found a bench in a half-circle of glossy-leaved rhododendrons overlooking the path and a slope leading down to a lake where ducks came paddling hopefully in search of bread. I was inclined to be self-conscious—for this was something new to me—of spreading my handkerchief on the wooden slats so that her green linen dress shouldn't be soiled.

She settled herself, looked at me, smiling, saying: "Well, Gordon?" and I launched into a description of my visit to the Blakes, an account that I had been mentally rehearsing on and off throughout the day. I didn't mention my experience coming back along the lane or my chat with Brother Harold. The time to speak of those would be later.

She listened without interruption, her eyes fixed intently on my face. When I had finished there was silence for a while. I took out my cigarettes, offering them to her and flicking my lighter. The ducks, disappointed, had sailed away to the far

28

side of the water. A boy and girl, their arms about each other's waists, her head on his shoulder, came slowly along the path. Joan watched them go before looking down again at the drawing I had laid across her knees.

"So Roddy is adopted," she said pensively. "And he's a twin. I didn't know that."

"One of identical twins," I added. "At least that's what the people in the nursing home told the Blakes."

She frowned. "I've never had anything to do with that sort of thing, but you'd think that with twins like that they'd try to place them both with the same parents. It doesn't seem right to separate them."

"It wasn't done through one of the approved adoption societies. From Blake's description of the place and the way they treated him I get the impression of a badly-run, perhaps shady nursing home, operating a kind of baby farm as a sideline."

I leaned back.

"Mrs. Blake had two babies of her own, both still-born. At the second confinement she had to have an operation. They told her that she wouldn't be able to have any more children. She took it very badly. That was when they decided upon adoption. Their doctor referred them to a legitimate adoption society but there were all sorts of snags. There was a long waiting list, and apparently Mr. Blake had to admit to having a police record—something to do with helping himself to scrap metal at the factory where he was working at the time. Also neither he nor his wife were regular church-goers. The society didn't seem very enthusiastic about letting them have a child. A friend put them on to the Harvey-Gorton Nursing Home at a place called Banford ——"

"I know the place," Joan put in. "It's not very far from Charidon." She picked up the drawing. "This is a remarkable effort for a boy of Rodney's age. If anything it's even better than the other one. A fine study. . . ."

A woman pushed a pram along the path, making some comment about the evening as she went by. On the lake two youths were fooling about in a rowing-boat, trying to splash each other, the craft rocking dangerously.

"Roddy has had his share of childish complaints," I said. "Mumps, measles, the usual things. And some that don't seem so usual. In August of last year he had a bad attack of tooth-ache that kept him awake a couple of nights with pain so intense that it brought black rings round his eyes. They took him to the dentist but there was nothing wrong, no apparent cause of the pain. All his teeth were sound.

29

"Two years ago he was walking across the lawn they have at the back of the bungalow and he fell over for no apparent reason. Mrs. Blake saw it happen. She said he fell sideways, almost as if something had run into him, pushing him off his feet. When she reached him she found he was unconscious. And even though it was only soft turf that had broken his fall, both of his legs and thighs came up in large areas of bruising. The doctor sent him to hospital so that tests could be made. But they were all negative. There was no explanation for the bruising."

I stopped then, waiting to see if Joan had any comment to make. When she stayed silent I dropped my cigarette and ground it under my heel before continuing.

"I think it could have been some kind of stigmata. If that's the right word. I think that there's a link of sorts between Roddy and his twin brother. The brother had an accident and Roddy came up in sympathetic bruises."

"A kind of rapport. . . ." She stared down at the drawing. "I suppose that could be the explanation. I've heard tell of such things but I never knew whether they were true or not." She glanced sideways. "You seem sure that the other twin is a boy."

"I think he's Roddy's make-believe playmate. Which means his name is Tony; short for Anthony, I suppose. And I'm guessing that this is a portrait of his mother or else some-one he knows very well."

She lifted delicately incredulous brows.

"You mean the drawings could have been passed across in the same way as the bruises and the toothache? I can't believe that, Gordon."

"Last night I rang up my brother in London. . . ." I waited for her to pass the usual comment.

"I didn't know you had a brother."

"Half-brother, to be exact. Same father, different mothers. He's nearly twenty years my senior. Harold Ferris-Seacombe. He introduced the hyphen about the same time he gave up being called plain 'Doctor' and became the consultant medical specialist at St. Vincent's. There's a rumour that he's in the running for a knighthood. He's on the committees of God knows how many charity organisations and he runs a forensic laboratory as a hobby. From time to time the police make use of his talents. He spent a couple of years in the States some time back. You may have seen his picture in the papers last week. He was one of the guests at a luncheon given at the American Embassy."

"Quite a celebrity," Joan remarked.

"We don't see very much of each other. Town mouse, country mouse; that sort of set-up. I'm very much the poor relation." I tried not to sound bitter. "By the time I came on the scene Brother Harold was well launched on his spectacular career. I had to make do with left-overs. At least I can say I've got where I am under my own steam. Where was I? Dragging him from his bathroom at half past eleven at night to answer questions about identical twins.

"He was inclined to be a bit cagey at first, saying that that sort of thing wasn't in his field. So I told him that I only wanted the information to satisfy my own curiosity and that he was the only one I could turn to for expert advice. He started off by treating me to a lecture on how identical twins come about. Apparently there are three ways in which they can develop. So far as I can make out the usual way is for the fertilised ovum to divide, forming a mass of cells called the blastula. From this, two gastrulae—whatever they might be—are formed, and these are the start of the twins. Identical twins are always, so he said, of the same sex. Which ties in with the Tony theory. They may also be conjoined; you know—Siamese. But that doesn't happen very often.

"He said there were very good grounds, based on evidence, to assume that there may sometimes be a link between identical twins. He quoted the instance of twin girls, one of whom had to have her appendix out, while her sister, at the other side of the country, had all the symptoms of appendicitis and much of the aftermath pain of the operation."

Joan nodded. "I've read about things like that. So if they really do happen then it could explain the bruises on Roddy's legs and maybe even his occasional ability to draw with his left hand. But that doesn't get us very far. . . ."

I thought I knew what was coming next.

"It couldn't possibly have anything to do with what happened to Thorne and the other boy," she said.

So then I told her what had happened to me on my walk back along the lane. I chose my words carefully and I deliberately kept my voice as matter-of-fact as possible.

"The Blakes said that Roddy was somewhere in the woods," I finished. "Just before the hallucination came I had the feeling that someone was watching me. I grant you that that could have been imagination. But what followed wasn't. I feel sure that Roddy was responsible for what happened. I think that he chose an abyss because in some way he had found out that I have a phobia about depths. He could have used the same sort of thing on Thorne and the other boy. Only then he put something terrifying behind them, so that they ran blindly and instinctively away from it. In my case it came in front. A warning, perhaps. Don't go any further, or else. . . ."

There was silence for a while. Then:

"I don't believe it," she whispered, her face ashen.

"I'm almost certain that his parents are afraid of him, although they didn't say as much. Mr. Blake couldn't keep his eyes off the window. I think he was afraid of being overheard. He went to great lengths to tell me he'd never raised his hand to the boy. I got the impression that he'd tried once and received some kind of warning."

"It just isn't possible," Joan said, her voice back to normal.

"It could be a kind of projected hypnotism. That's one explanation of the Indian rope trick. Or perhaps something to do with extrasensory perception. Why he should have the ability to be able to do it I have no idea. If we knew something about his real parents that might give a lead. If I didn't know what it was like from my own experience I'd feel about it the same as you."

"You're sure you couldn't have imagined it all?" she asked, and answered herself: "No. You're not like that. . . ."

"I've only to close my eyes now," I told her, "and I can see that damned gaping abyss as clear as can be. I dreamed about it last night, which didn't help matters any." I smiled at her. "You could say it has left a lasting impression."

She asked: "Have you another cigarette, Gordon?" She accepted a light and leaned back, answering my smile with an obvious effort. The colour was returning to her cheeks.

"If we were to tell anyone about it they just wouldn't believe. They'd say we were both out of our minds. . . ."

She stopped, the cigarette half-raised to her lips.

"If it's the way you think, then he was responsible for Thorne's death."

"Yes," I agreed steadily. "If it's the way I think."

"What are we going to do about it then, Gordon? We've got to do something! He could easily do the same thing again." She looked at me, eyes wide, dawning horror settling like a mask on her features. "And he's still only a child! He's going to grow up. . . . We can't let him go on without trying to stop him!"

"It's all only a theory at the moment," I told her. "But I think it's a theory that can be proved. Or at least, partly proved. If we could get something concrete to go on we could bring Brother Harold into it. But it's no use tackling him until we have substantial proof that he can check for himself."

"You can prove it?" Perplexity replaced horror. "How?"

32

She put one hand to her mouth. Then: "The other twin, you mean?"

"We know he exists and we know quite a lot about him. It shouldn't be too difficult to track him down."

I ticked the points off on my fingers.

"He lives in or near Charidon. His mother, or someone very close, is the woman in the drawing. He should have similar features to Roddy. Left-handed, an artist, and his name is Tony. Two years back he had an accident of some kind. Last August, a bad attack of toothache. Knowing all that we shouldn't have much trouble tracing him."

"Do you think Roddy knows about him?"

"There's no way of telling for sure. Certainly, the news that he is adopted and has a twin somewhere hasn't been broken to him. But we don't know his capabilities. I'm only guessing that he reached into my mind to find out about my pet phobia. But if he did, then he could equally well have looked into the Blakes' minds and found out the truth. In any case I would say that he is intelligent enough to know that someone is in contact with him. I think that the times he runs away he is trying to find this other person. The drawing of Charidon could have been sent as a guide. Why that particular moment should have been chosen, I don't know. Perhaps they aren't able to exchange words, only pictures, and under certain circumstances."

"So you're going to Charidon," Joan remarked quietly.

I nodded. "I've got to get to the bottom of all this."

"I know the place very well. And at least one of the people who live there." She gazed at the lake. "Would you like me to come with you, Gordon?"

"I was hoping you'd say that."

She smiled faintly. "Two respectable unmarried teachers going off on a holiday together. I wonder what the rest of the staff would have to say? When do we start?"

"We've got seven weeks to play about with but we don't know what lies ahead. The sooner the better, Joan. They're holding the inquest on Thorne on Monday. I suppose I'll have to attend. Will Tuesday morning be all right?"

"Any day will suit me. What if we aren't able to find him there, Gordon?"

"Then we move on to Banford. We know that the nursing home has packed up but there's bound to be someone we can talk to who've had dealings with the place. With a bit of luck we might be able to run down one of the old staff. The local tradespeople might give us the first lead. Or the doctors. They might be the best bet. I'll only have to mention Brother

33

Harold's name and they'll lean over backwards to be helpful."

"Roddy's real parents," she said.

"I have the feeling that they are the key to the whole thing," I told her. "Even if we do find Tony at Charidon and he fits into the picture, we'll still have to go on to Banford. If we can add the parents to the list, and if all four of them have the same odd talents in common, then we'll have something to lay in front of Brother Harold. What happens after that will be out of our hands."

4

Philby's theory that Thorne had been showing off when he met his death had come to be the generally accepted one. The inevitable verdict at the inquest was accidental death. I spoke my piece, this time going into the details of how Thorne had taken it upon himself to be one of the boys sent to collect the gear. At the coroner's request I added a few words, for what they were worth, on his behaviour at school. Slater took up the tale as eye-witness, and the verdict was followed by the usual expression of the court's sympathy to the parents. I was glad when it was all over.

There were only a few people travelling north on the Tuesday morning. We had the compartment to ourselves as far as Darlington. Settling herself facing me, Joan asked:

"Don't you lodge in the same house as Mr. Philby, Gordon?"

"His is the first face I see every morning."

"Wasn't he at all curious about where you were going?"

"Not particularly. He's off on his own holiday on Friday. A grand tour of the south coast. He was too busy planning routes to bother about me. And he was trying to sort out school representation for the funeral this morning. He did ask if I would be available. I felt guilty when I had to tell him I'd be out of town. Maybe he thought it was just an excuse I'd made up on the spur of the moment."

The suburbs thinned into country. The train rocked between fields.

"How long have you been teaching, Gordon?"

I had to think about that one. In a monotonous existence minutes become hours while months, in retrospect, have a habit of shrinking into days.

"I've been at Cookley for five years. Before that I suffered a couple of years in a primary school in Manchester. Which means that seven years of my thirty-two have been spent trying to stuff knowledge into mainly unreceptive heads."

"It sounds like you aren't keen on the work."

Which was true enough. It was more a question of bare tolerance than active dislike.

"It's à living, Joan. I'm afraid I haven't got what you might call a vocation."

She laughed at that.

"I don't suppose many of us have these days. Although we like to think otherwise. Mr. Chips and his over-dedicated existence belongs to the past."

"Or to the public schools where dedication isn't a luxury."

"What don't you like about it?"

And what was the answer to that? Now I came to think it seemed like I had never bothered to put the thing into words, not even for my own benefit. Did I dislike teaching? Not exactly. That wasn't it.

"It's always being on a platform, I suppose. You know. . . . Forty-odd pair of eyes watching you all the time. And I've never been all that keen on dishing out orders, not even to a bunch of school-kids. I'm not the stuff dictators are made of. A kind of inferiority complex?"

"I wouldn't say that," she said. "I know what you mean about being on a platform. I feel much the same. But you're a good teacher, Gordon. I've heard the others talking about you. And the boys seem to respect you. I get on with the girls well enough. The boys are sometimes a handful. Art is a sissy subject so far as they're concerned." She laughed again. "They call me 'Dolly'. I've never heard their name for you."

"I don't think they have one," I told her, and wondered if that was a good thing or a bad.

A white-overalled woman wheeled a trolley along the corridor; I bought coffee and foil-wrapped biscuits.

"Your half-brother," Joan said; "why do you always call him Brother Harold?"

"A relic of the past. When I was going to school he was already grown-up, in practice as a doctor. I always wanted to call him Uncle. He didn't like that. So he became Brother Harold every time I spoke to him."

Durham station was a place of reeking smoke, slanting

35

sunlight dulled by grimy glass, and a platform stacked with boxes and mail-bags.

"So you've been five years at Cookley," Joan observed as the train gathered speed again, lurching noisily over points. "I've been there for nearly two. It's funny we shouldn't have had much to do with each other till now."

"If we had to be labelled I'd be wearing a tag marked 'bad mixer, leave alone'. In any case, our paths rarely cross in the daily routine. And like you once said, I use the tradesmen's entrance while you find the main door handier. I'm glad we did get together at last. That's one thing I've got Master Blake to thank for——"

I stopped, mentally cursing my tongue for running away into something I had determined not to talk about until we reached our destination.

"I know," Joan said, quietly understanding. "I've spent the last three days going over it all in my mind. It doesn't do any good."

We changed trains at Newcastle-upon-Tyne and again at Hexham. Now we shared a compartment in a non-corridor, slow-chugging local with a couple of red-faced, leather-gaitered farmers who exchanged opinions about crops and livestock in a dialect all their own.

The train pulled into Charidon a few minutes before one. We were the only passengers to alight on the wooden-planked platform. The surrounding hills gave an impression of enfolding, protective cosiness. There was a narrow foot-bridge, a toy signal-box, beds of bright flowers, and a grizzled porter impatient to take our tickets. Beyond the gate a cinder slope led to a winding street that was oddly familiar the moment I laid eyes on it.

"Up there, behind the station"—Joan pointed—"is the hill that gives the best views. That's where I did my paintings last year."

The road climbed steadily upwards in a series of gentle curves towards successive layers of perspective-flattened hills with houses squatting comfortably in the hollows.

We had lunch at a small hotel, set in its own grounds, some distance beyond the station in the opposite direction to the village. Afterwards we sat over coffee in a pleasantly cool lounge with oak-panelled wall and a great air of out-of-this-world isolation. It was easy now to forget the purpose of our visit. I was tired after the journey; replete from the meal. It was an effort to keep my eyes open.

"I don't usually go in for this sort of thing," Joan remarked contentedly. "I suppose it's silly but I don't like going in hotels on my own. The rest of the people always seem to be gathered in groups and you feel left out. It's different now."

A bee, trapped between chintz curtain and window, buzzed somnolently. I felt my head nodding. Setting her cup down Joan yawned delicately, two fingers a token gesture over her mouth.

"We can't have this," I said, forcing myself awake.

She smiled. "It must be the air. I remember the last time I was here I used to drop off after dinner each day. Mrs. Foster used to have to wake me."

"You must have got to know her quite well."

"I stayed with her the best part of a week and I don't think she stopped talking the whole time. Except when I was out or asleep. She seemed to know everyone's business in the village. If there is a boy called Tony living here she'll know all about him."

And that drove the last vestige of sleep away.

We went into the reception hall. Our two cases stood against the wall.

"Will you be staying, sir?" the fresh-faced woman behind the desk wanted to know.

"We're not sure yet," I told her. "Is it far to Banford?"

"About twenty miles."

"Bus or train?"

"Both, sir. Although the buses give the better service."

Thanking her I knelt by my case, opening it, taking out the woman's portrait, wondering for a moment if it would be worth while asking the landlady if she recognised it, deciding that it would be too obvious and maybe rumour-inducing.

"Bring the other as well," Joan suggested over my shoulder.

I found it, handed them both up to her.

We walked down the road, past the station, towards the village. To the right, hills crept above the trees as the road dropped towards the first row of cottages. Joan pointed out a landmark.

"The Three Sisters."

The air, after the town and the journey, was sharp and fresh. We passed a garden that was a mass of lupins. From another came the peppery sweetness of stocks. Even the banks, the sloping verges, had been planted with flowers. A farm lorry lumbered by, the driver raising his hand in friendly acknowledgment of our standing to one side to let him pass. Two young men, bearded beyond their years, both wearing fiercely-scarlet shirts, each with a portfolio affair under their arms, one carrying a folded easel over his shoulder, swung past.

Turning to Joan to pass some comment about itinerant

37

artists, I saw that she had unrolled the drawing of the village and was studying it as she walked, glancing up from time to time as if checking the view-point. Then I saw why she had suggested we bring it with us.

She pointed as we rounded a bend.

"Straight ahead, Gordon; Mrs. Foster's cottage is the second in the row at the bottom. The drawing must have been done from somewhere along here."

I walked a little behind her, looking over her shoulder, until we reached a place where drawing and reality seemed to coincide. We were standing in front of a red-brick building with tall windows and a metal-railed tarmac surround. It didn't need the name, raised on a tablet over the door, to tell us that this was a school.

Opening the gate, hinges squealing, she went into the playground, walking backwards, the drawing held at eye-level, until she ended up with her back against one of the windows.

"So now we even know where he sits in class," she observed with satisfaction.

Rolling up the drawing she came back through the gate, watched now by a couple of curious-eyed children, a small boy and an even smaller girl, who had stopped on the other side of the road.

Joan smiled at them. "Do you go to school here?"

The boy nodded suspiciously. "Yes, miss."

"Do you know a boy called Tony?"

He pondered gravely, head on one side, while his companion scuffled small feet in the dust and peered up from under her lashes.

"Not anyone called Tony," he finally decided.

Joan bit her lip. "You're sure?"

"I don't know the names of all of them, miss," he offered anxiously.

"Of course you don't!" She smiled at him again. "Thank you for trying to help."

We walked on towards the cottages.

"I think it'll be best if I talk to Mrs. Foster on my own," Joan mused. "I'll tell her that I was just passing through and couldn't resist dropping in to see how she is. I'll show her the portrait and see if she recognises it. She knows I teach art, and Roddy's name isn't on it, so she'll probably think I did it. If she does recognise it then everything should be plain sailing."

"And if she doesn't?"

"Then the woman, whoever she is, can't live in Charidon.

38

So then I'll have to think of some excuse for asking about a boy called Tony."

She glanced at her watch.

"You'd better give me at least an hour, Gordon. Knowing Mrs. Foster she'll have the kettle on and the table laid right away, and be all set for a long chat. She'll have to know everything that's happened to me since last we met before I can even begin to show her the drawing. It's nearly three now. I'll tell her I'm meeting a friend at four o'clock."

We reached the gate. She pointed out the vase in the window. "It's still there." Then: "You'd better go on before I knock, otherwise she'll want to ask you inside as well. And I can talk better to her on my own." She smiled sunnily in case there was a sting I could find. "You know what women are."

I walked on alone. The cottages gave way to a row of small shops and then to a triangle of grass where children played, laughing and screaming. I stopped, lighting a cigarette, watching them covertly until I was sure that none of the boys bore any resemblance to Roddy. I was relieved in one way, feeling that if Tony did exist and my theory was right, then he would have the same odd character as Roddy and would not be interested in playing with other children.

Beyond the green was a small stone public house, another row of cottages with carefully-tended gardens, and a deserted and picturesque door-sagging smithy. Then came a half-a-dozen larger detached houses, each standing in its own grounds. There was a church by a cross-roads, a squat grey building with a stumpy tower and a lychgate, that looked as if it had been there since the beginning of time.

The clock in the church tower told me that I had only used up a quarter of Joan's hour. Sitting on the low stone wall that encircled the churchyard I lit another cigarette, leaning against the carved pillar of the lychgate letting the afternoon and the surroundings have their way with me.

Quite suddenly the whole purpose behind our visit to Charidon seemed unbelievable. It was impossible to imagine that an ordinary schoolboy in a far-off town should be possessed of powers bordering on the supernatural. It was unthinkable that he could in any way have been responsible for the death of another boy.

I had to force myself to relive the interview with the Blakes and the subsequent experience along the lane before I could even begin to accept the same things I had had to persuade Joan to believe. It was something, I suppose, that the nightmare-abyss was fading from memory. At one time I had thought to have it with me for the rest of my days.

At ten minutes to four I dropped to my feet to retrace my steps back through the village. There was no sign of Joan when I reached the cottage. I strolled on until I came to the school. In sight of the cottage door I lowered myself to the grassy bank. There was a light feathering of cloud over the odd hill formation called the Three Sisters. I heard the sound of a train chugging into the station, whistling with nostalgic mournfulness, starting off again.

Then the cottage door was open and Joan stood in the sunlight, talking to someone hidden in the shadows. Turning, she saw me and raised her hand, perhaps in proof of the excuse that a friend was waiting. The door closed and she came down the path into the lane and towards me. I rose to meet her. It was difficult to read her expression. There was perplexity rather than the achievement—satisfaction I had been hoping for.

"Well?" I asked eagerly.

"I'm not sure. . . ." We started to walk back slowly towards the inn. "I'm trying to sort it out in my mind. It doesn't fit. . . ."

"Two heads are generally better than one," I said tritely.

Taking a deep breath she slipped her arm through mine. I matched my stride to hers.

"She recognised the drawing. That's the first thing. It's of a Mrs. Latham who lives in one of the larger houses by the church. She's the vicar's sister. She has a daughter called Eileen who's fifteen. And she has an adopted son."

She paused.

"He's twelve. He's got very black hair and what Mrs. Foster called a 'foreign-looking' face. He doesn't mix with the other children; not even with his sister. His only interest in life seems to be drawing and painting. He's left-handed and he's got odd white scars on both arms. Mrs. Latham teaches music, the piano, but apparently when she suggested teaching him he told her he wasn't interested. But she made him take a few lessons—this was quite a few years back— and it was obvious he had no aptitude for music. But one day she came into the house from the garden, and there he was, seated at the piano, playing a Bach fugue that she was sure he'd never even heard before. He has a habit of leaving home for days at a time, refusing to say where he's been when he gets back. Two years ago he was thrown from a pony and badly shaken and bruised. . . ."

She paused again.

"It all fits so far," I said, keeping my voice steady.

"I haven't finished yet. According to Mrs. Foster he's never

40

had toothache. And his name isn't Tony, it's Peter. And he didn't come from a nursing home. He was dumped, in a basket, on the vicarage steps in September of 1953. The vicar found him, and being a bachelor, handed him over to his sister, Mrs. Latham, to look after while enquiries were being made. She and her husband adopted him some time later when the police were unable to trace where the child had come from."

She looked up at me.

"Two more things before you start trying to sort it out. Mrs. Latham isn't happy about Peter. She once confided to Mrs. Foster that she'd give her right arm if there was some way of getting rid of him. And the pony that threw him. It died the following day. Something of a mysterious affair. It was stabled in one of the farms in an isolated outbuilding. The stable was burned down, with the pony inside, and no one had been near it for several hours before."

We walked for a while in silence. I felt like a man who has seven draws up on his coupon, had missed a fortune by one result and buys several newspapers to make sure that the result of the last game is the same in every one. I had felt so certain that here in Charidon we would find a boy made up of the pieces of information I had assembled. The picture was here, almost complete. There were only three pieces that didn't fit. I set about trying to alter their shapes.

"Toothache is a very common thing. If Peter did have an attack there is no reason on earth why his mother should have mentioned it to Mrs. Foster."

"In August of last year," Joan said steadily, "when Roddy had his sympathetic attack, Mrs. Latham happened to be in hospital. Mrs. Foster went in each day to look after things and get the meals. She would have known first-hand if Peter had had a bad attack of toothache."

I let it go. I went now for the adoption, for that seemed to be the main difference, apart from their names, between the Tony I had been expecting to find and the Peter who had been presented in his place. I found a possible explanation, remote though it seemed.

"The people who adopted the other twin from the nursing home might, for some reason, have had second thoughts, and got rid of it by dumping it on the vicarage steps. I know it's unlikely, but it is an explanation."

"It's the most unlikely thing under the sun. People don't do that sort of thing." She frowned pensively. "Did Mr. Blake happen to tell you the exact date he adopted Roddy?"

"Yes. . . ." I thought back. "Some time in the middle of September, 1953. Either the fifteenth or the eighteenth. I forget which."

"The Lathams keep up Peter's birthday on the date he was found. September the fifth."

We stopped together, looking at each other. It took only a moment to work the thing out.

"Which means that Peter had been with the Lathams at least ten days before the Blakes adopted Roddy. And the nursing home people told Mr. Blake that the other twin had been taken only a couple of days before. So it can't be the same one. . . ."

"That's what I've been trying to sort out," Joan said. "There's only the one conclusion we can come to."

"Not twins," I discovered with dismay. "Triplets. Roddy, Peter and Tony. Three of them. Oh, Lord. . . ."

"That's the only way it can be," she agreed.

"I suppose we ought to take a look at this Peter," I said as we neared the inn.

"The Lathams, including Peter, are on holiday; touring Wales, according to Mrs. Foster."

I think I was relieved. "Like Roddy, he seems to have his own peculiar gift."

"You mean when they found him playing the piano?"

"I was thinking of the mystery fire that killed the pony."

"You think he was responsible for that." It wasn't a question and her level voice told me she must already have been thinking along the same lines.

"I'm ready to believe almost anything. I wish we could
——"

I stopped. "So now we're looking for another of them. Only this time we don't know much about him except that his name is Tony, he could look like Roddy, he had toothache last August and he's probably a gifted musician. If we could talk to your Mrs. Foster we might pick up a few more leads from Peter's behaviour. But we can't risk that."

"It would be all over the village before you could turn around," she agreed wryly.

We turned into the inn drive.

"So what do we do now, Joan?" I asked her. "Go straight on to Banford or stay the night here?"

She smiled. "I think I'd like a good night's sleep before tackling any more problem children."

I booked two single rooms and the landlady asked if we would like tea. She laid a small table for us in the lounge.

42

Apart from two morosely taciturn old gentlemen we seemed to be the only guests.

Afterwards we strolled in the garden. The sun was still hot but now its heat was tempered by a refreshing breeze. The path meandered aimlessly between flower-beds and rockeries, leading towards a terrace overlooking a rock-strewn slope that wasn't steep enough to set my phobia protesting and my head spinning.

Another path led from the terrace, out of the garden through a small wicket gate, climbing between trees towards the crest of a hill. And now the slope became steeper, falling away, a sheer drop into a rocky ravine, so that I found myself hugging the inside of the path, as far from the verge as possible, my feet ploughing through bracken and low gorse instead of being on the baked clay of the path.

Joan said suddenly: "I wonder what Roddy is doing now."

"He wasn't in school on Friday."

"I know; you told me, Gordon. That's why I was wondering where he was."

It was the utter stillness of the evening, not even a bird-sound, that brought back the memory of my walk from the Blakes' bungalow along the silent lane. There was the same uncanny feeling of expectancy now. When I felt the familiar probing of invisible eyes I tried to persuade myself that it had to be my imagination playing tricks. But the eerie sensation grew stronger. I felt Joan's hand clutch at my arm, heard her sharp intake of breath, and then I knew that she must be aware of the same sensation.

I knew what was coming. There was the nightmare horror of knowing that something indescribably evil was about to happen, and that I was powerless to do anything about it.

The scene in front of us started its anticipatory dancing and shifting. The shapes, the outlines of the trees and bushes, lost solidity and coherence, becoming tenuous shadows against the new scene that was coming through. Joan's fingers bit frantically into my arm.

Then the path was gone and there was the empty, horrifying loneliness of limitless space, and the vertigo-horror of the bottomless abyss at my feet. But this time it was different. Now it was even more vivid than before, and moving, the brink crumbling beneath my feet, forcing me back step by step.

Joan screamed shrilly, releasing my arm, shuddering away, hands held palms outward in front of her face as if warding away something evil. She stumbled away, screaming at each step.

Above my own terror I was able to remember the reality

43

ravine that bordered the path, invisible now, swept away by hallucination, but there just the same, waiting as she blundered blindly towards it.

I went after her, my arms out-stretched, swinging from side to side in frantic efforts to find her now invisible shape. I lurched full-face into something that wasn't there, something hard and rough and unyielding that drove the breath from my body. My fingers discovered the contours of a tree trunk. Fighting waves of terror and impotent urgency, I felt my way round it, guided by Joan's screaming.

It was only by luck that my hands found her waist. As I touched her she screamed again, louder than before, struggling, fighting to free herself from my grasp, her nails raking down my cheek. And then suddenly her body went limp in my arms, her screams were cut off, and in the same moment the emptiness was wiped away and the trees, the bushes and the path were back again.

Her body heavy against my breast, we were poised on the very brink of the ravine. The horror of the nightmare abyss still tore viciously at my nerves. I swayed, recovered, stumbled, dragging her with me, away from the verge. Gathering her up into my arms, I went back down the path towards the inn.

5

The landlady was more than shaken out of her customary rural composure by the collapse of one of her guests. Her babbled, shocked apologies gave the impression that in some obtuse way she felt responsible for what had happened. She fluttered anxiously with smelling salts and brandy while Joan, her eyes still closed, lay on the settee in the lounge where I had carried her.

"She was tired. . . ." I offered explanations as they came to mind. "And after the heat of the day and the long journey. . . . We shouldn't have gone climbing. She must have overdone things."

"Of course." She accepted the explanation with some relief. Her eyes went to my cheek and I reached up, finding thin lines of encrusted blood.

"A branch caught me," I said.

Joan's lids trembled; her eyes opened in a face from which every last vestige of colour had been washed away. She stared vacantly up at the ceiling, frowning slightly. Then her gaze found my face and her hands came clamping down on my arm.

"It's all right," I said, speaking slowly and distinctly. "It's all over."

I looked up at the landlady then, afraid of what Joan might say in the first moments of coming round, tempering as best I could dismissal with gratitude.

"Thank you very much for all your trouble. You've been more than kind. I think it might be best if I look after her myself now."

She went reluctantly, taking the smelling salts but leaving the brandy behind. I put the glass to Joan's lips. "Drink this." I held it there until she had gulped it down. As I took the glass away a wave of shuddering racked her, and I put my arm about her shoulders, holding her tightly, her face pressed against my breast. Then the tremors turned to tears, the reaction I had been expecting. I smoothed her hair, trying to soothe her, aware of the inadequacy of it all.

After a while the sobbing stopped and she pushed herself gently away, fumbling for her handkerchief. When I gave her mine she managed a watery smile.

"Sorry about that, Gordon . . . I must look a sight."

The brandy was bringing some of the colour back to her tear-stained face. She glanced a little fearfully in the direction of the door that led to the garden.

"It's all over," I said again.

She touched my cheek with wondering fingers. "Did I do that?"

"It could have been a branch. Neither of us was able to see what was happening. The skin's barely broken."

It would be best if she were to talk about it now; get it out of her system. Then perhaps she could start trying to forget.

"Not the sort of experience calculated to do the nerves any good," I remarked lightly.

"I panicked. . . ." She shivered. "I think I knew what was going to happen when everything started going misty. But I was expecting to see your gaping abyss . . . I didn't expect——" She broke off, shuddering afresh at the memory.

I put my hand on her shoulder. "Take it easy, Joan." And then: "You mean you didn't see the abyss?"

45

She shook her head. Her hair was silky soft against my cheek.

"A spider. . . ."

"A what?" I was incredulous.

"A huge bloated spider. Something that I knew just couldn't exist, and yet it was so real. . . . It stood almost as high as my waist, with long—feelers, reaching out towards me; a mouth with huge fangs, dripping. . . . It kept coming towards me. When I felt it touch me. . . ." She broke off. "I suppose I struggled. I didn't know it was you. It was you, Gordon?"

"Yes." I came slowly to me feet. "A spider. . . . So we both saw different things."

It was her turn to be incredulous. "You mean you didn't see it?"

I shook my head. "I had my old abyss back again, larger than life."

She stared up at me. "I don't understand."

"I think I do. Have you always been afraid of spiders, Joan?"

She smiled again, a little shamefacedly. "Always, for as long as I can remember. I've tried to get over it. . . ."

"And I've always been afraid of looking down into depths. Roddy must have been responsible for what we saw. . . ."

"I guessed that when it started. He must have followed us down here."

"Or else come on ahead. I don't think he deliberately chose which picture we were to see. I think that in some way he reached a mental finger into our minds, pressing the button labelled 'fear'. The things we saw we each made up ourselves. The things we have the greatest horror of."

I went to stand by the open door, looking across the garden towards the hill. I felt sure that was the explanation. And there was something else I felt sure about, only this was something I wasn't going to tell Joan. The first time it had happened to me it had only been a warning. But now, this time, it had been something very different. A place had been deliberately chosen. An attempt had been made to send us plunging into the ravine. We would both have been killed, or very badly maimed, on the rocks far below. There could have been another inquest; another verdict of accidental death.

Behind me, Joan asked anxiously: "What are you thinking about, Gordon?"

I turned to face her, searching for something to say in place of the truth. I found it, and another point worth bearing in mind against the future.

"The first time, when it happened to me, I had been thinking about Roddy just before. It was the same up the hill. We had both been talking about him only seconds before it started. It could be that there has to be a link between his mind and ours before he can press that button. I don't know . . . And it may be that he has to be somewhere close by; I don't know that either."

"Why has he followed us to Charidon?" she asked quietly.

I shook my head. "He may have been here already. He wasn't in class on Friday." Another thought struck me. "I wonder if he knows about Peter as well as Tony?"

Then the landlady was back again, relieved to see Joan smiling, commiserating with her, then remembering to tell us that dinner would be ready in twenty minutes.

Before we went upstairs to bed, a little after eleven, I made Joan drink two more brandies, hoping they would help her drop off to sleep quickly so that there would be no question of her lying awake, reliving the day.

On the landing she reached up to touch my cheek with soft fingers.

"I'm sorry, Gordon."

It was the most natural thing in the world for me to lower my head so that I could kiss her.

My bedroom was small, with low beams that all but grazed my head while I undressed. The window was open to the night, the curtain moving gently with the soft breeze. Moonlight spilled silver-blue across the floor and up the wall. I smoked a last cigarette standing looking out over the silent countryside. The hills, black and silver shapes, were so near I could have reached out and touched them.

There was no way of telling how long I'd been asleep. I woke up—or fancied I woke, for I could have been dreaming —pushing myself upright against the pillows, listening intently. It was as if someone had called my name from a long way away, the sound still echoing in my head. An odd feeling of urgent compulsion took me out of bed and to the window.

The moon was high now, almost overhead, only the carpet beneath the window holding two oblongs of moon-glow. I looked outside.

Immediately below the window was a small open area of crazy-paving, bounded by shadowy clumps of bushes. A figure stood to one side, the ghost-figure of a boy wearing a white shirt and dark trousers, shadow-dappled and indistinct, the upturned face a pale, featureless blur.

A voice drifted up to me, a memory of the voice that had brought me awake.

"Mr. Seacombe. . . ."

47

I leaned out, narrowing my eyes.

"Blake?"

"I didn't mean for it to happen that way, Mr. Seacombe. Please go away. Go back home. . . ."

"What are you doing out there?"

"Go back home again. . . ."

The voice died away; the figure melted into the darkness and was gone. I went back to bed. And next morning, in the full glory of the sunshine of a new day, I didn't speak of it to Joan because I couldn't be sure that it had happened, that it hadn't been a dream.

We caught the ten-fifteen bus outside the inn.

Banford was a small, hybrid sort of place, an odd mixture of market town and manufacturing centre. Leaving our cases at the bus depot we sat over coffee in a café, the first one we came to, with stained, marble-topped tables and not over-clean display cabinets that were a jumble of cigarette cartons and fiercely-iced cakes.

After her night's sleep Joan looked none the worse for her experience. She had changed to a daffodil-yellow frock that blended happily with her corn-coloured hair and the tan tinge the sun had brought to her small features.

"I suppose you'll just have to choose a doctor at random, Gordon," she asked.

"The first surgery we come to," I replied.

We didn't have to walk far. Joan spotted the brass plate on the door of the small terraced house five minutes after leaving the café. "F. Yarrow, M.D. Surgery: 10.00 a.m.—11. 30 a.m." I looked at my watch. We would just be in time to catch the doctor before he presumably set off on his rounds.

Dr. Yarrow was young, in his middle-thirties was my guess, with a thin, harassed-looking face and a shock of unruly black hair. There were no patients in the waiting room, and the surgery door stood open. In his shirt sleeves he was washing his hands at a sink in one corner.

"New faces," he commented, wiping his hands.

"Not potential patients I'm afraid, Doctor," I said.

He shrugged his shoulders into a blue jacket before glancing significantly at his watch.

"We will only take up a few minutes of your time," I told him quickly.

He regarded us from under suspicious brows. "Not representatives I hope?"

"Nothing like that. This is Miss Grey. My name is Seacombe. You may have heard of my brother, Harold Ferris-Seacombe."

48

"Mr. Ferris-Seacombe?" He had an engaging smile. "Endothelial venous thrombosis? The current *Lancet?"*

"More than likely. I know he contributes regularly to the medical journals."

"You'd better sit down," invited Dr. Yarrow cordially. "And how may I help you?"

"We are trying to unearth certain facts that my brother may use in his work," I started, which was, in a way, true enough. "Miss Grey and I are school-teachers. One of our pupils happens to be an adopted child, a twin. We are trying to trace the other twin."

I paused, inviting his comment.

He nodded. "Go on, Mr. Seacombe."

"They were adopted through a nursing home here in Banford. The place closed down some years back——"

"The Harvey-Gorton." He smiled faintly. "I know about it."

"We are hoping that we may be able to get in touch with either the late proprietors or a member of the staff. We thought that a local doctor would be the best person to tackle."

"Yes." Hands in pockets, Dr. Yarrow leaned against his desk. "I've been in practice here for five years. The Harvey-Gorton closed down the year before I came. But I've heard quite a lot about it since.

"It was run by a Mr. and Mrs. Hulton, and by all accounts they ran it pretty close to the law. If you know what I mean. They didn't have much of a staff. There was a cook, a Mrs. Faber, and her husband who acted as gardener and general handyman. A Miss Martha Young, a nurse of sorts, was the only other member of the staff. I think that quite a lot of local people must have known what was going on." He shrugged. "Nobody did anything about it; lack of proof, perhaps. There was talk of an enquiry when the place closed down but nothing came of it. Ostensibly it was a home for elderly people who could afford to pay little less than it would have cost them to spend their remaining years in a hotel.

"The way I see it, the Martha Young I mentioned was responsible for the adoption side-line. She had an affair, God knows who with, and a subsequent happy, or unhappy, event. The Hultons unofficially disposed of the unwanted child. That must have been how it started. The place closed down when Hulton died and his wife decided to call it a day. She left the district, as did the Fabers. I've no idea where any of them are now. But Miss Young was lucky enough to drop into a housekeeper-cum-nurse position looking after an elderly widower. His name's Foley, and he lives at Haverton

House, about a mile out of town on the main road. She may be able to help you.

"The home itself was sold just as it stood, complete with furniture, to a firm of hotel proprietors. Now it's called the Banford Temperance Hotel." He grinned. "And that's the full, sordid story."

"Which is more than I had been hoping for," I told him gratefully. "What kind of person is this Miss Young? Approachable?"

He grinned again. "Would you be talkative about your past if it had been as shady as hers?" He became serious. "I'm not Mr. Foley's doctor, but I have come up against Miss Young. She has a certain respect, perhaps in deference to her profession, for medical men. You have my permission to use my name if it will be of any help."

I thanked him again.

"Twins. . . ." he mused. "Perhaps something out of the usual?"

"I believe it is unusual for twins to be separated early on in life," I replied evasively.

He raised a dark eyebrow. "That wasn't what I meant. All right. But if you do come up with anything interesting you might let me know. Reflected glory and all that. Your brother is quite a big noise up in town."

Outside again, Joan took my arm. "That was a lucky break, Gordon."

"Two leads," I agreed.

"Two?"

"The nursing home was sold fully furnished. There's a good chance that the Hultons kept records and those same records may still be tucked away in some corner of the hotel."

"Not much hope of that," she said doubtfully. "Martha Young's the best lead."

"If we can get her to talk. And don't forget that all this happened eleven years ago. Which is a long time for anyone to remember."

We had lunch at a small hotel that seemed to cater mainly for the farming fraternity. The place was packed, and we had to share a table with a couple of garrulous farmers' wives. We ate in silence, forced, despite ourselves, to listen to an animated discussion upon a proposed scheme to bring sewage facilities to one of the outlying districts; a discussion, the personal ramifications of which did little to enhance the pleasure of the meal.

Afterwards, we found our way to Haverton House. It was a pleasant enough walk once we had left a cluster of small industrial plants behind. The road climbed steadily through a new estate where the postage-stamp gardens were still uncultivated. Haverton House stood alone, perhaps half a mile beyond the estate. When we reached the double, wrought-iron gates that opened on to a sweeping drive leading towards a grandly-porticoed door, I had certain misgivings. It is one thing to visit the owner of a house; quite another to call on a member of his staff. First impressions might be important; I didn't want to start off on the wrong foot with Miss Young.

"Front door, or tradesman's entrance?" I asked Joan.

She smiled gaily, seeming to be enjoying the novelty of the adventure.

"I suppose it all depends upon her status in the *ménage*. The elderly widower-unattached housekeeper arrangement could have all sorts of possibilities."

We made our way round the side of the house. In the yard a muddy-complexioned maid with bedraggled hair was shaking out a mat in a desultory fashion. She listened, gaping, to my request, then popped her head inside the kitchen, shrieking, "Miss Young! Folks fer you . . . !"

Martha Young had an intimidating, harshly-angular grey face topped with a pathetic incongruity of over-frizzed and patently dyed yellow hair. She wore the pretence of a nurse's uniform—a blue dress with white cuffs and collar and dangling breast-watch.

I said: "We've come on a rather delicate and personal matter. Dr. Yarrow suggested that you may be able to help us in an enquiry we're making."

Then I introduced myself and Joan, and threw in mention of Brother Harold for good measure. With no relaxing of her grim features she invited us to follow her inside.

We sat on uncomfortable, tall-backed chairs in a musty-smelling, over-furnished room. Now came the business of breaking through her shell and instilling some kind of confidence. I spoke slowly and carefully, trying to choose each word with care.

"Before I start, Miss Young, I have to say that anything you may tell me will not go any further. . . ." That didn't sound right. I qualified hastily: "At least so far as names and personalities are concerned. . . ." Had she understood? She nodded curtly without any change of expression, standing with her back to the window, hands clasped across the blue concavity of her waist. I launched into my story.

At the end, before she had time to speak, I added: "We

have no interest of any kind in the Harvey-Gorton Nursing Home or what went on there. All we are concerned with is trying to trace the people who adopted the first of the twin babies."

There was a long silence. Miss Young seemed to be making up her mind. I found it difficult to keep my eyes on her intimidating gaze.

I said hesitantly, in an attempt to break the silence: "I know that it's a long time ago, but——"

"I recall the occasion very well, Mr. Seacombe," she said coldly. "They were the only twins that passed through our—Mrs. Hulton's hands. But I am in no position to tell you much about it that you don't already seem to know. They were about a year old when they were brought in. As you say, they were adopted within a few days of each other by different people. At the time I thought it a great pity that they should have been split up in that way. I said as much to Mrs. Hulton. She told me that the man who took the first one had been adamant in refusing to take both. And when we later tried to contact him, the people who had taken the second baby asking if we could get the first one back, we were unable to locate him. I cannot remember his name."

"Do you remember anything about the people who brought them in?"

"As it happened I was present at the time. Mrs. Hulton was always very careful when taking in children. She always made a point of making sure that everything was as it should be." I wondered just what that meant. "A woman brought them in; a middle-aged woman and a farmer's wife by her appearance and speech. But that is only my personal assessment. She told us that their mother was dead, that she was the aunt, and that she had been taking care of them but had found them too much to cope with. She refused to give her name, or that of the parents. But when Mrs. Hulton insisted upon some kind of reference she mentioned the doctor who had recommended her to the Home. That is all I can tell you, Mr. Seacombe."

Which was little enough. I tried to disguise my disappointment. At least there was still one potential lead.

"Can you remember the doctor's name, Miss Young?"

Concentration brought no change to her mask-like expression.

"It was unfamiliar to me, and so obviously not the name of one of the local doctors. But Mrs. Hulton accepted it without question. An unusual name. . . ." Her lips moved silently while she tested syllables. "Marsh. . . . That was part of it.

Yes." Certainty but no triumph at the discovery. "Tidmarsh."

Somewhere in the house a bell rang softly as I came to my feet, thankfully sparing the formality of protracted gratitude. She ushered us out, this time through the front door.

On the step she asked; "If your enquiries are successful will that mean that the children will come together?"

"It is more than likely," I replied cautiously.

She seemed in no great hurry to answer the bell.

"I'm pleased, Mr. Seacombe. I hope you are successful. They should never have been parted in the first place." She closed the door.

"I wonder what it would take to make her smile?" I remarked to Joan as we went down the drive. Perhaps it was an unkind thing to say. It could be that Miss Young had little in life to smile about.

"She couldn't always have been like that," Joan said wisely. She looked back at the house, a lonely, grey inhospitable-looking place. "I feel sorry for her, Gordon. I think she must have taken it badly when the babies were separated. At least she did do her best to help us."

"Dr. Tidmarsh; whoever he may be. And if that is his name. She sounded certain enough, but when people have to take their minds back over the years they can come up with mistakes. It's little enough to go on."

She took my arm as we swung into the road. "Another visit to Dr. Yarrow?"

I nodded: "He'll be the best one to ask. I don't remember seeing any mention of an evening surgery on his plate, though."

"There wasn't."

"I shouldn't think he lives on the premises. Doctors usually go in for larger houses than that."

"The hotel then?"

"Two birds with the one stone," I told her. "I mean, we've got to find somewhere to stay the night. We can have another chat with Yarrow tomorrow morning."

6

The Banford Temperance Hotel was an unlovely building with a yellow-stone porch, off-yellow curtains to the windows, and an air of solid, Victorian boarding-house respectability.

We signed the register and the aquiline-faced, beehive-haired receptionist revolved the book, read the entries, inspected the empty floor at our feet and said: "No luggage?" in a tone compounded of suspicion and artificial refinement.

"At the bus station," I explained.

Two keys were laid in front of us. "Faive and seven. Will you be partaking of tea?"

"A happy thought," I agreed gravely, avoiding Joan's eye. There was no time like the present.

"I wonder if it would be possible for us to have a word with the proprietor?"

"The manager," she corrected, eyebrows reaching for the ginger hair-line.

"The manager, then?"

"Mr. Payne?"

"Mr. Payne," I said patiently.

We were shown into a small office. Mr. Payne was white-haired, ponderously-jowled, and had a habit of latching his thumbs into the pockets of his blue waistcoat. He reeked of some kind of disinfectant, and listened to my story with many interruptions and steadily-growing mistrust.

"An unusual request, Mr.—er—."

I reminded him of my name for the third time.

"Yes. . . . You have proof of your—er—intentions?"

I could see his point. When you run an hotel you can't be too careful. Especially with guests who come without luggage and start off by asking permission to search through any articles of furniture the hotel might have inherited from the previous owners.

I suggested that Dr. Yarrow would probably vouch for us. I also gave him the phone numbers of both St. Vincent's Hospital and Mr. Gregg's private address. He was impressed but not satisfied. I hoped he wouldn't take me up on the headmaster's reference. He didn't. Reaching for the phone he said: "Myrtle. Put me through to Dr. Yarrow. You'll find his number in the book."

Five minutes later he was preparing to help us in our search. I made a mental note to apologise to and thank the doctor the next time we met.

"This desk," said Mr. Payne, "and that bureau were here when we took over. We emptied them. Yes. The attics." He approved his suggestion. "Most certainly the attics. There is quite a lot of stuff stored up there. So far as I can recall nothing was destroyed. Keep a thing seven years and you will find a use for it." An idea came to him. "It will be seven years since we took possession, Mr.—er. Quite a coincidence." We laughed politely. Then he led the way along passages and up stairs.

The "attics" was one long room extending the width of the building. Furniture was piled to one side. So far as I could see there was nothing resembling a filing cabinet. He indicated a pile of cardboard boxes. I dropped to my knees on the dusty floor and busied myself untying knots. Joan helped while Mr. Payne watched from the centre of the room.

We found what we were looking for in a boot-box; a small notebook filled with dates, names and addresses. I flicked through the pages. There it was. "5 September 1953. Admitted: twins, (male). Age: approx. twelve months." On the facing leaf was the entry that clinched the thing. "18 September 1953. Mr. Blake, Gorton Cottage, Cookley." Which meant the entry before that was the one we were after. "16 September 1953. Mr. Brereton, Lowton Villa, Kendly."

"Brereton," Joan said over my shoulder as I jotted down the details.

"You've found what you were looking for?" asked Mr. Payne with some surprise. I think that until that moment he had still harboured doubts of our intentions. He came to breathe heavily over my other shoulder. "Kendly. That's quite near. About ten miles away."

Downstairs again he showed us where we could clean up before partaking of tea. It seemed now that he was all out to make up for his earlier lack of enthusiasm. He came to me in beaming good humour where I waited at the dining-room door for Joan to come down the stairs.

"A thought came to me, Mr.—er." He gestured vaguely in the direction of the reception hall. "I assume it will be your intention to go to Kendly?"

"That's our next move," I agreed.

"I see that you haven't a car. Kendly is a mere handful of

houses and farms, with no regular bus service. You will find it difficult to get out there. It struck me that I may be of help. On Thursdays I always send a van out that way, to collect fresh vegetables. I prefer to buy direct from the producers rather than pay the exorbitant prices demanded in the local market-place. I would be only too pleased to offer you a lift."

"That's very thoughtful of you," I agreed doubtfully, picturing an uncomfortable and perhaps far from clean journey in the rear of a bucketing lorry.

He smiled at my tone. "Perhaps 'van' is a misnomer. A stationwagon, in fact; driven by Dodd, my handyman. A comfortable car driven by an experienced er—driver."

That was different. "If it won't be putting you to any trouble. . . ."

He raised repudiating hands. "A pleasure, Mr.—er. Shall we say ten o'clock?"

Later that evening Joan and I strolled through the town, going in the opposite direction from that we had taken on our way to talk to Miss Young. This seemed to be the older part of the place, unspoiled as yet by factories or ribbon-development. Closely-packed shops gave way to terraced houses and then to larger villas. There was a park and a red-brick, doll's house hospital, and then the open country. We stopped by a small stone bridge that spanned a stream of slow-running, brown water. There was a cluster of farm buildings to one side; a tall briar hedge to the other. Joan rested her elbows on the wall, gazing down into the fascination of running water.

She said: "When you were talking to Miss Young, Gordon; did it cross your mind to mention that they are triplets, not twins, to see what her reaction would be?"

"I'm afraid it didn't," I confessed.

"Or to ask if she'd noticed anything odd about the babies?"

"They were only in the Home for about ten days, Joan. And don't forget that we've both been teaching Roddy for a year without noticing anything out of the ordinary about him."

"Babies always laugh a lot," she mused. "Looking back, I can't ever once remember seeing Roddy smile. But you don't pay all that much attention to the way a schoolboy behaves. Babies are different. You expect them to smile. If they don't, you get to thinking something's wrong. You know what I'm trying to say."

"I know," I agreed, and then, although the evening was warm, for some reason I shivered violently.

"Someone walking over my grave," I told her lightly when

56

she glanced up with widening eyes. I took out my cigarettes and offered them to her. There was no danger here; no ravine. . . . Only a bridge across a shallow stream, a dusty road and a farm. He wouldn't try anything here. I found myself staring at the briar hedge.

"I wonder what kind of people the Breretons are?" Joan asked pensively.

"Lonely people by all accounts." There were deep shadows between a barn and a shed. "Kendly doesn't even own a bus service."

"We're not going to walk all that way?" She sounded dismayed. "It's ten miles according to Mr. Payne."

I laughed at her consternation. "Not to worry. Transport laid on. An estate car will be waiting for us at ten o'clock tomorrow morning. With the compliments of Mr. Payne and an experienced driver called Dodd who's going to the wilds to collect vegetables."

She blew an exaggerated sigh of relief. "It's not that I don't like walking, but ten miles if it's going to be as hot as today. . . ."

"Too much of a good thing," I agreed, and looked at my watch. "We'd better be making our way back. Dinner is partaken of at eight."

Joan giggled in an unteacherlike manner. "I wonder how long it took her to cultivate that refained accent?"

And idea came to her as we were making our way back. "A car to take us out there, Gordon. That's all very well. But how do we get back again? We don't know how long we'll be with the Breretons. We can't expect Dodd to wait for us. They'll want the vegetables at the hotel well before lunchtime."

"I hadn't thought about that," I had to admit ruefully.

"Can you drive?"

"I've still got my licence. But it's ages since I've driven a car. Why?"

We passed a garage on our way out where they were advertising a drive-hire service. I mean, we may have lots more running-about to do."

I chose a small black saloon. With Joan sitting contentedly enough by my side I drove it back to the hotel with great caution and some uneasiness. I was even rustier than I'd thought.

When Mr. Payne came to see if the dinner had been to our satisfaction I explained what I had done. I was also honest enough to confess that I wasn't all that happy about the arrangement. He was both sympathetic and understanding.

"I have never learned to drive myself, Mr.—er, but I believe that it is an art once learned, never forgotten. In any case, you will find little traffic on our country roads. A wise move on your part ... I have to admit that I hadn't considered your return journey. It would not do at all, not at all, to have two of my guests stranded out in the wilds." His laugh boomed through the room.

Thursday morning was another of bright sunshine. We left for Kendly shortly after half past nine. The road led past the sombre house where Miss Young nursed and kept house for her elderly widower. I was beginning to get the feel of the car, accelerating adventurously but unwisely, taking an unexpected corner too quickly, then having to brake suddenly at a sign: "Caution. Dangerous Hill." We dropped steeply, swinging at the bottom through a narrow-arched railway bridge, the engine roaring and echoing momentarily in the confined space. Then we were climbing up into the sunlight again.

There was no mention of Kendly on any of the sign-posts we passed. I stopped to make enquiries at a cottage, and an old man with dangling braces told me that we were, in fact, already in Kendly, and the house we wanted was perhaps quarter of a mile ahead, off the main road. . . . "Hid-like, so's you can't see it from road, but there's a lane'll take you right to the front door."

We found the turning, and as we drove along the narrow lane I said: "And how do we play this one, Joan?"

"The mixture as before," she rejoined; "Conscientious school-teachers trying to re-unite parted twins. Unless you have a better idea."

I hadn't. After all, that was partly the truth.

Lowton Villa was tucked away in a half-circle of sheltering trees. It was larger than I had imagined, a dignified-looking house with half-timbered walls, pseudo-mullioned windows and a lawn that was a marvel of green velvet. It was a few moments before our knock was answered.

A tall gentleman with polished silver hair brushed into careful wings over each aristocratic ear surveyed us with a dignity that matched his surroundings. A dignity that was perhaps marred by the floral, frilled apron that incongruously adorned his waist, and the plate poised delicately upon one upturned palm. His grey suit was a miracle of tailoring; his pale lavender tie and matching breast-pocket handkerchief the epitome of discretion. His eyes took in our faces, Joan's yellow frock and the waiting car in one assessing gaze.

"This, then, is the day of which I have been warned," said

58

he, before we had time to introduce ourselves. "But I must admit to some slight feeling of disappointment. I had been led to believe that some sort of fancy-dress would be employed. Not that I have any fault to find with your attire, Madame. . . ." He bowed gracefully in Joan's direction. "Or your appearance as a whole. On the contrary. However"—he sighed—"I had hoped to be confronted with an unveiled Aphrodite, rising from the foam, one hand extended, clutching a wealth of crisp fivers. But I suppose the line has to be drawn somewhere. You have but to name your product and I shall unhesitatingly speak the formula. Is it to be whiter than white? Or is yours the powder that does little more than wash whiter than the rest?"

It would be the easiest thing in the world to fall into his flowery way of speech. I fought down the temptation while Joan threw back her head and laughed.

"I'm afraid we have no connection with any soap firm," I told him. "We are nothing more than school-teachers."

He showed no great surprise.

"Your wire came—let me see—on Saturday. I hadn't expected it to be followed by a personal visit. It is kind of you to take time out to explain in greater detail. You, Madame"—his plate revolved in Joan's direction—"must therefore be the matron. Things have certainly improved since my school-days. As I recall, the matrons with whom I had dealings were for the greater part forbidding females with hirsute upper lips, an unfeeling way of slapping sticking-plaster on painful abrasions, and with invariable penchants for assistant-headmasters."

I took advantage of his pause for breath.

"I'm afraid you are mistaking us for someone else, sir. We come from a school in Cookley."

"Cookley?" The plate sank to waist level. "Then you haven't come to talk about my grandson?"

"Would you be Mr. Brereton?"

"I would indeed."

"Then it is quite possible that it is your grandson we would like to discuss with you."

"In that case. . . ." He stepped invitingly aside. "I was in process of preparing my first sustenance of the day. It would give me great pleasure to offer you doubtful coffee and whatever we may come across in the wealth of cupboards at our disposal."

We followed him to a kitchen of spotless white enamel, gleaming chrome and polished surfaces that might have been lifted bodily from the pages of a glossy magazine.

"I am in sole charge of the establishment," our host informed us, "my son and his wife being on holiday in Greece, and the maid—I use the term in its loosest sense—having a day off."

Laying his plate on the table he eyed a coffee percolator with small enthusiasm.

"May I be of help?" Joan asked tentatively.

Removing his apron he handed it to her with a gesture.

"You will earn my lifelong devotion," he assured her magnificently.

Drawing a chair to the table he invited me to be seated. Before joining me, the careful silver wings of his hair had to be smoothed into place, and a tie that required no attention adjusted with precise finger-tips.

"My name is Seacombe," I informed him, fighting and temporarily losing the urge to fall into his way of speaking. "The lady ministering to your creature comforts is Miss Grey."

He made a small ceremony of shaking hands. Then he took the opportunity of instructing her in the kitchen lay-out.

"You will find cake in the container to your right; biscuits in the cupboard above your head. The controls beneath operate the television apparatus. The radio is next door to the refrigerator, where you will find my daily milk ration. The coffee is already out. I think that covers all possible contingencies."

He turned a rueful gaze in my direction.

"A place for everything, and everything in its place. The outward manifestation of an over-regimented existence. Have you heard of my son, Mr. Seacombe?"

"I don't think so, sir."

"R. Harris Brereton. *The Elementary Principles of Child Psychology.*"

"I've read it," I told him. It had been on the list of Gregg's compulsory reading. A "spoil the rod, spare the child" doctrine that had made me writhe. Over-tolerance carried to nauseating limit. I had no intention of being drawn into a discussion upon the merits or otherwise of the work.

"I have a boy in my form, Mr. Brereton. His name is Rodney Blake. He was adopted from a nursing home in Banford eleven years ago. We are trying to locate his twin brother who was adopted a few days earlier."

"And you have reason to think that my grandson may be this brother?"

An odour of coffee started to permeate the room. Spoons rattled cosily in saucers.

"Yes, Mr. Brereton."

"You may be right. All the facts seem to indicate that you are correct. My grandson was adopted by Harris eleven years ago from a place in Banford. The people there told him at the time that he was one of twins and tried to persuade him to take both. But Harris refused. One child was all he needed."

His voice had lost all its former flamboyance, becoming the slightly unsteady voice of an old man.

"You must understand that once Harris has made up his mind upon a course of action it is impossible to divert him from it. He has no children of his own; an unfortunate position for a child psychologist, about to write a volume about upbringing, to find himself in. Do you follow?"

"Yes, sir," I replied. Joan brought cups to the table. She set a plate of biscuits between us. It remained untouched.

"What is your grandson like in appearance?" I asked him. A description of features could lead to a description of mannerisms, perhaps of certain peculiarities.

Mr. Brereton said: "If you will excuse me," and went out of the kitchen. Joan pushed the sugar bowl towards me, and I helped myself automatically.

"Adopted just so the author of a book would be able to say he had a son of his own," Joan said in a low voice.

"That's how it seems. At least, that seems to be the impression he's trying to give."

Mr. Brereton returned with a bulky folder. Seating himself, he laid it unopened on the table.

"I'll try to explain." His flair for words seemed to have deserted him. Now he had to pause, searching for the right expressions. "Even for school-teachers it will take a lot of understanding. So far as Harris was concerned, the boy was merely part of a means to an end. That seems a cold-blooded thing to say, but I see no point in trying to disguise my feelings. In many ways he was an odd child. He had no time for the usual toys. At the age of five he was sent to a kindergarten. Then to boarding school. He has been there ever since. The last time I saw him was some three years ago when he returned here for a short stay when changing from a junior school to a senior."

He laid his hands on the folder.

"You might say this is a summary of his existence. Reports, records, letters from his teachers. . . . Harris has an arrangement with the school so that he can keep check on the boy's progress. He keeps him there even during the holidays, but apparently my grandson finds that no great hardship. He is given a free rein in the physic and chemistry laboratories.

The latest report that came, barely a week ago, points out in glowing terms that he has a great future as a physicist."

Producing a pair of heavy, black-rimmed spectacles, Mr. Brereton set them on his face before opening the folder.

"He doesn't seem to have any interest in sports or organised activities of any kind. That means no photographs of cricket or football elevens. But there is this. . . ."

"This" was a photograph of a group of perhaps a hundred serious-faced boys, arranged in the inevitable tiers, the front row squatting uncomfortably cross-legged. Rodney Blake's face stared unsmilingly up at me from the centre of the third row, the sweep of pitch-black hair, the high bones and hollow cheeks unmistakable. I laid my finger on it.

"Yes," said Mr. Brereton. "That's Simon."

And because I had been so sure that the name would be "Tony" my head jerked up and I echoed: "Simon?" incredulously. Joan put her cup down quickly, clattering in the saucer.

"You sound surprised," Mr. Brereton remarked. His eyes went from my face to Joan's coffee-flooded saucer.

The first piece of the new puzzle was the wrong shape. And the other pieces?

"I suppose that if Simon had any sort of illness, however slight, the school would keep you informed?" I suggested to Mr. Brereton.

He nodded slowly. "The matron is a very efficient and conscientious woman."

"Did he happen to have a bad attack of toothache last August?"

Mr. Brereton looked hard at me before lowering his eyes to the folder and leafing through papers.

"Last August. Here we are. Treated for small acid burn left hand. That's all. No mention of toothache. Why do you ask, Mr. Seacombe?"

He would have to have an explanation of some kind; there were more questions still to be answered.

"We know now that my pupil and your grandson are twins. We think there may be a kind of——" What was the right expression? "A kind of sympathy between them."

"I see. . . ." He didn't seem very sure.

"Is Simon right or left-handed?"

He had to think. "He's a south-paw, as our American cousins have it." He smiled faintly.

"And does he happen to have scars on his arms?"

"You seem well-informed, Mr. Seacombe. I take it that your pupil is similarly endowed?"

I nodded: "I haven't seen them for myself. His parents tell me that both his arms have white scars reaching from wrist to elbow."

"Simon," Mr. Brereton stated, "is scarred only on one arm. The right. Harris was very curious about it. A specialist said that it was clearly the result of some kind of surgery." He added significantly: "Done very shortly after birth. Does that convey anything to you, Mr. Seacombe?"

"I'm not sure. . . ." The puzzle was becoming even more confusing. The word "surgery" had opened up a fresh field of thought. I needed time. . . .

"Did anything unusual happen to him two years ago?" Joan asked suddenly.

He looked at her, adjusted his glasses and bent over the folder again, searching through the miscellany, finding type-written slips, reading, rejecting, shaking his head. . . .

"Nothing so far. Wait, though . . . there's something here. 'Treated for severe bruising of both thighs. Simon unable to offer any explanation for injuries. Had not been participating in any kind of sport. No accident of any kind. Denies that another boy responsible.' "

He glanced up. "Another sympathy-link for us?"

"Another link," I agreed. Then: "Has he ever run away from school?"

"I gather that Rodney Blake must have the same failing. Yes, Mr. Seacombe; at frequent intervals. But he always returns under his own steam, refusing to say where he's been, ready to accept his punishment. In point of fact the last item in his dossier—as Harris insists upon calling it—is the wire that came last Saturday informing us that he has skipped once again."

For all I felt inadequate to cope on the spot with this new complication of facts, a suspicion was beginning to form in my mind. There was one last thing I had to know. But was it the sort of thing a school matron would think of including in a written report?

"Like Simon," I said, "Rodney is a boy who keeps himself to himself. He has no friends. According to his parents he invented a playmate for himself. . . ."

There was no need to go any further.

"That takes us back to his first school," said Mr. Brereton, busy in the folder again. "Here we are. Mention of recurrent nightmares. Boy waking up screaming. A suggestion that psychiatric treatment might benefit. . . ."

He permitted a smile to cross his features.

"A suggestion that Harris took very badly. There was a

63

brisk interchange of correspondence. That was when Simon's make-believe companion came to light. Complete with name. The same name, apparently, he shouted aloud during his nightmares. The matron wrote asking if he knew anyone called. . . ." He waited.

"Tony," I supplied.

"Yes," said Mr. Brereton, leaning back and removing his glasses. "Tony. And that, you know, strikes me as being the oddest link of all."

The last piece of an old picture; the start of a new. Rodney, Peter and Simon. And somewhere else, another boy called Tony. That was the only way it could be. Not three of them. Four.

"I think"—Mr. Brereton intruded on my thoughts—"that there is much more to this than meets the eye. If you will forgive the use of the hackneyed expression." His former flamboyance of speech seemed to be returning. "With all due respects to sympathetic school-teachers as a whole I can't see two of them making a long journey merely in an attempt to reunite separated twins. And when certain unusual facts come to light during the course of their investigations one gets the impression that perhaps everything isn't quite as it should be in the State of Denmark. Don't you think I deserve taking into your confidence? After all, my grandson is involved."

Thankfully, a phone shrilled, and with an apology he went to answer it. At least it would give us a few minutes in which to decide how much to tell him. I looked at Joan. She was staring down at her cup.

She asked in a low voice: "Four of them, Gordon?"

"We can't be certain of that."

"Quads. . . ." she marvelled softly. "That's if they were all born at the same time. But in that case, wouldn't we have heard about them before? Wouldn't it have been in all the papers?"

"Twelve years ago," I reminded her. "Even if there had been anything about it in the papers we'd have forgotten by now."

Mr. Brereton returned, looking puzzled.

"There's a Mr. Payne on the line, Mr. Seacombe. He sounds very upset. I think you'd better have a word with him."

The phone was in the hall. Mr. Payne's voice, worry and relief struggling for supremacy, babbled almost incoherently over the line.

"Thank God, Mr. Seacombe. I was worried in case it was worse than it is. After what you said I was afraid that you

64

may have changed your mind. I didn't see Dodd start out. I've been imagining the worst; I had to make certain. . . . It was my suggestion, you see; if you had been in it, then I would have felt responsible. The police have only just this minute called me up. But they hadn't the full report. They don't know how it could have happened. No other vehicles involved. All they could tell me was that the driver had been killed. They didn't know whether there were any passengers. . . ."

After a while, the story finally clear, I return to the kitchen to face Joan's enquiring gaze. Mr. Brereton was tactfully busying himself replacing papers in the folder.

"There's been an accident," I said. "At the railway bridge. Dodd, the hotel handyman, has been killed. They don't know how it happened. Mr. Payne has worried in case we'd changed our minds and gone with him."

I watched the colour drain from Joan's face.

"If we hadn't hired that car, Gordon. . . ."

"We were lucky," I said as steadily as I was capable of.

"A shocking affair," Mr. Brereton said in a hushed voice. "Terrible. . . . I knew Dodd quite well. He comes—used to come this way at least twice every week. He must know the road like the palm of his hand. I can't understand it. He was a most careful driver. . . ."

And then a picture came to build itself in my mind: a boy climbing to a roof to throw himself off to his death. Another picture as the first faded: an abyss that moved its crumbling verge under my feet, forcing me back to where a real ravine waited. And yet another. . . . A car hurtling down a hill, the driver's face a mask of senseless fear, hurtling down to smash against the side of the bridge. . . .

Another inquest, there would be; another verdict of accidental death. And if we hadn't changed our minds, there would have been three bodies instead of just the one. . . .

I knew it was useless trying to hide my face so that Joan shouldn't read its expression. She would know as well as I did how the accident had been caused. And why it had been caused.

"He must have done it," she breathed in horror. "He must have thought we were in the car. . . ."

Brereton said: "I don't know what all this is about, but I think it's time you told me just what is going on."

7

"I think I could use some more coffee," was all Mr. Brereton had to say when I had finished. "How about you? No"—as Joan made to rise—"permit me."

Bringing the percolator to the table, he refilled the cups and then set it down carefully. He regarded it in silence for a few moments, then:

"Quite a story. One that strains credulity to the breaking-point. I think that I am prepared to accept it. For one thing, little though I have seen of him, I have always had the feeling that Simon was not as other children. For another, I feel that I have had proof enough of the strange links that exist between the boys. A coincidence set you off on the trail. It has led to another coincidence; the death of Dodd.

"It would appear, Seacombe, that at least one of the children is possessed of extraordinary powers. Powers that again I am prepared to accept, assuming them to be some kind of development from certain thought-projectory faculties that one hears mentioned from time to time. I am also ready to accept your theory that there are four of them. Or even more. . . ."

He slanted a silver-grey eyebrow in my direction.

"Had you considered that possibility?"

"We haven't come up with anything that suggests there are more than four," I told him.

"No. Four it shall be. And up until now you have been trying to cope on your own?"

"That's about it, sir."

"While appreciative of the implied deference," said Mr. Brereton plaintively, "I would much rather you didn't call me 'sir.' It makes me feel older than I am. For what it's worth, my full name is Bartholomew Ignatius, which offers a surprisingly large variety of alternatives. I have always felt most strongly that a child should have some say at its christening. At school I was called 'Iggy' by my enemies, and 'Berty' by my friends. In latter life, fortunately, 'Bart' has come to be the accepted abbreviation."

I was grateful now for the anti-climax of his affected manner of speech. That it was affected I felt sure. I saw it as part of a self-imposed defensive armour against an over-bearing son with a rigidly narrow outlook. We spent a few light minutes enlarging upon the earlier, more formal introductions.

"Gordon," said he, "and Joan. Yes. Now where were we? You were about to tell me how you had been trying to cope on your own."

"We have nothing to go on save suspicion based upon coincidences," I explained. "Our idea was first to try to find Rodney's twin brother—at that time we thought there were only the two of them—and then the real parents. It seemed reasonable to suppose that they might all share the same peculiarities. If they did, then we would have something concrete to set in front of Brother Harold."

"Brother Harold being Mr. Ferris-Seacombe?"

"Yes."

"Sensible enough," Bart approved. "As I see it, that was all you could do. Unless you were prepared to make fools of yourselves. And now?"

"We've learned a whole lot more, but we still haven't got anything substantial."

"I'm inclined to agree with you, Gordon. Let us try to put ourselves in your brother's shoes. First, the links. I understand that such sympathy attachments between identical twins are not uncommon, although certainly not to the extent of those you have demonstrated. Your brother, in his medical wisdom, would brush such evidence aside. Let us take Rodney's apparent ability to induce thought-pictures. You have both had first-hand experience of this. But undoubtedly your brother would suggest that you had merely suffered some kind of hallucination. The death of the schoolboy and Dodd's accident would certainly not be acceptable as evidence. As you say, we have nothing substantial to lay before responsible authority. Our next move is clear; we investigate the next lead."

It seemed that he was taking the thing out of our hands.

"Dr. Tidmarsh," I said with some resentment.

He smiled gently at my tone.

"My grandson is involved, Gordon. Oddly enough, I think a great deal of him. Does that surprise you? Perhaps it does. He was never at any time what one might call a lovable child. But neither was Harris."

Of Rodney: "We wished we'd never took him," the Blakes had mourned.

"I'd give my right arm if I hadn't adopted him," Mrs. Latham had said of Peter.

It seemed that Bart was different. But then he had had little to do with his adopted grandson.

"Three heads are better than one," he said tritely. "And I do have a certain standing. Connections could easily become important. The Chief Constable happens to be a personal friend of mine."

I glanced at Joan. She was looking down at the table.

"We had no intention of trying to exclude you," I said lamely. But I had to find an excuse for my apparent boorishness. There was one all ready. "But you must realise it could be dangerous."

"That thought had occurred to me," he replied grimly. "Oddly enough, I have been trying to imagine what kind of picture would be produced if mental fingers, as you so aptly describe them, were to reach inside my mind for the button marked 'fear'. I can think of nothing. So far as I am aware I have no special fear, no phobia. It could be quite an enlightening experience. We must wait and see."

His tone almost gave the impression that he was looking forward to the experience. I found it difficult to imagine a man who harboured no fears at all.

"Dr. Tidmarsh," I reminded him, returning to the pre-diversion point.

He nodded. "I have never heard the name before. Let us hope that Dr. Yarrow is better informed. But for the moment. . . ." He paused. "When dealing with a problem of some complexity I have always found it a great help to get the facts down on paper."

A letter was taken from the folder and placed face down on the table. An elegant silver pencil was produced. Four match-stick men were drawn in a row.

"There we are. Right; the first one. What do we know about him? Hard facts, not supposition." His smile was disarming.

"Rodney Blake," I said. This wasn't the first time I had come to realise just how little I knew about one of my pupils. "Lives at Cookley. Excellent in English; mediocre in all other subjects. You know what he looks like. And that's about all we know about him."

"Don't forget the scars," Bart reminded, his pencil busy. "I find them most intriguing."

"Scars on both arms, then," I supplied. And added for good measure: "Right-handed."

"And the next one?"

"Peter Latham. Lives at Charidon. Left-handed; scars again on both arms. A talented artist. That's the lot. Apart from the fact that he may have the ability to start a fire from a distance away."

"But which we don't know for sure. Right. The next one I can fill in myself. Simon Brereton. Speciality: physics and chemistry. Left-handed; scar on right arm only. Which makes him different from the other two. And now we have to put a question mark under the last one. We can only assume that his name is Tony."

"And we think he may have had a bad attack of toothache last August," I added.

"Which again is only supposition. But a reasonable one at that. And it would also appear that he may be the gifted musician of the family. Remember Peter's sudden and inexplicable ability to play the piano?"

He pored over the diagrams. "One scar, two scars. There must be a reason why Simon has only the one. It has been attributed to surgery almost certainly performed very shortly after birth. We can assume that all the scars were caused in that same way at the same time. So what do we deduce from that?"

"Some kind of malformation that had to be corrected," I hazarded. "Birthmarks, possibly."

The answer didn't satisfy him.

"I don't think so. This must have been something in the nature of an emergency operation. Something that had to be done there and then."

I knew then what he was trying to make me say. But this was something I knew very little about. Such things did happen, but only rarely, usually making headlines in the papers. And so far as I knew the operations usually took place some time after birth, as soon as the babies were strong enough to stand the surgery.

"Are you trying to say that they had to be separated from each other?" I asked.

Instead of replying he folded the paper, tearing down the creases, producing four separate pictures of match-stick men, the knaves from some surrealistic pack of playing cards.

"Let us move them round," he said, "so—matching scar to scar. That puts Peter and Rodney in the centre with Simon and Tony on the wings as it were. And for the unknown quantity of Tony to fit into the pattern means that he will have one scar, on his left arm. And I would go even further and say that he will be right-handed. Does that make sense to you, Gordon, Joan?"

It could have been like that. They could have been born joined together from wrist to elbow. Not in a tight group, for then all would have had two scars, and Simon had only the one, but in a string. I could think of no other way in which to picture it to myself.

A string. . . .

Joan said quietly: "Like a row of paper dolls, joined arm to arm. . . ."

"Siamese quadruplets," Bart agreed. "I suppose we can call them that. Linked physically as well as mentally. Three cushions of flesh to be cut. Perhaps stitches. . . ." He stroked his chin. "A doctor, of course. . . . A doctor delivers quads and then performs the immediate surgery of separation. A unique event. And yet, you know, no one seems to know anything about it."

I looked at Joan. "When we first worked out that they might be quads we wondered why we hadn't heard about it. But it was twelve years ago, and we could easily have read it at the time and then forgotten. But if they had been joined, Siamese children. . . ."

"Glaring headlines. A seven-day wonder." Bart pointed to the television set. "Had we got those things twelve years back? I forget. But if we had, the screens would have been full of it. Pictures of everyone concerned would have been splashed in every paper in the country. It would have been something that none of us would have forgotten. Which means it wasn't there for us to read about and remember.

"What happened must have been kept a closely-guarded secret. If the slightest whisper had got about the reporters and the cameramen would have been there in their hundreds. The doctor kept his mouth shut. So did the parents. They must have known that publicity would certainly have brought financial rewards on a large scale. The doctor and the midwife— if there was a midwife—would have become famous. But nobody so much as breathed a word. And that, to say the least, is odd. Damned odd."

The coffee had grown cold and scummy in my cup. I stirred it for something to do, not intending to drink it. Joan gathered up the four sketches, fanned them, dropped them like a discarded poker hand.

"Or have we been letting our imaginations run riot?" Bart wondered into the silence.

He looked at the clock on the wall, a sleek affair of silver and enamel, with slender prongs for fingers and chrome dashes instead of numerals; a clock that would have been more in keeping as part of some complex electronic device.

70

"Almost half past eleven," he said unnecessarily, for Joan and I had both automatically turned to follow his gaze. "Perhaps we have left it too late to catch Yarrow before he leaves his surgery." He hoisted himself to his feet, flexing elegantly-slim shoulders. "I can but try."

When he had gone into the hall, pausing—habit-driven, perhaps—at the mirror by the door to check his appearance, Joan asked: "What do you think, Gordon?"

An odd sense of loyalty to the absent Bart made me shake my head. "I'm out of my depth, Joan. I don't know what to say."

I didn't tell her that I thought he was enjoying himself in his own way. That because he had had nothing to do with what had gone before, and hadn't seen, as I had, the crumpled body of a dying schoolboy, he was treating the whole thing as a kind of adventure, a welcome relief from the boredom of a lonely existence. That was what I thought. And perhaps, at that time, I was right.

"No luck," he announced from the door. "Missed him by five minutes. But some anonymous adenoidal female took a message. She will ask him to call in here sometime this afternoon."

He swung his glasses in a way that reminded me of Philby.

"I suggest that until we have spoken with Yarrow we try to forget the matter in hand. I resume my position as a host with two welcome guests to be entertained. But a host temporarily bereft of domestic staff. Fortunately lunch will present no great problem. There is a large variety of cupboards and receptacles, all stocked to bursting point with an assortment of cans. It will simply be a matter of choosing the right ones. In the meantime there is a garden I can show you. A very nice garden. Harris panned it with what I may call a scientific approach to the local contours. There are paths and unexpected vistas. A lake, even."

"Cans," remarked Joan, smiling and coming to her feet, "are all right in an emergency. I'm sure that if we were to look round we would find vegetables and meat. It isn't too late to get a real meal under way. That's if you have no objections?"

He had been hoping, I felt sure, for Joan to come up with just that suggestion. And he was as profuse, as I had known he would be, with his gratitude. He followed her to the gleaming lengths of tables, cookers and sinks.

"Are you sure you will be able to cope with all this?" He pointed out dials and switches.

"I'll find my way round," she assured him patiently.

When he was satisfied he led me out to the garden.

71

A terrace, bounded by a low stone wall, ran the width of the house. Wide steps dropped down to a lawn. There was a white statue of a dryad of some kind that crouched, gazing with empty eyes across the garden towards the distant hills. The ivy on the plinth had been trimmed to an artistic shape.

"A most attractive young lady," he remarked. He was looking at the undraped dryad. "Joan," he added.

"Yes," I said.

"Peace"—we were passing a rose-bed—"these." His hand touched the petals. "Are you interested in roses?"

"I'm afraid I know very little about them. These look very nice."

We trod a weed-free gravel path. Neat verges, geometric curves.

"A lovely view," I commented, looking at the hills. Trees and bushes had been planted in carefully descending lines, framing the distant slopes.

Coming to a place where a carved stone bench faced a half-circle of flowering bushes and the inevitable pre-selected vista, he stopped, producing a slim gold cigarette case. The case also held a lighter. There was no breeze from which the flame had to be shielded.

"You don't think I'm taking too much on myself?" he asked suddenly.

"No," I told him. "No." And I could think of nothing to add.

"This," one hand, cigarette between two fingers, swept to take in the garden, pointed towards the house, "and this. Harris'. Gardeners and maids." He looked at the glowing tip of his cigarette. "And Simon, too. Do you understand?"

"I think so."

"Harris has everything worked out. A young man has things to do. An old man—that's how he thinks of me—has his last years to live out. Living them should be a sufficiency in itself. I'm talking nonsense."

"No," I said again.

He rested his hands on the back of the bench; slender white hands that could have belonged to a woman.

"Simon. I've been thinking about him. If there is something wrong, if authority does have to step in, what will happen to him?"

That was something that had been at the back of my mind; something I had been trying not to think about. I shook my head dumbly.

"You see, one of them has killed. They could be all the

72

same. That other one—Peter—you say there was a pony. There could have been other things. Simon, too. . . .

"If they can prove to their satisfaction that Rodney was responsible for the death of that other boy, what will they do with him? And the others? Lock him—them, away somewhere? Or would the doctors, the scientists have their way with them?"

The cigarette burned unheeded between his fingers. My thoughts reached ahead of his. I knew the conclusion he was going to reach. Perhaps, despite myself, I had thought about it before, subconsciously.

"Something very different. . . ." He was thinking aloud rather than talking to me. "Something that authority has never had to cope with before. As alien as if they had come from some other world. How would we receive invaders from another planet if ever they came? If they came and killed . . . ?"

He wouldn't have heard me if I had tried to find an answer.

"Survival. Self-protection. The dominant instinct." He let the cigarette fall to the ground. "Dispose of the invaders before they do more damage, before more arrive. Dispose of the children before they become men."

He stared down at his hands.

"But it might not be like that at all."

"No," I said, and moved a little away from him, towards the end of the bench, resting one hand on the carved protuberance of a stone flower.

The branches of the trees were still, frozen to a wax-like immobility. The low screen of bushes and the hills they helped frame had lost perspective, becoming the painted backdrop of a stage. Nothing in the garden, or beyond, seemed to move.

Something started to stir in my mind. There was the old sensation of probing eyes. My hand clenched tightly on the stone ornament in anticipation of what I knew was to happen.

But there was no growing haziness to the scene, no melting and altering of shapes. This was something different. I could feel, sense, rather, the mental fingers probing into my thoughts, coiling, writhing as if seeking some focal point.

Contentment, reassurance, a feeling of well-being came flooding. The soothing hand of a mother for her child. The enclosing protective comfort of the family fireside while the gale batters futilely at the shuttered windows. The utter knowledge that all is well, that there is nothing to fear. But there was something else. . . . The fingers reached and probed. Sensations came and dissolved. And I knew, how I don't know,

73

that Rodney Blake was somewhere out among the trees, and that he was trying to tell me something.

Then it was all over. The fingers had gone, leaving in their place the terrible hollow emptiness of nothing. There was a timeless moment before I was able to take over again, my own thoughts gradually returning to fill the vacuum, my own personality taking hold.

Bart's gaze was hard on my face. I wondered how long he had been watching me, how long it had lasted. He knew that something had happened. I tried to explain how it had been. It was almost impossible to put into words. How does one describe a rainbow to a man who has never seen?

We walked slowly back to the house.

8

Dr. Yarrow arrived a few minutes after three. Bart opened the door to him, ushering him into the lounge where we had taken our after-lunch coffee. From the badinage that took place while they came along the hall it was obvious they were old friends. He was surprised to see us.

"Hullo? The private investigators. You seem to be getting around. And what brings you here to Kendly? Let me see, the last time I saw you you were bound for Haverton House and Miss Young. Any luck?"

"The trail led ultimately to Mr. Brereton," I told him, and he swung on Bart. "Not—?"

"Simon," Bart agreed. "Harris' adopted boy."

"I'm damned!" the other ejaculated. "It's a small world." He refused the offer of a drink—"On my rounds, you know"— and draped his lankiness across the arm and back of an easy chair.

'So what can I do for you this time?" The question was directed somewhere between Joan and me, but Bart answered it.

"Tidmarsh. Does the name mean anything to you?"

The doctor tried it for flavour. "Tidmarsh. No; I can't say it does. And I won't ask why you want to know."

"He's a doctor," Joan supplied.

74

"Dr. Tidmarsh. . . ." He plucked thoughtfully at his nether lip. Then: "You don't mean Old Toddidoc?"

"Who?" Bart wondered.

"Never heard of him? That's not unlikely now I come to think. His fame hasn't spread this far south. He keeps to the rural districts. I wouldn't have heard of him myself but for Dr. Pringle. You see, I took over my practice from a Dr. Pringle, and he has a brother, also a doctor, with a practice way out in the wilds. He's had several clashes with Old Toddidoc but has never been able to pin anything on him. It's 'Tod', by the way, not 'Tid'. Todmarsh. And the country folk call him 'doctor', even though he isn't qualified. A quack. Quite a local character; clerical rig and rides a tricycle. Rural witch-doctor, first class. Home-brewed potions and cow-dung poultices. You know the sort of thing." He grinned wryly. "Trouble is, they often work. Come to think, I haven't heard of him for some time."

"We think he was the one responsible for the twins being taken to the nursing home," I said. "At least, that's according to Miss Young. Only she didn't know him; she even got the name wrong."

"It could easily have been him. And likely as not our Miss Young wouldn't have heard of him. Like I said, he always takes damn good care to keep away from civilisation in the shape of Banford. And Miss Young always kept herself very much to herself."

"Can you tell us anything about him?" Bart put in.

"He may be dead for all I know. It must be at least a couple of years since I heard anything about him. And he was no chicken. I gather you want to try to get in touch with him?"

"Your perception," Bart remarked with gentle irony, "positively amazes me."

Yarrow grinned cheerfully. "You're an old rogue. So you've decided to join up with the private detectives. Wait till Harris gets to hear. I have the feeling that he won't be too enthusiastic if you do manage to unearth Simon's real parents."

"Harris," said Bart coldly, "can go to hell."

"And you might try going to Breston."

"Is that the best you can do?"

The doctor swung one leg over the other, exposing a length of hairy shin.

"Damn it, man! What do you expect? In any case, I wouldn't want to make things too easy for you and spoil the fun of the chase."

75

He became serious.

"The last I heard he was still living in Breston. Exactly where, I've no idea. But it's only a small place; you shouldn't have too much trouble."

"And if he happens to be dead?"

"You want jam on it," retorted Dr. Yarrow. "There was talk of a housekeeper. I don't know her name, but by all accounts she was about the same age as Old Toddidoc himself. So you never can tell."

"And that's all?"

"I ought to charge it up to professional services." Yarrow came to his feet. "And while I'm here, how's that chest of yours?"

"There's nothing wrong with my chest," Bart told him huffily.

The other fisted his shoulder affectionately. "Well, watch it. And your arteries. You're not as young as——"

"I've heard all that before."

"Good hunting," Dr. Harrow wished us generally from the door.

"An excellent doctor," Bart informed us a few minutes later when he returned from seeing his guest off the premises, "but with a deplorable, over-hearty manner. He is still very young. Age, one trusts, will bring a sobering influence. At least he has given us a lead of sorts." He glanced at his watch. "Ten minutes to clean up"—he was already as immaculate as ever—"and I shall be ready."

"How far is it to Breston?" I asked anxiously. I was getting used to the feel of a car again, but there was still a long way to go before I would be able to take the wheel with confidence. And knowing what had happened to the experienced Dodd wasn't going to help matters any.

He frowned. "Let me see. About thirty miles. Certainly no more. A half-hour run. . . ."

At least an hour, I thought.

"Is the car clean?" he wondered anxiously from the door, brushing his lapels with fastidious fingers. "The upholstery, I mean?"

There were, it seemed, two distinct sides to Bartholomew Brereton. I was getting to know both of them very well.

I drove back along the narrow lane that led to the main road, Joan at my side, Bart, with the precaution of a blanket to protect his suit, in the rear seat. It wasn't a pleasant thought that we would have to pass the place where Dodd had been killed, but there was no way of avoiding it.

76

We were silent until I had negotiated the railway-arch. There was no sign of the wrecked station-wagon, but on the dusty road—I tried not to look—patches of oil and smears of what could have been blood. I changed down clumsily to climb the hill. At the top Bart leaned forward to impart directions.

"Back to Banford, Gordon, then take the right-hand road at the market square. Incidentally, our way will take us through Charidon."

"Charidon," I echoed, and paused. "I wonder——"

"What is it, Gordon?" Joan asked.

"Another coincidence. It's been bothering me for some time. I was wondering if we could do anything about it."

Bart insinuated his face between us.

"Coincidences seem to be the order of the day. And what is this latest one?"

"You had a wire saying that Simon had run away from school again. I think you said it came on Saturday?"

He nodded. "That's right. He went over the wall on Friday evening."

"Rodney Blake wasn't in class on the Friday morning, which was unusual. They could have taken it into their heads to run away at the same time."

"An interesting thought," he observed.

"And you were wondering if Peter Latham had done the same," Joan said. "But he's away anyway; on holiday."

"Mrs. Latham and your Mrs. Foster seemed to be on good terms with each other," I suggested. "Don't you think there's maybe a chance that Mrs. Latham might send her a post-card? And if anything unusual had happened, wouldn't she mention it?"

"She'd had one card already. From Shrewsbury, I think. But I didn't read it and Mrs. Foster didn't say anything."

She added: "But of course it wouldn't be polite of me if I were to pass through Charidon again without stopping for a while to have another chat with her."

We reached the market square. I nursed the car over-cautiously through two streams of converging traffic, feathering clutch and accelerator, grating the gears harshly to the derision of the ruddy-faced driver of a farm-lorry. Thankfully, the righthand turn took us out almost immediately into open country.

"And if it does turn out that Peter has also slipped away," said Bart, resuming the conversation as if the complications of the market square had never existed, "then it seems to me that they could all quite easily be making for the same place. A sort of rendezvous. Or is that carrying the thing too far?"

"If they're not all heading for the same place there seems no sense in them all leaving at the same time."

"A gathering of the clans." There was no humour in his tone.

The road wound its way through spreading fields and gradually rising hills. I drove slowly, the needle hovering round the thirty mark, my nerves taut with anticipation, my foot ready to stamp on the brake at the first sign of anything out of the ordinary.

Neither Joan nor Bart fretted at our snail-like progress. When we had to pass under another railway bridge I felt the sudden tensing of Joan's body, the relaxing as we came out into the sun again.

I recognised the Three Sisters long before Charidon itself came into view. At first they were immediately ahead, swinging gradually to one side, taking up their familiar position as we passed the inn where Joan and I had stayed the night, and then the station with its cinder slope. I pulled up outside Mrs. Foster's cottage.

"I won't be longer than I can help," Joan promised as I reached over to open the door for her. We watched her walk up the path. Bart offered his cigarette case over the back of her vacated seat.

"Not calculated to do the old nerves any good," he murmured sympathetically. Looking at my damp palms and fingers that were inclined to tremble, I nodded.

"Simon," he remarked flicking his lighter for me, "always seems to choose week-ends or holidays for his excursions."

"I don't know about Rodney. I think he must choose the same times, otherwise I'm sure I'd have noticed his absences."

"So far as I can recall, the longest he stayed away was ten days. That was during the summer break last year."

I looked at the dash-board clock. A quarter to five. A pound to a penny Mrs. Foster was laying the tea-table for Joan's benefit.

"Breston's only a small place," Bart said, misreading my thoughts. "No cafés. Only the odd wayside cottage where you can get teas with Hovis. You know the sort of thing. But there's a decent pub where they do cuts off the cold joint and a fairish cheese. I wonder how long it'll take us to locate Old Toddidoc?"

He leaned back, not expecting a reply. Resting my elbows on the wheel I stared absently through the windscreen, watching a small girl throwing a ball for a black and white dog.

"So you had the impression that he was trying to get some

sort of message through to you," Bart remarked inconsequently, perhaps for something to say.

I nodded without speaking.

"But you couldn't be sure."

"The first time it happened," I said, thinking aloud, "along the lane, it was terrifying enough, but that was all. It was a nasty experience that left me badly shaken for a time. But I soon got over it; now I can barely remember. Before it came I'd been thinking about Rodney. The second time, when Joan saw it too, we'd been talking about him just before. And it was different. It's hard to explain. More vivid, more alive. And with sense of purpose. And it was evil."

I turned to look at him, resting my arm along the back of the seat.

"The first was a warning. The second was a positive attempt to kill. Then something else happened. I haven't said anything about it before because I can't be sure it really did happen."

I told him about the dream.

"A midnight visitation," he mused. "It could have been a dream. On the other hand——" He shrugged.

"There was no sense of fear with it. No feelings of any kind. And now, this last time——"

"Different again," Bart said.

"The very reverse of evil. As far from it as you can get."

"We'd been talking about him then," Bart said slowly. "Remember? Or at least I had. I'd been worrying about what might happen if authority took over."

I turned away to watch the dog, paws scrabbling in the dust, go scurrying after the ball. Were we trying to find significance where there was none? I wondered if perhaps the message, if there was a message, had been intended for me at all. It could have been meant for Bart. I had felt so certain that Rodney had been out there watching us. But it could have been Simon. Or both of them.

The sound of the cottage door closing brought me from a reverie that bordered on fantasy. I opened the car door as Joan came down the path.

"Well?" I asked as she settled herself, tucking the yellow frock about her knees, patting her hair into shape.

"She had another card from Mrs. Latham this morning, posted in Llanberis. Peter left them on Sunday. They were camping on the Denbigh Moors and when they woke he'd gone. She didn't seem all that worried on the card. Mrs. Foster told me that he'd done the same sort of thing on his

79

holiday last year. She asked Mrs. Foster to keep an eye open for him in case he made his way back home."

"So now all three of them are on the move," Bart said.

I reached for the starter, but she hadn't finished.

"I thought it might be a good idea if I asked her if she knew Doctor Todmarsh. She said she did, that he used to come to Charidon from time to time. He lanced a boil for her some three years ago."

"I wonder," Bart said darkly, "what Dr. Pringle would say if he knew about that?" And then: "So apparently he isn't afraid of using a scalpel. That's interesting."

"He died two years ago," Joan said simply. "So I don't suppose Dr. Pringle would mind one way or another."

"Damn!" Bart said explosively. "Sorry, my dear. So that leaves us out on a limb."

"Not quite. She told me where he used to live; the Toll House, just this side of Breston. And his housekeeper was a Mrs. Biddle. But she doesn't know what became of her when he died."

I reached for the starter again. The child gathered her dog into protective arms until we had gone by. Half an hour later saw us on the outskirts of Breston. The Toll House stood alone, its octagonal shape unmistakable.

"My turn to stretch my legs," said Bart.

A stocky man with fiery red hair and corduroys fastened with a wide leather belt opened the door to him. They spoke together for a few minutes and then Bart made his way back to the car, followed by the curious gaze of the Toll House tenant.

"One thing about the country," he informed us, seating himself after first rearranging his blanket, "everybody seems to know everyone else's business. Mrs. Biddle is a patient in the Banford Cottage Hospital. But she has a daughter, a Mrs. Fox. Mrs. Biddle went to live with her when Old Toddi-doc died. Rosemary Cottage, Pym's Lane, about quarter of a mile up the road. And Mrs. Fox seems to have a local reputation."

We had more trouble finding Rosemary Cottage than we had the Toll House. But then the latter had the right sort of name. Mrs. Fox lived in a dilapidated house that was despondent with neglect. A battered pram, one wheel missing, sagged by the front door. Children's toys littered the unkempt oblong of grass.

Bart inspected, shuddered and became pensive. Producing his wallet he extracted four five-pound notes and replaced them loose in the folder, ends carefully projecting a little, before returning it to his pocket.

He said: "I think you had better stay in the car, Joan. I have the impression that Mrs. Fox will react more favourably to an all-male delegation."

He paused with his hand on the door.

"It always pays to have one's facts at one's finger-tips. We are here to ask Mrs. Fox if her mother knows anything about twins that were taken to a Banford nursing home by an unknown woman, on the recommendation of Dr. Todmarsh eleven years ago. I think that puts the thing in a nutshell. And I suggest that you leave the talking to me, Gordon."

"Yes, sir," I said.

"And if she's the kind of woman I think she is," he added, "then I intend to leave most of the talking to her." He patted his pocket. "And this."

I followed him up a concrete path with cracks through which coarse grass had forced its way. Somewhere in the background a baby was screaming its head off. There was no knocker to the paint-peeled door; no letter-box even. Bart hammered with the edge of his clenched fist.

Mrs. Fox had greasy black hair that was a straggling frame for a far from clean face that still bore the echoes of a rude kind of beauty. A cigarette hung from her loose-lipped mouth all the while she was speaking. It was difficult to assess her age. Her eyes were as old as the hills. I put her to be in her mid-thirties. As it turned out I was ten years on the wrong side.

All of Bart's charm was insufficient to warrant our being invited inside.

"Mam ain't 'ere," she said sourly. "She's in 'ospital."

"I'm sorry to hear that. I understand that for a time she was housekeeper to a Dr. Todmarsh?"

"What's that got to do with you?"

He produced the wallet, absently it seemed, using it to stroke the side of his face. Her eyes found and avidly followed the exposed half-inch of blue-grey crispness.

"All we need is a little information," he told her courteously. "We could obtain it from your mother herself. But it would be a great pity"—he looked at her over the top of the wallet—"to have to bother her in hospital."

Mrs. Fox, her gaze fixed to the wallet, agreed that it would indeed be a pity.

"It is about something that happened eleven years ago. But

of course, you would be little more than a child. Perhaps you won't be able to remember."

"Eleven years ago." She nodded wisely. "I know what you've come about. I was fourteen; I remember right enough."

Ash broke and flaked unheeded down the front of her once-white blouse.

"Many's the time I've said to Mam that one day folks would come askin' questions. I expected it long afore this. Maybe the police—but you ain't them?"

"Good heavens, no!" Bart was vehement in denial. "This is a purely private affair, Mrs. Fox. No one will suffer as a result of our enquiries."

And he left it at that. As he had promised he left her to do the talking, all in her own way, not even interrupting when her story became hard to follow, and when it became obvious that what she was telling us seemed to have nothing to do with what we had come to find out. And all the while the baby kept up a dismal wailing from the rear of the house.

"It'll be about the Pulners' brat. You'll want to know where it came from. Well, it come from Werkley Ridge, that's a small-'oldin' way up in the 'ills. Mam an' Dad was both workin' for the Pulners then, an' we was livin' in the cottage on the 'oldin'. There was the two women, Miss Emily an' Miss Elizabeth, an' when their old man pegged out they run the place on their own till Stanley Pulner came on the scene and got hitched to Miss Emily. He were a Yank, so 'e said.

"Well, he went an' died of a 'eart attack while he was deliverin' vegetables down at Brayminister. That left the two women on their own again. Mrs. Pulner, she 'ad the kid later the same year. Dr. Pringle saw to it, but she died just the same; she never were what you might call strong.

"That left Miss Elizabeth on 'er own. Mam 'elped 'er look after the kid, but in the end she decided it were too much for 'er, so she asked Mam to 'elp 'er get shut of it. Mam brought it 'ome with 'er for a couple of nights. Maybe she 'ad some sort of idea of keepin' it 'erself; I don't know. Anyway, she took it away the mornin' after an' came back without it. I can remember that because it were the first time Mam 'ad ever been away from the village.

"I didn't know what was goin' on, but I got it out of Mam afterwards. She'd took the kid to Stapley-on-the-Sea an' dumped it in a shelter on the prom. Why she did it that way instead of takin' it to a proper place I'll never know. An' that's all there is to it. The kid was the Pulners', but they're both dead now, so that's finished. An' Mam's dyin'."

82

Bart looked at me and I shrugged helplessly.

"You haven't mentioned Dr. Todmarsh," he said to her.

She sniffed. "Old Toddidoc? 'e didn't 'ave anythin' to do with it. Not that 'e weren't up at Werkley every day while Mrs. Pulner was expectin'. But then 'e were 'er uncle. Dr. Pringle, what's a real doctor, 'e looked after things."

He slid the notes from the wallet and they were swallowed in the front of her blouse.

"Thank you very much for your trouble, Mrs. Fox." He sounded weary. He half-turned to go.

"Do you happen to remember what the baby looked like?" I asked her.

"Makin' sure it's the right one?" She grinned at me. "I remember all right. Once seen never forgot. Foreign-lookin' like 'is old man. Hair black as ink and ridges-like under 'is eyes. Never smiled the once, or made a sound, all the while 'e were at our place. No wonder Miss Elizabeth wanted shut of it. Enough to give you the creeps."

"Did you notice if he had any marks on him?" I asked. "Birthmarks? Scars?"

She grinned again. "You've got the right one, all right, mister. 'E 'ad a white scar on one of 'is arms; I forget which. I asked Mam about it, an' she said it was because of somethin' Dr. Pringle 'ad 'ad to do just after it were born."

Bart asked steadily: "How many children did Mrs. Pulner have?"

"I've told you all that," she cried impatiently, ready to close the door. "She only ever 'ad the one."

We walked back to the car.

It was as if we had built up a pyramid of facts, brick by brick with only two pieces—the real parents and a boy called Tony—needed to complete it. Now it seemed we had found those last two pieces. But putting them into place had brought the whole thing crashing to the ground.

I drove slowly along the lane away from the village, leaving the last straggle of cottages behind, until I came to a place where the verge widened at the entrance to a field. Swinging on to the grass, I braked, switched off the engine and leaned back. Bart, after treating Joan to a resumé of Mrs. Fox's story, had lapsed into a brooding silence, sitting bolt upright against the back of his seat, arms folded, chin on chest.

The pieces of the puzzle had to be reassembled. With one exception they all fitted into place. It was almost certain that the child Mrs. Biddle had taken to Stapley-on-the-Sea was the last one of the four. If Mrs. Pulner had had quadruplets instead of only the one child, the picture would have been complete so far as it went. Our next moves would have been obvious. Find out what had become of the last one, and if his name was Tony. Then the Pulners themselves. . . . Stanley Pulner, the "foreign-looking" father, had been an American. Brother Harold, with his connections with the American Embassy, should be able to help there.

If only there had been four instead of just the one.

No matter what Mrs. Fox had told us, there must have been four. That was the only possible answer. It was obvious that for some reason the multiple births had been kept secret. It stood to reason that Mrs. Fox, a schoolgirl at the time, wouldn't have been let into that secret.

And who else was there?

Old Toddidoc was dead. But Dr. Pringle was still alive, and so was Mrs. Biddle. But dying, according to her daughter. And what had happened to Miss Elizabeth? Mrs. Fox hadn't said what had become of her. We hadn't thought to ask.

So there was the background. Two sisters, ordinary country-women it seemed, had run a small-holding up in the hills after the death of their father. Then along had come a stranger and married one of them. That had been the start of it all; Stanley Pulner's arrival. He had to be the one responsible for the birth of the four strange children. I swivelled in my seat so that I could lean against the door and look at Bart.

"Two taken to a nursing home," he said, "by a woman. That'll be either Miss Elizabeth or Mrs. Biddle. Number three dumped on the vicarage steps by person or persons unknown. The last one left in a promenade shelter by Mrs. Biddle. And all, seemingly, about the same time. We should have asked Mrs. Fox if she remembered the exact date."

"Not after eleven years," I said.

"Four of them, no matter what she told us. There's no getting away from that. But I think she was telling us the truth as she knew it. Something went on in a farmhouse bedroom that she didn't know about. Something damned queer. Dr. Pringle delivered quadruplets, separated them, and then went back to his practice without saying a word. And everyone else concerned kept their mouths shut. Mrs. Biddle lied to her daughter. Life goes on with four babies kept hidden away, looked after by Miss Elizabeth and Mrs. Biddle. And then one fine day they decide to get rid of them. Just like that. Two to Banford, one to Charidon, one to Stapley. That's the only way it could have been."

Something had been worrying me; there was another small piece of the puzzle that was the wrong shape.

"Yarrow told us that Dr. Pringle had been gunning for Old Toddidoc. Yet he delivered the children, and according to Mrs. Fox, Old Toddidoc was also on the scene. In any case, we know he knew what was going on because he was behind the two who were taken to the nursing home. I can't see a qualified doctor working hand-in-glove with a quack he had been trying to run off the road."

"Perhaps that's why he kept quiet about the whole thing," Bart suggested with little conviction.

"Do you know him at all? Pringle, I mean?"

He shook his head. "Only by repute. From Yarrow."

"And Werkley Ridge?"

He shook his head again. "Never heard of the place."

"Mrs. Fox didn't tell us what became of Miss Elizabeth. She could still be living there."

Joan put in: "At least we know where Mrs. Biddle is."

"A plethora of leads." Bart smiled for the first time since leaving Rosemary Cottage. "It becomes a matter of priorities. A visit to Stapley-on-the-Sea and a chat with the local police. Stapley, as its name suggests, is way out on the coast. How far? Say forty miles. Tomorrow, I think.

"And then we must get in touch with Dr. Pringle. Yarrow will have to be our go-between there." He was clearly enjoying himself again. "We can't approach the doctor directly. Professional ethics apart from anything else precludes the direct approach. But one doctor may discuss patients with another."

He rubbed the side of his nose.

"Yarrow may need a reason before he agrees to co-operate. We may have to take him into our confidence. Or part of it, at least. A bridge to be crossed when we come to it. The help of a medical man might prove useful. But I have the feeling that the fewer people who know what is going on, the better.

"Then, as Joan says, we have Mrs. Biddle. Right on our doorstep in the Banford Hospital. Which leaves only Miss Elizabeth. And while we are in this part of the world I think it would be a good idea if we were to try to find Werkley Ridge."

I felt that he had forgotten the most important lead of all. I reminded him of Stanley Pulner.

"A dead-end, surely," he remarked.

"He could be the key to the whole thing. You forget Brother Harold and his various connections. He has friends in the Metropolitan Police and also at the American Embassy. According to Mrs. Fox, Pulner was an American."

"You can't set official machinery in motion without first giving sufficient reason," he pointed out.

"He'll have to know sooner or later."

"The link with authority." He lost his smile.

"I won't tell him more than is necessary," I promised, and pressed the starter. "Right or left?"

He leaned forward, assessing the view.

"To the right, one would imagine. Mrs. Fox described the place as being up in the hills. They seem to lie in that direction. I should stop at the first signs of habitation we come to and make enquiries."

The first signs of habitation in a countryside that was becoming wilder each mile we went was a small farm by a cross-roads. But the farmer was a newcomer to the district. He had heard of Werkley and that was all. He gestured vaguely "It'll be somewhere over yonder, I think."

Three miles then of empty lanes with no passing traffic. Poor looking fields gave way to a desolation of moorland and scrub. Hedges and fences disappeared; the road surface became rough. Hills, low-lying green and brown billows, crept in on either hand. There was a sudden oasis, a farm nestling in an unexpected green valley. Leaving the car I walked up a grassy lane that was hard-rutted from the winter passage of wheels.

An elderly man, brick-red-faced and with little hair, coarse flannel shirt wide to the waist, sleeves rolled tightly about thick, oak-brown arms, leaned on a spade to watch my approach.

"Werkley?" He straightened laboriously, pointing ahead. "Ay. About five miles up the road and then you take a left-'and turn." He eyed me warily. "Likely you'll be wantin' Brass Farm or Maybrick?"

"We're looking for a small-holding called Werkley Ridge."

He regarded me even more closely now, not taking his eyes from my face while he dragged a rag from his pocket and used it to wipe first his hands then his forehead. It seemed that the wiping was unnecessary; something to do while he gave himself time to consider.

"Do you know the place?" I asked.

He nodded heavily. "Ay. But you're wasting your time. There ain't no small-'olding there now. Hasn't been for six years or more. The whole place 'as gone to rack an' ruin." A thought came to him. "You weren't thinkin' of buyin'?"

"No. We're looking for someone called Miss Elizabeth." Had Mrs. Fox told us her surname? I couldn't remember. But he knew who I meant.

"You won't find 'er. She left years ago. Nobody lives up there now."

"Have you any idea where she went to?"

He picked up his spade. "She just went. Without tellin' anyone she was even goin'."

I lurched my way back along the ruts. It took me a few minutes to reverse the car.

Bart said: "I suppose that was too much to hope for." Then: "You'll stay at my place, of course. We can pick up your luggage from the hotel on our way back through Banford."

It was nearly eight o'clock by the time we arrived back at Kendly. After dinner I rang Brother Harold, first trying his home and when there was no reply, the hospital. It was a few minutes before he came to the phone.

"Gordon? A pleasant surprise to hear from you so soon after our last talk." All the condescension of an older brother for a younger.

I offered the usual sort of apologies for dragging him away from whatever he had been doing. A consultation, seemingly. . . .

"But threatening to become prolonged. I welcomed the

excuse to get away. And what is it this time? More information about twins?"

"Not exactly." That was true enough. How much would I have to tell him? How much had I told him the last time we had spoken together? I couldn't remember; it had been a life-time ago. Time enough for him to be told the truth when we had finished assembling facts. Now there was an old man and his fears of the intervention of authority to be considered. An evil hour to be postponed for as long as possible. And there was always the hope that things might not turn out as bad as we imagined.

So: "This is about one of my pupils; an adopted child. I've been trying to trace his real parents. I've managed to find out a little about his father, but one doesn't like to leave it at that."

He rose to the bait, vaguely worded as it was.

"You want to be able to present him with a ready-made family. Aunts, uncles, grandparents. All very understandable and commendable." Brotherly condescension again. "I never realised that teachers took such an interest in their pupils. Of course, you are working with the authority of the people who adopted him?"

"Yes. His real father is an American."

His laugh came over the wire. "I thought it might be something like that. The old G. I. bride story."

"This is much later than the war. They had the child twelve years ago. But he could have been in the country some time before that. His name is Stanley Pulner."

"Hold the line while I make a note." It was going to be easier than I had thought. But then Brother Harold always had been pleased to demonstrate the usefulness of his wide variety of connections. "Stanley Pulner. Arrived in England at least thirteen years ago. Is that all you can tell me about him?"

Like father, like son. Sons, rather. . . .

"Very black hair; sallow-complexioned; high cheek-bones. That's about all I can tell you."

"Little enough. But it's something to go on. Pulner isn't a common name. All right, Gordon; I'll do what I can. I don't suppose you're in any great hurry for the information?"

"I'd like to get it cleared up as soon as possible," I told him, "but please don't put yourself out. I appreciate that you have little enough spare time as it is."

"You're speaking from Cookley?"

"No. I'm up in Northumberland."

"Are you really?" He was surprised. "Then you'd better

I leaned sideways, resting one elbow on the wall, looking past the delicate lines of Joan's profile, the harder, Grecian angles of Bart's. There had to be some reason, some explanation for the strange children. Those sort of things just didn't happen accidentally. The mother seemed to have been an ordinary woman. The father was the unknown quantity. Somewhere in his past had to be the incident that had made him capable of breeding a new kind of creature. Mutants, were they? I had read of plants that had become altered, mutated —was that the right word?—by radio-activity. If plants, then animals. And we were still animals ourselves. Man the mammal. The genus of Primates. With a brain that we still hadn't learned to use properly. Was that the difference between the children and ourselves? Had they learned the use of that part of the brain that we left idle?

I felt the sudden tensing of Joan's body against mine, heard her sharp intake of breath. Both she and Bart were staring out across the garden. My pulse hesitating, then racing, I swung to follow the direction of their eyes.

A small figure was emerging from the shadows of the dark curtain of trees, coming slowly, wraith-like, into the silver flood of the lawn. Rodney—it was Rodney, I felt sure—wore the same open-necked white shirt, sleeves buttoned to the wrists, as he had when he had looked up at me from the moonlight of another garden. His face, as he came nearer, was as calmly expressionless now as it had been then. It hadn't been a dream, that other time.

I heard Bart's exclamation, knew what he was thinking, said: "No. . . ." putting my hand on Joan's. It was cold. "It's Rodney."

When he reached the centre of the lawn, a dozen paces from us, he stopped, looking back towards the darkness behind, the darkness that gave birth to a second figure, a duplicate of the first in every respect save for the clothes it wore. Some kind of flannel suit, I could see, as this second boy came across the grass to join the first, with the faint outlines of an emblem, a school badge, on the breast pocket.

Bart whispered: "Simon," in a tone of certainty. He would be able to recognise the badge, the school uniform.

It was a strange, almost shocking thing, seeing them standing there together, side by side. Before, in my mind, there had been Rodney—flesh and blood—and three shadows, nebulous beings, three fantasy boys that I knew must exist, but still, for all that, had been unable to picture. But now, here they were, two of them seen together, the first positive, visual proof that there were more than the one.

And they stood there, waiting. . . .

Waiting for one of us to be the first to speak?

A meeting of enemies under a flag of truce in some strange no-man's-land.

And what was there to say to them?

I put the blackboard behind me, my desk in front, and Blake standing in the classroom.

"What's all this about, Blake?" I asked sharply.

His voice came thinly but clearly. With something in it that could have been contempt.

"Go away, Mr. Seacombe. Before anything else happens. You don't know anything about it."

"About what?"

"You go back to Cookley and everything will be all right," he said, and then the other, Simon, spoke. But not to me.

"Make them go away, Gramps," he said, and there was certainly urgency in his tone. "Tell them to go away."

Bart said: "Come up here, Simon, and talk to me properly."

A conversation in a dream.

And then the dream became a nightmare.

They swung on their heels together, as at some pre-arranged signal, and ran back towards the trees. Bart called after them, but they took no notice.

And something came smashing into my mind. The night exploded into a million fiery shards, and the explosion was inside my head. Stark horror, physical in its impact, battered, pounding at my skull, driving reason away, blinding, slashing off everything save the overwhelming thunder of utter, limitless horror.

The fury sent me slewing round, lifting me, it seemed, off my feet, hurling me backwards as if I had been caught in the blast of a bomb-burst. Before the blindness, the blood-red curtain of darkness swooped down, I had a momentary glimpse of Joan, hands pressed to the sides of her face, mouth opened in a soundless scream, whirling away from the balustrade, clutched in the vortex of a tornado. Then everything was lost in the torment of unendurable, remorseless mind-shattering horror.

There was no way of telling how long it lasted, how long the fear-waves pounded, how long the pile-driving hammer thudded in the rivets of terror. There was no abrupt cessation, no sudden return to normality as had happened the other times. Gradually the agony eased. Feeling returned, then sight, then some semblance of reason. I was crouched against the rough wall between two of the French windows, my grassy lane that was hard-rutted from the winter passage of wheels.

An elderly man, brick-red-faced and with little hair, coarse flannel shirt wide to the waist, sleeves rolled tightly about thick, oak-brown arms, leaned on a spade to watch my approach.

"Werkley?" He straightened laboriously, pointing ahead. "Ay. About five miles up the road and then you take a left-'and turn." He eyed me warily. "Likely you'll be wantin' Brass Farm or Maybrick?"

"We're looking for a small-holding called Werkley Ridge."

He regarded me even more closely now, not taking his eyes from my face while he dragged a rag from his pocket and used it to wipe first his hands then his forehead. It seemed that the wiping was unnecessary; something to do while he gave himself time to consider.

"Do you know the place?" I asked.

He nodded heavily. "Ay. But you're wasting your time. There ain't no small-'olding there now. Hasn't been for six years or more. The whole place 'as gone to rack an' ruin." A thought came to him. "You weren't thinkin' of buyin'?"

"No. We're looking for someone called Miss Elizabeth." Had Mrs. Fox told us her surname? I couldn't remember. But he knew who I meant.

"You won't find 'er. She left years ago. Nobody lives up there now."

"Have you any idea where she went to?"

He picked up his spade. "She just went. Without tellin' anyone she was even goin'."

I lurched my way back along the ruts. It took me a few minutes to reverse the car.

Bart said: "I suppose that was too much to hope for." Then: "You'll stay at my place, of course. We can pick up your luggage from the hotel on our way back through Banford."

It was nearly eight o'clock by the time we arrived back at Kendly. After dinner I rang Brother Harold, first trying his home and when there was no reply, the hospital. It was a few minutes before he came to the phone.

"Gordon? A pleasant surprise to hear from you so soon after our last talk." All the condescension of an older brother for a younger.

I offered the usual sort of apologies for dragging him away from whatever he had been doing. A consultation, seemingly. . . .

"But threatening to become prolonged. I welcomed the

87

excuse to get away. And what is it this time? More information about twins?"

"Not exactly." That was true enough. How much would I have to tell him? How much had I told him the last time we had spoken together? I couldn't remember; it had been a life-time ago. Time enough for him to be told the truth when we had finished assembling facts. Now there was an old man and his fears of the intervention of authority to be considered. An evil hour to be postponed for as long as possible. And there was always the hope that things might not turn out as bad as we imagined.

So: "This is about one of my pupils; an adopted child. I've been trying to trace his real parents. I've managed to find out a little about his father, but one doesn't like to leave it at that."

He rose to the bait, vaguely worded as it was.

"You want to be able to present him with a ready-made family. Aunts, uncles, grandparents. All very understandable and commendable." Brotherly condescension again. "I never realised that teachers took such an interest in their pupils. Of course, you are working with the authority of the people who adopted him?"

"Yes. His real father is an American."

His laugh came over the wire. "I thought it might be something like that. The old G. I. bride story."

"This is much later than the war. They had the child twelve years ago. But he could have been in the country some time before that. His name is Stanley Pulner."

"Hold the line while I make a note." It was going to be easier than I had thought. But then Brother Harold always had been pleased to demonstrate the usefulness of his wide variety of connections. "Stanley Pulner. Arrived in England at least thirteen years ago. Is that all you can tell me about him?"

Like father, like son. Sons, rather. . . .

"Very black hair; sallow-complexioned; high cheek-bones. That's about all I can tell you."

"Little enough. But it's something to go on. Pulner isn't a common name. All right, Gordon; I'll do what I can. I don't suppose you're in any great hurry for the information?"

"I'd like to get it cleared up as soon as possible," I told him, "but please don't put yourself out. I appreciate that you have little enough spare time as it is."

"You're speaking from Cookley?"

"No. I'm up in Northumberland."

"Are you really?" He was surprised. "Then you'd better

let me have a phone number where I can contact you."

I gave it to him and added the address for good measure.

"Brereton, Lowton Villa, Kendly," he repeated. "Having nice weather up there?"

"As nice as it comes," I replied.

"I find myself envying you. London at this time of year has little to offer. I am hoping to get away for a few days later on. . . ."

We exchanged pleasantries for a few minutes and then he rang off. Replacing the receiver, a thought came to me. I looked up the number of the Banford Cottage Hospital and dialled it.

"I'm enquiring after a Mrs. Biddle."

"Which ward, please?"

"I'm afraid I don't know."

"Hold the line." There was a pause. "Ward Seven. Mrs. Biddle. No change."

I went back to the kitchen were Joan was washing the dinner things, Bart, frilled apron back in place, drying and stacking with a slow dignity. It was an odd little domestic scene. A kitchen was no suitable background for him. With his suave, impeccable elegance he would have been more at home in the hushed and reverent lounge of some exclusive men's club.

"All under control," I told their backs. "Brother Harold has agreed to co-operate."

"Good," Bart remarked evenly, without turning round.

"And without asking questions."

"Good," he said again, but in a very different tone.

"And Mrs. Biddle is still alive. I rang the hospital to make sure."

"A precaution that I must confess to having overlooked." He slanted a silver-grey brow over a matching shoulder. "We must pay her a visit as soon as possible. Let us hope that her memory isn't failing and that she is still capable of talking."

Removing his apron he folded it neatly before stowing it away in a drawer. Then, when Joan had wiped her hands, he took the towel from her, hung it up to dry, then stepped back to survey the sink and surrounds with careful eyes.

"Jenny," he observed with little enthusiasm, "will be back tomorrow. Jenny being the maid. She was trained by my daughter-in-law."

We went through to the lounge. We had dawdled over dinner and now it was a quarter to ten and dusk. Bart went to the window, made to draw the curtains, thought better of it

89

and drifted aimlessly back to the centre of the room. Joan had seated herself in one corner, picking up a magazine and flicking idly through its pages. Bart tapped the television set, shook his head at the empty screen and took out his cigarette case. I knew how he was feeling. I had the same restlessness myself. And Joan was turning the pages with a speed that precluded reading.

"A turn in the garden?" he invited, having passed round the cigarettes. Joan laid her book thankfully aside. We followed him into the hall and into another lounge, a room I hadn't seen before, with French windows that opened on to the terrace.

The moon was a mottled copper and silver disc, hanging low over the trees, framed in a motionless feather of cloud. A breeze had come with the dusk, stirring the branches, leaves rustling softly. The garden was a mystery of silver pools and dappled shadow. There was an unearthly quality to it that I found a little disturbing. But then I had spent most of my life in the town. The moon I knew was the lifeless white circle that reflected cold slate roofs and tall blackened chimneys.

We leaned over the stone balustrade, Joan with her arm tucked through mine. Her hair gathered up the moonlight, condensing it, giving her an ethereal beauty that matched the mystery of the garden. I was conscious of a curious air of expectancy. But there was no sense of foreboding.

"The one taken to Stapley," Bart said suddenly, breaking the spell; "it should be easy enough to track him down. A shelter on the promenade. Some innocent visitor probably had a shock. And then almost certainly a police station. And the police, whatever else they may do, keep exhaustive records. We'll have no trouble there. . . ." His teeth gleamed whitely. "I think I mentioned that the Chief Constable is a friend of mine. Your august brother isn't the only one to have connections in the right places."

"Connections can be useful," I said.

"And then we'll have the four of them. Names and addresses. A list of their peculiarities. And if your brother is successful. . . ."

"We add the father to the children. Perhaps then we'll find the answer to it all."

"And we wipe our hands of the whole thing. Forget personalities. Let authority take over." He crushed out his cigarette in a shower of golden sparks. "I suppose——"

"The father may have been just an ordinary man," I said. "But you don't think he was."

90

hands clasped to my ears, face buried between my knees. The world was suddenly empty and still.

After a while I managed to pull myself to my feet, swaying, holding on to the wall. Joan was a crumpled heap at the far end of the terrace. There was no sign of Bart.

I staggered drunkenly towards her, dropping to my knees at her side, fear—fear of my own making now—a tight hard knot in the pit of my stomach.

She was still breathing. Her face was white marble, her eyes closed, but her breast rose and fell steadily beneath the yellow linen. Gathering her into my arms I stumbled back through the open window into the lounge. She stirred as I laid her on a settee. When her eyes opened, horror glazing them almost immediately, I held her close as I had done once before while shuddering racked her body.

When she seemed to have recovered a little I laid her gently back against the cushions. She stared up at me. "What was it, Gordon?" And then, her eyes searching: "Bart?"

It took me some time to find him. He was lying on the gravel at the foot of the terrace steps. There was blood on his hands and down one side of his face. But he was still alive, and so far as I could tell, no bones were broken. He was too heavy for me to lift.

I raced back through the house to the hall and the telephone. The methodical mind responsible for the planning of the house had seen to it that a list of names and numbers—friends mainly, it seemed—was ready to hand. Both Dr. Yarrow's surgery and private numbers were there. It was nearly midnight. I rang his home number.

10

I left the lounge open so that the staircase was in view. Joan, white-faced still, silent, shivering from time to time despite the blanket I had draped about her shoulders, sat by my side on the settee. When I saw Yarrow coming down from the bedroom to where we had earlier carried Bart I had a glass of whisky poured out ready for him.

Putting his case on the sideboard he accepted it with a

curt nod, dropping wearily into one of the easy chairs. He wore a dark overcoat over blue and white striped pyjamas that were too short in the leg for his ungainly lankiness. Bony ankles terminated in red carpet slippers. He had wasted no time answering my call.

"He should be all right now," he informed us. "Sleeping. I gave him a sedative. But he's had a rough do." His eyes were puzzled over the top of his glass.

"It doesn't make sense. Nothing wrong with his heart. For his age, the old boy's in good shape all round. There's no reason why he should have had an attack like that."

He was clearly leading up to the question that any doctor would ask under the circumstances. And he would want an explanation that would match the symptoms.

"When he first came round," he brooded, "he seemed to be delirious for a few minutes. Babbling about his grandson and someone called 'Rodney'. I couldn't make any sense of it." Balancing his glass on the chair arm he regarded us closely. "Come to that, you don't look so good yourself, Seacombe. And neither does Miss Grey."

"We've been worried about him," I said inadequately.

Leaving his glass he came to his feet to take Joan's wrist between long high-knuckled fingers, putting the other palm on her forehead. Black eyebrows lifted in surprise. "What the devil's been going on here?"

It seemed to me, tired as I was, and worried, barely capable of rational thought, that the only thing to do was tell him the truth. In any case, we had already half-decided to take him into our confidence.

"It's a long story," I said, "and it's getting on for one o' clock in the morning."

"You're not the only one that's tired. But I've got a patient upstairs. I want to know what happened to him."

So I told him.

When I had finished he leaned back and folded his arms, his face a mask of disbelief, chin thrusting aggressively from between the upturned collar of his pyjamas. A lock of hair fell over his forehead and he shook it from his eyes with an impatient gesture. It was a few moments before he spoke.

"Of all the impossible. . . ." He seemed to be thinking aloud. His eyes went to the ceiling. "Something certainly took all the stuffing out of him. . . ." Then came down to Joan. "And Miss Grey has all the symptoms of shock." He shrugged. "All right, Seacombe; I'll go along with you for the time being. I won't even comment on it until he's well enough to tell me himself what happened. With all due respects I know nothing about either of you. Apart from what you have told me yourselves."

And his tone told us that he wasn't prepared to accept even that.

"Fair enough," I said. "In any case, Bart was considering telling you the story before this happened."

There was no change in his expression.

"Was he, now. For any particular reason?"

"We were going to ask you to help us again."

"I see. Well, we'll leave it at that." He picked up his case. "I've had more than enough for one night. Thanks for the drink."

I went with him to the front door.

"And thank you for coming so promptly."

"You're welcome." He spoke curtly. "I'll be round about ten to have another look at him. He should be all right for the time being. There's no need for either of you to sit up with him. By the looks of you, you could both use some sleep."

But he couldn't let it go at that.

"You'd have me believe that one schoolboy killed another without so much as touching him? And that the same boy was responsible for Dodd's accident?"

"Yes," I said.

"And he and the old man's grandson were the cause of that?" He pointed back up the stairs.

"Let Bart tell you himself," I said.

"I'll do just that. Keep him in bed till I come."

He walked down the drive to his car.

I didn't get the chance to obey his last instruction. It was half past nine before I woke the following morning. In the kitchen I found Joan preparing breakfast, Bart watching the breaking of eggs into the frying-pan with a benevolent and approving gaze, looking little the worse—apart from a deepening of the lines from eyes to mouth—for his previous night's experience. He had changed to a blue suit with matching shirt and tie, and there was an aroma of after-shave lotion. There was a scrape down one side of his face, and exchanging greetings he spread his hands—red gravel-rashed—for my inspection.

"I must have slid head-first down the steps. It could have been much worse. I don't want to go through anything like that again. At least I have some idea now what they can do when they set their minds to it."

He smiled without any great humour. "If I had any doubts

before, and I don't think I did, they've certainly all gone now. Joan tells me you had to tell Yarrow what it's all about."

"I don't think he believed a word I told him."

"You can't blame him. I can hardly believe myself that——" He broke off, his features suddenly puckering, so that it seemed he was on the verge of breaking down. While I went towards him again he fought and regained control. "It's all right. It's just that I can't believe Simon would try to harm me. . . ."

He shook my hand away with small irritation. "I'll feel better when I've had something to eat. That reminds me——" He looked round enquiringly. "Jenny?"

Joan said: "She arrived a few minutes after I got down. I'm afraid we didn't hit it off together. I told her that I would be looking after you for a while and she made it clear she resented my presence. I suggested she get on with her housework. She was too surprised to argue. I hope I did right." She wafted two plates of sizzling egg and bacon to the table.

Bart made no attempt to disguise his admiration.

"I am not," he declared pontifically, his old self returning, "what one might call 'old'. Don't be misled by my outward appearance. Beneath this slightly withered cloak of flesh burns the spirit of a young man, a widower these ten years. A man who has been at the mercy of his resident relatives and their choice in domestic staff for the same length of time. A man, moreover, to whom a wife who would be the bulwark between himself and the aforementioned staff, would be little less than a God-send. Let us forget the disparity in our ages. You know what I am trying to say."

He applied himself to his breakfast without waiting for a reply.

"I'm afraid that she is already spoken for," I told him.

He sighed heavily over a fork-load of bacon. "I was afraid that might be the case." He swivelled to watch Joan refilling the frying-pan. "Your mind is fully made up?"

What had started off as an essay in badinage suddenly, at least so far as I was concerned—and Joan too, I hoped, became something very different.

She paused for a few moments before turning to smile at me.

"Quite made up," she assured us both.

As proposals go it was probably one of the most unromantic and certainly unpremeditated that ever a girl has received. It was a moment about which I felt something should be done. Despite the frying-pan I took her in my arms and made a thoroughly good job of kissing her, an operation that was watched by Bart with dawning understanding.

"Good heavens!" he exclaimed, fork poised. "Do I understand that the whole thing has come to fruition here and now?"

"Beneath his cloak of flesh," Joan said demurely, "he's inclined to be rather shy. I could have wished for more romantic surroundings. But a girl can't have everything. Where was I? Oh, yes; one egg or two, Gordon?"

Dr. Yarrow, arriving a few minutes after ten, was admitted by the ginger-haired, dark-faced Jenny.

"I thought I told you to keep him in bed," he said accusingly to me from the kitchen door.

"It would take a better man than Gordon," Bart remarked placidly, reaching for the last slice of toast, "or you, for that matter, to keep me in bed when there's nothing wrong with me."

"There was plenty wrong with you last night," Yarrow retorted. "Put down that toast and give me your wrist. I must say you look more your usual self. I remember telling you once what would happen if you got over-excited."

"Is that what you call it?" Bart recovered his toast. "I thought Gordon had told you all about it."

"He told me a story of sorts."

"And you didn't believe him?"

"No," Yarrow said bluntly. "I didn't. Although I must confess that it kept me awake for some time." He nodded acceptance to Joan's mute offer of coffee. "I know a little about human nature. It was obvious someone had knocked the stuffing out of you. I couldn't figure out why Seacombe had come up with such an explanation. Two schoolboys were responsible for what happened to you . . . I mean, ask yourself. . . ."

Bart said steadily: "Between us we've collected nearly all the evidence we need to set the thing in front of responsible authority. And that is something we shall certainly do when we have tracked down the last of the four and learned something about their father. That's how true the story is."

Yarrow set down his cup with exaggerated care. "Responsible authority being the police. You'll have to watch your step, Bart."

"Not the police," I put in. "My brother."

"I see. And even though, according to you, Bart, Simon is one of them." He passed nervous fingers through his thick

97

thatch of hair. "I was under the impression that you thought the world of the boy?"

"Simon being one of them doesn't make any difference." Bart stared at his plate. "They've got to be stopped. All the evidence points to their being responsible for at least two deaths. For all we know there may be more. And don't forget that I've had personal experience of what they can do."

Yarrow turned still-sceptical eyes in my direction. "How long did this—this attack last?"

I knew what he meant. "I don't know. Perhaps only a few seconds."

"It's totally beyond comprehension." He shook his head. "All right; I grant you that such things, but on a much smaller scale, may be possible. Hallucinations can be artificially induced. Add mass hypnosis and a touch of extrasensory perception, and one can believe almost anything. So long as one reads about it in a technical paper. But it's very different when you come across it first-hand. What about the people who adopted them? Don't they know what's going on?"

"Gordon has talked to Rodney's people," Bart said. "The impression he got was that they knew he was different from other children and were afraid of him. Mrs. Latham says she wished she'd never adopted Peter. I've always felt that Simon was different too, even though I've had little enough to do with him."

"You've said as much to me several times. I'll go along with you for the time being. Seacombe said you were thinking of asking me to help again. . . ."

"We want to find out from Dr. Pringle just what did happen up at Werkley Ridge. But it would be useless approaching him directly."

"I see that. All right." He came to his feet. "I'll call him now. You want to listen in?"

We followed him into the hall. Jenny, busy with vacuum cleaner in the lounge, stopped work to watch with coldly inquisitive eyes. Bart seemed to find some pleasure in closing the door on her. Yarrow dialled the number without having to look it up.

"Pringle? Yarrow here. . . . I'm fine. You . . . ? Oh, busy as usual. . . . Look, I wonder if you could help me? I believe you attended the confinement of a Mrs. Pulner at Werkley Ridge some twelve years ago. . . . That's right. . . . No, nothing like that. To satisfy my own curiosity, that's all. . . ." He grimaced silently. "Thanks. . . ."

98

"Looking up his records," he relayed to us, hand over mouthpiece.

"Hullo? . . . I see. . . . Yes. . . . Like that, eh? Thanks, Pringle. . . . Holidays? You're joking, of course. You tried getting hold of a decent locum? . . . Thanks again." He rang off.

"Pringle was called to Mrs. Pulner on 16 August 1952. But not to the actual confinement. That child had been born the day before. She was in a shocking state when he got there. She died before the ambulance arrived. He later signed the death certificate. Everything was above-board. And he saw the child; healthy enough, he says. Child, Bart; not children. There was only the one. So where do you go from there?"

"To the Cottage Hospital," Bart rejoined grimly. "To talk to Mrs. Biddle."

"Pringle's no fool," Yarrow said. "He's as conscientious as they come. He wouldn't have put his name to the certificate if he had any suspicions at all that things weren't as they should be."

He looked at his watch. "As luck has it I've got to pass the hospital this morning. If you've made up your mind to interview the unofficial midwife I may as well come with you. You any idea which ward she's in?"

I thought. "Seven, I believe."

"Women's Medical. Sister Ross. She's a tartar. The patient may be on the seriously-ill list but if you're not relatives she won't admit you unless you can give a damned good reason. I'll do what I can." He nodded at me. "And you might try mentioning your brother's name." He grinned reminiscently. "It worked the oracle with me."

"Talking of influential connections," Bart remarked, and reached for the phone.

"Colonel Winter," he said a few seconds later. "Bartholomew Brereton here. . . . Gerald? Bart. Look, old man, I've got a school-teacher here who's trying to trace the parentage of an adopted child. Apparently it was dumped in a shelter at Stapley-on-the-Sea eleven years ago. We propose paying a visit to your mob at Stapley. I don't suppose we'll meet with any snags?" He listened, smiling to his satisfaction. "I'm greatly indebted to you, Gerald. I'll do as much for you one day."

"The Chief Constable," he informed us, not without some smugness, replacing the phone. "Shall we go?"

At the Cottage Hospital Dr. Yarrow's presence took us past the porter's lodge and as far as the corridor leading to Women's Medical. There Sister Ross, grey-haired, only small, but with a starched, over-officious pugnacity that more than made up for her lack of stature, presented the anticipated obstacle.

"Mrs. Biddle is on the danger list, Doctor, which means, as you well know, that she may be visited at any time. But only by near relatives. So far no one has been to see her. Which is just as well. She has to be kept very quiet. I cannot admit outsiders under any circumstances. . . ."

She was very firm, refusing to be swayed by Yarrow's persuasions, mention of Brother Harold cutting no ice at all.

Bart said smoothly: "We appreciate your concern for your patient, Sister, but this is a matter of some urgency. In point of fact I have already spoken to the Chief Constable."

She was startled at that. "The police . . . ?"

Yarrow looked uncomfortable. Bart smiled benignly down at her from his height.

"In that case"—she decided ungraciously—"only for a few minutes. And certainly not all of you."

Joan said: "Perhaps I'd better be the one. She may find it easier to talk to another woman."

"And if Sister has no objection," Yarrow added, "I'd better come with you."

Sister Ross opened the ward door. "The bed in the far corner. It is already screened. And under no circumstances must you excite the patient." She had the last word. "I hold you responsible, Doctor Yarrow."

Bart and I found our way outside again. In silence we sat in the car and waited. It was a quarter of an hour before they came walking down the steps and across the sun-filled yard to join us. I held the door open for Joan. Yarrow, with his car waiting, rested his elbows on the top of the open window. For a few moments he regarded us without speaking. There may have been resentment in his gaze. Certainly there was something in his dark eyes that hadn't been there before.

"Apologies, I suppose," he started. "You, Bart, and you too, Seacombe, I'm not sure I go along with the story yet. I need time to think about it. But part of it's true enough. God knows what Pringle would say if he knew. . . ."

Joan, not far from tears, said: "She's very ill, Gordon. On our way out the sister told us it's cancer. But she was able to talk. I think she had been worrying about it. She smiled at us when we left. . . ."

I put my arm round her shoulders.

"That damned old rogue Toddidoc is behind it all," Yarrow said. "He saw to the actual confinement. He was Mrs.

Pulner's uncle and apparently she refused to have anyone but him to look after her. He delivered four babies, linked by pads of flesh on the forearm. And he separated them there and then. In all fairness he didn't want the job, but Mrs. Pulner, weak from loss of blood, became hysterical, and he was afraid of what might happen if he didn't fall in with her wishes. I think he probably panicked.

"He stayed the night at Werkley, but next morning it was obvious that Mrs. Pulner was in a bad way and getting worse. He knew enough about medicine to realise this was something he couldn't cope with. And if she were to die there and then, he would find himself up to the ears in trouble of the worst sort. So he and Mrs. Biddle put their heads together. While she phoned Dr. Pringle he tucked three of the children away in the attic to hide the evidence of his kitchen-table surgery, leaving only the one out, as proof of the confinement, but carefully wrapped up to disguise the bandages on its arm. Then he got the hell out of it as fast as his tricycle would take him. Along came Pringle, and you know the rest. . . ."

"I felt sure," Bart remarked with every degree of satisfaction, "that it must be something like that. Are you satisfied now?" And then, suddenly anxious: "You will keep it all to yourself? At least for the time being?"

Yarrow shook his head slowly. "I don't know what the devil to do. By rights, I ought to get in touch with Pringle. I've never come across anything of the kind before. As a doctor ——"

"We're going to Stapley now," Bart told him. "There should be no difficulty in tracing the last one of the four. Gordon here has already started work on the father. We may even get some sort of reply today. Then the whole thing will be finished so far as we are concerned. You can be present when we set it all down on paper."

He looked at me. "That's how we'll have to do it. Write it all down. Then I suppose it will mean a trip up to London." He turned back to Yarrow. "It might be a good idea if you were to come with us when we do go. Will that help salve your professional conscience?"

"My professional conscience, as you call it, is only concerned with what took place at the confinement," the other rejoined heatedly. "I've no intention of letting myself be dragged into something that is little more than wild theory and supposition, and in any case is too damned fantastic to be taken seriously by anyone in their right mind."

"All right." Bart held up a pacifying hand. "I apologise.

You've made your point. Then will you let us take it through to the end before starting anything?"

"It's waited twelve years; a few more days can't make any difference. And I'm not sure Pringle can do anything when he does learn the truth. It'll most likely be a matter of letting sleeping dogs lie."

He smiled. "They can't do anything to Old Toddidoc, and that's for sure. They might want to take a look at the children though. . . ." He whistled softly. "Siamese quadruplets. . . . Four of them, born in a row, joined arm to arm. It takes some believing. And then separated by a quack. God!—he was lucky to get away with it. They must have been tough little brats."

"Tough," Bart echoed. "Yes, I suppose they must have been."

I thought he was about to say more but he changed his mind.

Yarrow straightened. "I'll go along with you again. And for God's sake, take it easy, Bart. You had a rougher do last night than you realise. I'll look in on you sometime this evening."

We watched him stride back to his car.

If it hadn't been for the tiredness prickle at the back of my eyes and the tenseness of nerves that refused to let any movement be automatic, I would have enjoyed the drive to the coast. Bart, his blanket folded beneath him, his head pillowed on his hands, slept most of the way. We reached Stapley-on-the-Sea shortly after half past twelve. At the police station, a cheerful-looking, yellow-brick building set in a quadrangle of trees, the desk sergeant was expecting us. At the mention of Bart's name he became briskly businesslike.

"Colonel Winter phoned earlier, sir. I think we have the information you are after. I made a note of it here. Male child, approximately ten months old, found in one of the promenade kiosks by a Miss Peters on the evening of 3 September 1953. Description: Dark hair and complexion. Healthy. Distinguishing marks: scar on left forearm. Will that be the one, sir?"

"I'm amazed," said Bart, "that you were able to locate it from the few words I had with the Chief Constable. That's the one all right."

"We were almost certain, sir. Stapley isn't the sort of place where unwanted babies are dumped regularly. We have no dance halls or night clubs. It makes a difference, you know. . . ."

"It must," Bart agreed gravely.

"According to our records there was only the one child found abandoned in the summer of 'fifty-three. Which made it easy to trace."

He waited for Bart's smile.

"It was brought to us, and we passed it on to the local orphanage asylum while the usual enquiries were made. Unfortunately we were unable to trace the mother. I have already phoned the institution. The child was adopted in June of 1954 by a Mr. and Mrs. Gregory. I have made a note of their address at the time. Brownleas, Haydon. Haydon is a small village some distance the other side of Brayminster."

"You have been most helpful, Sergeant——?"

"Upton, sir."

"Sergeant Upton. And efficient. I shall make a point of telling the Chief Constable so the next time we meet."

"That's very kind of you, sir."

A constable, typing at a desk, glanced up and then looked quickly back at his work, but not quickly enough to hide his private smirk.

Outside again, Bart, looking very pleased with himself, said: "Scar on left arm. Just as we worked it out. So now we've almost got the last one." He rubbed his hands. "Lunch first, I think, and then a trip out to—what was the name?—Haydon. It might be a good idea if we were to provide ourselves with a large-scale map of the district."

We bought the map after lunch at a hotel. Stapley was a bright place, red with buildings that seemed newly-washed, green with continual avenues of trees, colourful with crowded pavements of holiday-makers. We had to wait our turn for a table to become vacant at the hotel, and buying the map meant first having to wait in a queue before we could get to the counter. There was a further delay while Bart found a shop that sold his own particular brand of cigarettes.

Back in the car I spread the map across my knees and studied it, Joan's head satisfyingly close to mine, Bart leaning forward from the back seat to point out Brayminster for my benefit and then trace the winding third-class road that led to Haydon. As the sergeant had told us, Haydon lay perhaps five miles out of the cathedral city, and according to the contour markings, fairly high up in the hills. Refolding the map, tiredness came sweeping over me, perhaps the outcome of a heavy meal on top of only half a night's quota of sleep followed by what had been for me a long and tiring drive. I yawned loudly and uncontrollably.

Bart was immediately solicitous. "You look done in, Gordon. Would you like me to take the wheel for a time?"

The suggestion was more than welcome. All the same. . . .

"Are you sure——?" I started, but he was already on his way to change places. So I sat comfortably in the back and watched him nose away from the kerb into the almost solid line of traffic with a deceptive ease that roused my envy. Then I relaxed. Boarding houses and trees flowed smoothly by. Children, brown-skinned natives, laughed their way, buckets and spades in hands, to the waiting beach. The pavements emptied as we reached the outskirts. Boarding houses thinned to the larger, more select hotels, interspersed with tennis courts and golf courses. The sun was warm, the day golden, and I was very tired. Closing my eyes I dozed.

When I woke again we were progressing in a series of jerks, hemmed in by tightly-packed traffic, along a narrow street between tall, black-and-white fronted houses that leaned forwards until they threatened to meet overhead. Ahead were the twin spires of the cathedral, slanting grandly to the sky, a picture that I recognised although I had never been to the place before.

Seeing me awake Joan said unnecessarily: "Brayminster, Gordon." And then, smiling: "Did you have a good sleep?"

Bart's sagging shoulders, his tensed grip on the wheel, shouted his weariness aloud. I was angry with myself. It had been my intention to take back the wheel from him at Breston. Instead I had let him drive the whole fifty miles, a short enough distance for a young man, or even an elderly man accustomed to driving and in good health. But he was neither of those. When we had cleared the traffic and the road widened so that there was safe room in which to pull up, I leaned forward to tap his shoulder. "I'll take over again, Bart."

He made no protest. We made the change in silence. As we moved away Joan said quietly: "He wouldn't let me wake you."

At an unsignposted junction I stopped to consult the map again. Bart, I was pleased to see, was already fast asleep again. But I didn't like his pallor or the deeply-etched lines that bisected his cheeks. He was still asleep when we finally reached Haydon. I drew up outside what appeared to be the only public house in the place. Haydon was little more than a series of rows of flat-fronted cottages, a sombre church and a small cluster of shops. Grey and brown were the dominating colours; the harsh greys of the roofs and the dull browns of the spreading hills. There were a few trees, all

104

bent in the same tortured angle, shuddering away from the winter north-westerlies.

The public house was closed. Sleeping, I had forgotten the passage of time. It was nearly half past four. With a word to Joan I walked towards the shops. One of them was the inevitable combined sub post-office and general store, the windows a clutter of the dusty conglomeration of the years. This seemed the most likely place to enquire for a house called Brownleas.

The plump-featured woman who peered through the grille, sandwiched between a stack of canned fruit and an open bag of some kind of grain, was eager enough to be of assistance.

"You goes up the road a spell an' then takes the first lane on the right. Brownleas is at the top. You can't miss it. It'll be Mr. Hoyle you'll be after. I knows he's home; he were in here not twenty minutes since."

So the search wasn't to end at Haydon after all. I had had the feeling ever since leaving the police station that things seemed to be going too smoothly. But this was a post office. Perhaps the woman here was responsible in part of the local deliveries. If the Gregorys had left the district altogether then there might be a forwarding address still on record.

"I'm very anxious to get in touch with Mr. Gregory," I started.

Her features worked vigorously, eyebrows shooting up in startled surprise, eyes gleaming, mouth gaping momentarily. I was the ignorant stranger who knew nothing of what had been happening. She was inclined to be scornful.

"You mean you don't know nothing about them?"

I shook my head. "I'm afraid not." It was obvious now from her changing expression, from this new tone of her voice, that here was something more than just a family leaving a house and moving elsewhere. Here was a story that had to be told, and told slowly and carefully, right from the start, so that not one moment of tragedy should be overlooked. She folded her arms on the counter, her face close to the diamond mesh of rusty wire.

"I remember them coming to Haydon like it were yesterday. As nice a couple as you could hope to meet. . . ."

"I thought there was a child?" I interposed quickly, and received an impatient frown for the interruption.

"They didn't get him till they'd been here maybe a year. Mr. Gregory, he built a kiln in his garden; you know, for baking pottery. She used to do the painting on it. Nice stuff, it

105

were; I've still got some of it in the back. Then they used to parcel it up an' post it off.

"He had a little beard, trimmed to a point, and he always wore an open shirt and short pants, year in, year out. She were pretty enough in her own way; a bit washed-out to my way of thinking. In between painting she used to give lessons on the piano. . . ."

If nothing was to come of all this, then it was so much wasted information. "What happened?" I asked, but she refused to be hurried. There were no customers waiting to be served; all the time in the world was at her disposal.

"I don't know what got into them to want to adopt the kid. She didn't even tell me what she were going to do. One evening, in she comes, as pleased as Punch, with the baby in her arms.

" 'Look what I've got, Mrs. Jarrett,' she says. . . ."

I fretted impatiently through a word-by-word repetition of a meaningless conversation that had taken place eleven years ago. I had a mental picture of a young, arty-crafty couple. Now all I wanted to know was what had become of them and the child they had adopted. That it was the last one of the four, the one we had traced from Stapley, there could be no doubt. . . .

"And a regular little devil he turned out to be," Mrs. Jarrett was saying. "I've had a lot to do with kids in my time, but never a one like him. No one took to him; not even the other children. He were something more than just plain naughty. They couldn't do a mortal thing with him. . . ."

And then the same thing that I had heard twice before: "Mrs. Gregory used to say that they regretted the day they ever took him in."

The same pattern. "What happened?" I asked, and now she reluctantly acknowledged my impatience.

"He committed suicide," she breathed awesomely, watching my face, eager for the pleasure of my shocked reaction.

Shocked I was, but not in the way she intended.

"You mean Tony?" She didn't deny the use of his name, or query my knowing it, although she hadn't mentioned it herself.

"Not him!" she retorted vexedly at the anticlimax of my misunderstanding. "His father! Mr. Gregory. Hung himself from a tree. At the inquest they said he must've been out of his mind."

And that wasn't the end of it.

"She took it real bad as you might imagine, but she kept on

at the house. And then one day she came in here to post a letter. Tony would be about seven at the time.

" 'I can't go on like this any longer,' she tells me. 'I'm sending Tony away to a school. It's the only thing. . . .' Then she starts crying. Everyone knew he were too much for her, and for the rest of us, come to that. So I tells her she's doing the right thing."

It seemed then that the story was to end with another lead.

"Can you remember which school she sent him to?"

We had come to the second moment of awe.

"He didn't go to no school at all. Not that we knows of, anyway." She savoured this second climax. "That very same night the house burned down, with her inside. Nobody knows how it started. They found what was left of her, but never a sign of the boy. A lot of folks say he must've been inside as well, for all they never found a trace. Whichever way it was we've never seen anything of him since. The house stood as it was for a while, and then Mr. Hoyle came along and had it rebuilt. If you came here looking for the Gregorys, then you've had a wasted journey. . . ."

I walked back to where Joan waited by the car, Bart yawning and stretching himself awake. I had to tell them that it would be a waste of time going to Brownleas. I had to explain how the only lead to the last of the four had finished in a dead-end.

A woman had died in a blazing house, and a pony had perished in a burning stable. A schoolboy had thrown himself from a roof, and a man had hung himself from a tree. This seemed to be a pattern with no beginning and no ending. A pattern of death.

It was a long drive, and a silent one, back to Kendly. For the first time since hiring the car I found myself driving automatically, without first having to consider each gear change, without trying to anticipate what might lie behind each oncoming corner.

I was exhausted, and perhaps that was part of it. Perhaps too there was an odd sense of relief in the knowledge that our failure to find Tony meant that the complication of presenting the facts to Brother Harold would have to be postponed or even abandoned.

I felt sure, driving with the evening sun aslant the windscreen, that his enquiries about Pulner would come to nothing. It had been a waste of time to ask his help in the first place. . . . One American amongst millions; a hopeless task.

Now there was nothing left for us to do. Acceptance of that fact brought an anaesthetic calmness and resignation.

After dinner we went into the lounge with the windows that overlooked the garden. I was able to sit placidly while Bart wandered restlessly from window to bookcase and back to window again. Joan, seeming to sense my new mood, sat silently at my side on the settee. And I think I knew, before Bart broke the silence, what he was going to say. And I knew —with the I-have-done-all-this-before feeling of a dream— what we would say in return, and how things would be arranged.

"Miss Elizabeth," he said suddenly, turning from staring out at the garden. "That's the only lead we have left. Apart from Pulner——"

"I don't for one moment think that Brother Harold will come up with anything," I observed steadily.

"I think the same. I was never hopeful from the start." He looked at Joan. "Mrs. Biddle might be the only one who knows what became of Miss Elizabeth."

"There was no time to ask questions," she replied simply. "Sister was becoming impatient."

"We must talk to her again," he stated in a tone that brooked no denial. "And we can't afford to waste any time. Tomorrow may be too late."

"You want to go to the hospital now," I said.

"Now." He glanced urgently at his watch. "Nearly half past nine. The place will be bedded down for the night. But that doesn't matter. I'll find some way of getting to her. There's no point your coming, Gordon. . . ."

It was a play I was watching; a play with two characters and an audience of one. Soon the curtain would fall on one scene and rise on another. I waited for Joan to speak her part, but Bart took the lines for her.

"I think you'd better come with me, Joan. She knows you now. It will be better than a stranger. . . ."

Not characters on a stage, but puppets moving woodenly to the bidding of invisible strings. Through the open French windows the dusk-heavy garden was another artificial scene on another stage. It was cooler now than it had been, with a light mist collecting in the hollows between the trees.

Joan was uneasy about the proposed arrangement.

"One of us will have to stay here," I reminded her. "Don't forget that Dr. Yarrow promised to look in some time this evening."

Standing in the porch, I watched them drive away. Then I went back inside a house that had become filled with a curious, but not wholly frightening, sense of expectancy. The mist was thickening, tendrils reached out across the lawn. Shivering a little, I closed the windows and returned to the settee. The minutes ticked by. The windows that I had just closed opened slowly and silently, under their own volition it seemed, for Rodney Blake, standing there, watching me, had his arms at his sides.

11

Thin face; tar-black hair drooping across the hollow-templed forehead; cheek-bones so pronounced that contrast drove the eyes deep into the skull. He could have been only one of the four. Seeing two together had brought the others into being, so that all of them were vividly alive. But he wore a crumpled white shirt with the sleeves buttoned to the wrists, and so I knew he had to be Rodney.

Up until a few days ago we had been teacher and pupil. Now a very different relationship existed. I was afraid of him; not so much of the boy himself as for the unknown quantity he represented. On his part there was a kind of tolerant condescension; the amused tolerance of a superior being for one of his inferior. Glass beads for the natives. . . .

Afterwards, I felt that his visit had been prompted by nothing more than childish devilment, a spreading of derisory fingers to the nose, an irrepressible urge to show off. Whatever else he might be it seemed there was still a streak of the ordinary, mischievous schoolboy in him.

He had come to show off, to demonstrate some of his powers and gloat over our futility against them. Even the way in which he came—the windows that had seemed to open of their own accord—was part of the demonstration. As if he were saying: "This is just one of the things I can do. . . ."

And at the start he used a strange language of his own, an odd kind of phraseology, letting me know that this was the way they communicated with each other and that our language was inadequate for their needs.

He used their private way of speaking when—although I sensed that something was about to happen—I was startled to my feet by the uncanny moving of the doors and his ghost-like appearance out of the misty night to stand in the opening.

If he had ever learned to smile he would have smiled then, a sneering, supercilious smirk. His features remained as impassive as they had always been, but the intent was there just the same, in the tone of his voice.

"Not this time. There's nothing to be afraid of this time. Nothing is going to happen to you. Tony-me is sleeping. If I wake that part I will think it to Simon-me at the Pillory and to me at home, and then I will think it here so that I can go before it reaches."

Senseless jargon it seemed at the time. But thinking about it afterwards I was able to remember every word and understand what he had been telling me.

I said the first thing that came to mind.

"What are you doing here? What do you want?"

He regarded me steadily. "Just to talk to you."

"What about?"

He made the ghost of a shrug and for a moment was an ordinary boy, lost for words. "Oh—things."

But his watchful eyes said something different. "Here I am," they said. "Don't you want to find out what I can do?"

The thing was knowing where to start, which questions to ask first. This was the first real contact I'd had with him since—since I had called him back from the classroom door, ordering him to put his drawing on my desk. The morning when. . . .

"You were responsible for what happened to Thorne," I said.

The off-hand shrug again. "It was how it happened. Tony-me was big, and——" He broke off; started afresh. "Tony was with me when Thorne knocked me over, so Tony felt the hurt too. That's why it happened."

And while I was trying to make sense out of it:

"I didn't want anything else to happen. I thought the police coming and that they would ask me questions, so I let Peter in big so that there wasn't much room for Tony."

It was because I already had some idea of the links that existed between the four that I was able to understand a little of what he was saying. I tried putting it into my own words to see how they sounded.

"When Thorne hurt you, Tony felt pain at the same time. So he put a picture into Thorne's mind and he killed himself trying to run away from it. And then you were afraid that when the police asked you questions Tony would know what

110

was going on and might try the same with them if they became at all suspicious. . . ." Was I making any kind of sense? "So you linked with Peter instead, and he made you draw that sketch of Charidon."

I wondered how long we'd been talking. It was too early yet to listen for the sound of the car returning. Let Yarrow have five minutes with Rodney and he'd soon change his mind about impossible stories. Rodney had waited until I was alone before coming; perhaps he had even arranged that I should be alone. Did that mean he had no intention of talking to the others?

"Not to the others," he observed, although I hadn't spoken. And he added: "They'll soon be back. She's dead, you know."

I didn't ask how he knew. There was a certainty in his voice that told me he was speaking the truth. So he intended leaving before they returned. Ten minutes to the hospital—if Bart put his foot down, and I thought he would—a few minutes of enquiry, ten minutes back. Little enough time now in which to learn something of the four. For all I knew this might be the only opportunity I would have of learning anything about them. Questions teemed in my mind. I went for the one that seemed the most urgent.

"Where is Tony now?"

He didn't even bother to shake his head. His sardonic gaze was the only answer I got.

"Look, Blake," I said earnestly; "you can't go on the way you have been. You must have sense enough to realise that. We don't want you—any of you—to come to any harm. What we're trying to do is only for your own good. Quite a few of us know what you've been doing. In time, other people will find out too. People who matter—you understand? They will——"

What would they do to them? I didn't know.

"The longer you carry on like this, the worse it will be for you in the end. We only want to help you."

He called my bluff, making no attempt to disguise the sneer in his voice.

"Nobody can do anything to me. I'm not afraid of anyone. Nobody can hurt me."

Not "us"—but "me". And that struck me as odd. I had been talking about them as a whole, and he had answered only for himself. And that didn't seem to make sense; not when they were so closely linked that what happened to one must certainly effect the rest. Surely, under those circumstances, he would be as much concerned about his brothers as he was for himself. There wasn't time to try to work that out now. . . .

111

"You helped kill Thorne," I said steadily. "And Dodd. Four people know about it already. No matter what you——"

He wasn't even bothering to listen to me. His eyes narrowed, he stared over my shoulder.

"They're coming back." He was talking to himself, I think. "One, two—three. The other is with them."

I moved towards him then, with some idea of stopping him from leaving. But he moved so quickly that by the time I had crossed the room and reached the terrace he was down the steps and running across the moonlit lawn towards the mist and the shadows. When I called he ignored me. He vanished without a backward glance.

Then I went back through the house and opened the front door. Car lights swung into sight down the lane. I felt no surprise at seeing the lights of a second car following. The first pulled into the drive; the second stopped in the lane. Joan and Bart waited for Yarrow, and they came up the drive together.

"Our tame medico was just coming out of his place as we passed," Bart briefly explained, "so we waved him into the convoy." And with a change of tone. "We had no luck at the hospital, Gordon. Mrs. Biddle was dead when we got there. She died earlier this afternoon."

"I know——" I started without thinking, and bit the words off in time.

"So another lead peters out," I said instead.

Yarrow said coldly: "I wondered where you'd been. What on earth made you want to go bothering the old lady again?"

"We had no luck at Haydon," Bart retorted equally coldly, seemingly nettled by the tone. "But we still have Pulner to follow up. It's unlikely that Gordon's brother will come up with anything. Miss Elizabeth is the only other person who might be able to tell us anything about him, and Mrs. Biddle seemed the only one who might be able to tell us what became of her." He waited for the other to precede him into the hall. "Does that make things clear?"

"Abundantly so," Yarrow observed drily.

In the lounge he went into a semi-professional routine, checking Bart's pulse, listening to his heart then clicking his tongue and passing caustic remarks about old men tearing about the countryside like madmen when they ought to be resting in bed. While Bart busied himself at the decantered sideboard he flung himself into an easy chair, one leg cocked awkwardly over the arm. Yarrow always seemed to have trouble disposing of his ungainly limbs.

Joan, murmuring something about the evening becom-

112

ing cooler, hot drinks and sandwiches, vanished in the direction of the kitchen. I followed a few minutes later, not so much because I wanted to be alone with her—although under any other circumstances that would have been reason enough —but because I wanted to think, and the lounge was crackling with a resumption of earlier arguments.

Arranging cups and saucers on a tray Joan remarked: "You've been very quiet since we got back, Gordon." We hadn't reached the stage of using the usual engaged-couple endearments. But then we had had little enough time alone together since achieving that status.

"I had a visitor while you were away," I told her. She looked up quickly, pupils dilated.

"They came back again? Gordon, they didn't——?"

I reassured her anxiety. "Only the one; Rodney. And nothing happened. He just dropped in for a chat." I told her about the conversation.

"And that's all?" she marvelled.

"I'm sure that he just came to show off. And gloat. He boasted that there was nothing we could do to stop them."

I added an afterthought: "He seems to be able to read thoughts and move things without touching them. Telekinesis, I think it's called."

"Do they know?" she nodded in the direction of the lounge.

I shook my head. "It would be a waste of time telling Yarrow. He only deals in first-hand facts. And Bart, he's worried sick about Simon, although he doesn't say much about it. If I tell him that Rodney admits to Thorne's death it will only make matters worse. Suspicion's bad enough; knowing for certain a whole lot worse. I'll only tell him if it becomes necessary."

"Yes." She turned back to her work.

What had Rodney said? "Nothing to be afraid of this time. Tony-me is sleeping. . . ."

Tony-me. One word he had made of it.

"If I wake that part I will think it to Simon-me at the Pillory. . . ." Tony-me; Simon-me. And what or where in God's name was the "Pillory"?

"——And to me at home, and then here, so that I can go before it reaches."

Gibberish. But I thought I knew what "it" was. And some kind of relay system was suggested. "It" wouldn't start unless Tony awoke. If he did, the others would pass the message along until it finally reached Rodney.

"To me at home," he had said. Not Rodney himself because home for him was Cookley. So it had to be either Simon

113

or Peter. Simon's home, surely, was here at Kendly. That left Peter Latham. And he lived at Charidon.

I went along the hall that was filled with the argumentative buzz from the lounge. "So if I imagined it," Bart was saying indignantly, "then so did the others. I suppose you'll call that mass hypnosis." Opening the front door, I went out to the car. The road-map was in the glove compartment. Back in the kitchen I spread it open on the table. Joan, perhaps sensing something from my eagerness, left off work again to peer over my shoulder. I took a few seconds off to explain my theory. Then she helped by laying the back of the bread-saw along the line from Kendly to Charidon.

The children communicated with each other by thought. Was a straight line still the shortest distance between two points where thought-waves were concerned? We followed the back of the blade across the contours. The Pillory was a horse-shoe grouping of hills, smack on the straight line that led to. . . .

"So that's where Tony is," Joan said, in a matter-of-fact voice, as if there could be no doubt about it.

I folded the map and slipped it into my pocket. Then I waited until she had finished loading the tray so that I could carry it through to the lounge. She followed with a plate of sandwiches. Bart and Yarrow had lapsed into the truce of a brooding silence. I wondered if Yarrow's concern for his patient had anything to do with his obstinacy in refusing to accept our story. Most likely he was one of those earthy realists who will go to any lengths to find rational explanations for anything that smacks of abnormality, supernatural or otherwise. Which in a doctor is probably an admirable trait.

I said: "The boys all seem to run away at the same time. It seems reasonable to suppose they all make for the same place."

"We've gone over all that before," Bart said impatiently. I had the feeling he'd just lost a battle to Yarrow.

"I think I know where that place is," I said.

There was an odd little silence. Yarrow stared at me very hard. Bart leaned forward. "You do? Where?"

"Werkley Ridge," I told them, and I thought: This will mean that I'll have to tell Bart about the visit after all.

But it didn't. He found another reason for Werkley being the place. Or perhaps he was clutching at a straw.

"Of course!" He slapped his knee. "Where they were born. The only place where they were ever together. We should have thought of that before."

Yarrow was unimpressed by the reasoning.

"I'll grant you that there may be links between identical twins that will try to bring them together. In identical quads it may be even more developed. But it is only the wildest supposition to think that they would home on their birthplace. God damn it, man! They were only twelve months old when they left Werkley Ridge. They won't be able to remember a damned thing about the place, least of all where it is."

Bart refused to be swerved. "They aren't ordinary children."

The other drew in his chin with a resigned, here-we-go-again gesture, made as if to speak, caught Joan's eye and shrugged heavily instead.

"Sandwiches?" she invited generally, oiling the water. "Cheese this side, boiled ham the other. The best I could do, I'm afraid."

I dealt plates like a pack of cards.

Yarrow was still resigned. "I suppose this will mean another trip."

Bart, choosing himself a sandwich, grunted in reply.

"Tomorrow"—the doctor reflected—"let me see; Saturday. No morning surgery. I suppose I could forego my week-end round of golf. Can you find room for another passenger in that beetle-car of yours, Seacombe?"

"I thought wild-goose chases weren't your line of country," Bart commented drily.

"They're not. But my patients are. And you, God help me, are one of them. The most obstinate and unco-operative of the damned lot."

Which was, I felt, a poor enough excuse for wanting to accompany us. Perhaps Dr. Yarrow wasn't all that narrow-minded and dogmatic after all.

He left a few minutes before eleven. At Bart's suggestion I rang Brother Harold's home to see if he had anything for us. He hadn't; he wasn't even hopeful.

"I gave the American Embassy a ring immediately after your call, Gordon. They said they'd do what they could. The trouble is, the information you were able to give me is very little to go on. If you had the exact date of arrival it would make things infinitely easier. As it is. . . ." I felt his shrug over the phone.

"Thanks a lot, anyway," I told him.

I was a long time getting to sleep that night. Perhaps it was because I had passed from the stage of physical exhaustion to that of mental, or maybe it was because I had so much to think about. Whatever the cause I lay and stared at the ceiling and relived over and over the conversation with Rodney Blake. I had made enough sense out of it already to work out where Tony might be living. Could I take that same process of reasoning a step further?

I could, and after a while, I did. Understanding came so swiftly that I found myself sitting up in bed, hands pressed tightly to my temples as if that would help me think the clearer.

There was a pattern. There was the "I" who was Peter, the "I" who was Simon, the "I" who was Tony and the "I" who was Rodney himself. When he had said "Nobody can do anything to me" it was exactly the same as if he had said "Nobody can do anything to us". The links between them were something much more than an ability to transmit thought and sensation. Something much more. A link that was as solid as if it were made of flesh and bone.

This was dual personality carried to its incredible extreme. Doctor Jekyll working in his surgery at the same time as the evil Mr. Hyde prowled the night streets. Hyde looking through Jekyll's eyes into a microscope at the same time that Jekyll was watching through Hyde's eyes the back-street slut marked down as his next victim. At the same time; that was the difference. Not one man with two interchangeable personalities, but one man with two separate personalities, each housed in a separate body. One man who was two.

And four boys who were one. The Rodney-me part with a talent for writing; Simon-me—physics and chemistry, according to Bart; Peter-me who was an artist. And Tony-me, musician, and other things. The part responsible for the killings. The evil quarter of the multiple personality. The dominant part. . . .

When I had talked with Rodney I hadn't been speaking to one boy but to four. No—three. One part had been sleeping. The part that would have hurt me if it had had the opportunity.

Each piece in this new picture fitted smoothly into place. I felt certain that I had reasoned my way to the truth. Incredible as the solution seemed, it fitted all the facts.

And having worked everything out to my satisfaction I lay back on the pillows, closed my eyes and went out like a light.

12

Waking from a dreamless sleep to a room golden with sunshine was not the abrupt return to reality that I had become accustomed to the past few days, but a drifting into that pleasant half-and-half existence, neither asleep nor fully awake, where nothing seems of any great importance and thoughts fall into place without any trouble at all.

The ormolu clock on the bedside table pointed filigree fingers to ten o'clock. Completely relaxed, I lay and listened to the comfortable sounds of the house underneath. Understanding had brought a feeling of security. Know your enemy. . . . I felt I knew a great deal about the enemy now. To better understand a problem, Bart had once said, put it down on paper. And he had come up with the first important truth. Paper dolls in a row. But how could one draw on paper four separate things that were only the one? Draw and fold? No; they would still be four different things. It was a difficult concept even to hold in mind. I found an analogy of sorts that helped. And would probably help Joan to understand when I came to tell her. I would have to tell her. But not the others. Yarrow would treat my theory with ridicule and contempt. Bart—he might accept it. But Simon was part of this thing that had four separate lives.

In the hall Jenny, dour-faced, polishing a mirror, grunted in reply to my greeting and comment about the weather. But in the kitchen Joan, the table laid ready, pan waiting on stove, responded very differently.

After a while she disengaged herself, patted her hair back into place and turned back to the stove to set the pan spluttering.

She said: "I overslept as well; I've only been down about a quarter of an hour. I looked in on Bart but he was sleeping like a baby. I hadn't the heart to disturb him."

"He needs all the rest he can get," I said. "Yarrow's right, of course; he shouldn't be gallivanting round the country. Not after what happened. He was lucky. We all were, come to that."

"Like that time at Charidon," she said calmly enough. "Only that was different."

I thought that I knew the backgrounds to each attack that had been launched. But first I had to explain, or try to explain, the theory that I had worked out. She listened without stopping work. But she only partly understood what I was saying.

"You mean that they are linked in some way all the time, not just occasionally; that each of them knows all the time what the others are thinking or doing?"

"It's more than that." I brought out my analogy. "Imagine you live under water and don't know anything about the world above the surface. All right. Now, one day, someone in this world you know nothing about tucks his thumb across his palm and dabbles four fingers in the water. All you see are four separate things, alive, but unconnected. You have no way of telling that they are in fact all part of the same thing. You see four separate creatures when there is actually only the one. That's what the children are like. We see them as four different boys. But it's not like that at all."

She was silent for a few minutes. Water gurgled in the drain below the open window.

"He's up," she said absently. Then: "Four different things can't be one, Gordon. It's impossible."

"It's impossible according to our concept of life. This is something different. A new kind of life, if you like. Try to think of it in terms of ourselves. Each of us is a mixture of a whole lot of things, basically good and evil. Mostly we keep the evil traits out of sight. But they're there all the same. A good person may change completely if something happens to his mind. Remember Jekyll and Hyde? A story based on medical fact. The sort of thing that could happen. Does happen, come to that. There's an operation—I think they call it a frontal lobotomy—by which something is done to the brain so that the character changes. A criminal becomes a respected member of society. But the man he becomes as a result of the operation must have been there all the time. Do you see?"

She didn't, and I tried again.

"Go right back to the time of birth. Go farther back still. Remember what Brother Harold told me when I asked him about identical twins?"

She shook her head. "You didn't explain very much about it."

"They start off by being a single fertilised cell. That cell is the nucleus of a human being. It's got everything necessary

118

to form the new character. Part of it is evil, part is good. Then the cell divides. Each new cell forms a group called the blastula. And each group contains the same mixture of good and bad. But supposing all the good goes into one group, and all the evil into the other. And supposing that instead of separating completely the two groups of cells remained joined, and are born that way. . . ."

"Siamese twins."

"But with a difference. Not two babies joined together and surgically parted to form two separate entities, but only the one baby, divided into two halves, capable of existing separately, but still only the one. Now do you see?"

"I think so," she agreed doubtfully.

"It was the way Rodney used words that gave me the first clue. He used 'I' instead of 'We'. There was no such thing as 'Them', meaning the other three. He spoke of the 'Tony-part' and 'Simon-me'. Just as we might say: part of me wants to do something, but the other part doesn't."

She shook her head. "I still can't see it clearly, Gordon. I can visualise the fingers in the water, but only because I know they're linked out of sight."

"That's how the four children are linked; out of sight."

"Supposing something serious was to happen to one of them? Supposing one of them was to die? If you're right, what would happen to the other three?"

"Cut off one finger," I said, "and the others would still go on living."

But I wasn't so certain about that as I would have her believe. Analogies are all very well when you're trying to visualise something. But they don't always match up with the full circumstances.

"Everything that has happened so far can be made to fit the theory," I told her. "They have four brains between them; it's reasonable to suppose that their faculties will be multiplied accordingly. That could explain their unusual powers. The various natural talents have been distributed between them, magnified again. Each of them is brilliant at one subject. Three of them seem to be 'good.' One of them has collected all the evil traits, Tony. And evil being the dominant characteristic, he is the one who rules the roost. Or tries to. The others gang up on him at times. Like when Rodney came to see me last night. He made sure that nothing would happen to me.

"That first time when I saw the abyss; it was terrifying but not dangerous. Rodney must have known that I was on to something so he tried to warn me off. Then he followed us to

Charidon. Tony got at us there, through Rodney, and that was a deliberate attempt to kill. And so was the time when we were out on the terrace. It would have been successful then if Rodney and Simon hadn't started to run away before it came. They knew it was coming. Part of the composite creature wanted to kill us; part didn't. But how often do we do things 'despite ourselves', as we say?"

"You may be right." Joan brought a loaded plate to the table and I drew up a chair.

She said: "I was thinking; when the children run away they still have to eat. Where do they get food from, Gordon?"

Which was something I hadn't thought about.

Then Bart's voice boomed genially from the hall. "Good morning to you, Jenny. And how are you this fine morning?" I didn't catch her reply. Perhaps she hadn't offered one.

He was his usual self, debonair as always, now wearing a tweed jacket that could have come from nowhere else but the Highlands. A red silk scarf replaced his tie, tucked carefully into the neck of a white silk shirt. There was a faint dusting of talc on his chin, and this he discovered and fastidiously removed in front of the mirror by the door, where he had paused for his customary inspection after first greetings had been exchanged.

He had an appetite that put mine to shame. He was still eating when I went back upstairs to collect the map I had left on the dressing-table. This time I would be travelling a different road to Werkley. Two routes seemed likely; one through Charidon, the other via Brayminster, two sides of an ellipse with little to choose between them where mileage was concerned. I decided upon the former because at least I knew my way as far as Charidon.

I found the place where I had asked the farmer the way to Werkley Ridge. "Five miles up the road and take the left-hand turn" he had said. It was as well I remembered. Werkley wasn't marked on the map. But some five miles along the road a dotted line led away into the hills, to a narrow valley with only the one entrance. At least I knew now where I would be making for.

It was nearly half past eleven before we got under way. Bart, in his usual place in the back, his blanket thoughtfully augmented with a cushion, guided me first to Yarrow's home. The doctor, dressed in high-necked pullover, floppy jacket and not over-clean slacks, was waiting for us at his gate, glancing significantly at his watch as I drew up. We had arranged to collect him at eleven.

"I took your advice," Bart told him virtuously, "and got

in some extra sleep. Sorry we're late. Where on earth did you rake that rig-out from?"

I drove back through the market square and turned into a road that had become familiar. In the back Yarrow and Bart wrangled happily without any mention of the purpose of the trip. But there was still an undeniable undercurrent of tension.

Passing through Charidon, nearly twelve o'clock now, Yarrow said: "Let me see; you've been to Werkley before. I suppose there's a pub of some kind where we can get a decent meal?"

"We didn't actually go into the place itself," I told him. "It can't be very big, though; it's not marked on the map."

We were beyond the village now, on the left-hand fork past the church, a road that was strange to me, the sign-posts pointing to a place called Korfe. Harvesting was in full swing in some of the fields.

Five miles beyond Korfe we met the Breston road and I was back on familiar territory. There were the spreading moorlands, the patches of scrub, the dun-coloured billows of hills. We were climbing steadily, and from time to time, despite the warmth of the sun, the breeze blew suddenly cold.

"You're certain this is the right road?" Yarrow asked anxiously.

We were passing the isolated small-holding in its hidden green valley.

"This is as far as we came last time," I said. "It was the farmer here who told me that Werkley Ridge was empty."

Yarrow's worry about it being the right road was occasioned by his anxiety about a place to eat. "We don't all lie in bed till midday. I had breakfast at eight. It's getting on for half past twelve and this road seems to be leading away from civilisation."

"Werkley," Joan suggested, "can't be very far ahead now. And in any case, we've just passed a hotel. You were too busy looking the other way. We can always come back again."

We reached Werkley ten minutes later, and I almost drove straight through before realising, when there seemed nothing ahead save trees and hills, that two rows of dilapidated cottages and a small public house was all the village consisted of. Reversing clumsily I edged off the road on to a cobbled verge.

"The Farmer's Pride"—the name was painted in white, ill-formed letters above the narrow doorway—was made up of two cottages joined together and an extra storey added, no pretence having been made to match the stone walls of the old with the more recent red-brick additions. But the wood-work was brightly painted, the cobbles weeded, and there were colourful curtains to the narrow windows.

There was an antiseptic, soft-soap scrubbed appearance about the interior. A white-topped counter ran the length of the narrow room. There were two beer pumps, a barrel covered with a clean cloth, three shelves laden with bottles. The landlord was a brisk, dapper-looking man with sleek black hair and a small black moustache. That he was in his shirt-sleeves detracted not at all from his business-like, well-dressed appearance. One felt that his jacket had been removed solely in deference to his surroundings and not because he preferred it that way.

Two men, farmers by their dress, leaned against the far side of the counter, breaking off a low conversation to watch our entrance. One was hatless, his hair a rough grey thatch. The other wore an old battered felt with the rim turned down.

The beer was as good as any I had tasted elsewhere. Sherry was carefully measured and poured for Joan. Yarrow thawed over his tankard sufficiently to broach the matter of food.

"We do dinners for some of the labourers," said the land-lord, "farm-hands, you know. The wife will be seeing to it now. I don't see why she shouldn't be able to fix you up. . . . All of you?"

"All of us," agreed Bart a little flatly, perhaps not feeling too happy at the prospect of a meal that had been intended for farm-workers.

"Another four. Very good, sir. That's if you don't mind waiting a while?"

"All the time in the world," said Bart with small maliciousness and a sideways glance at Yarrow.

"I'll have a word with Elsie," said the landlord, vanishing into the shadows of a doorway.

"Not a local man, I would say," Bart commented conversationally. He looked round with approval. "Nice little place. Clean." Meeting the gaze of the two farmers he nodded genially. "Good morning, gentlemen."

They returned the greeting but made no effort to strike up a conversation. Felt Hat was burly, with a pleasant, dark brown face that was a mesh of wrinkles, and surprisingly bright blue eyes. His companion was morose-looking, wiry, and had a whispy, brown-stained white moustache. He was the one who pointedly turned his back on us after Bart's conversational gambit.

The landlord returned. He was still smiling, but now I had the impression his smile had the appearance of being fixed.

Behind him, in the gloom, a woman's head bobbed as she tried to look over his shoulder.

He said: "It will be ready in half an hour. I'm sorry about the delay but Elsie had only been preparing for three." He threw a quick glance in the direction of the silent farmers. "There is a garden out at the back. Perhaps——?" He lifted a counter-flap in such obvious invitation that it would have been almost impossible for us to have refused even if we had been so inclined. We followed him along a stone-flagged passage with doors leading off on either side. There was no sign of the owner of the bobbing head. The garden was a narrow strip of lawn bounded by bushes and a couple of rustic benches.

"This is usually private." He swept his hand vaguely. "The garden, I mean. But I thought you might prefer privacy. My name is Cole, by the way; Albert Cole."

"A pleasure to make your acquaintance, Mr. Cole," Bart said grandly. "Not a local man, I take it?"

"Manchester; both the wife and me." He put one hand on his chest. "Asthma. The doctor told me to get out in the country. We bought this place on spec, as you might say. We get more than enough fresh air up here."

He leaned sideways against the door so that he could look up the passage and keep an eye on the bar. He was patently ill-at-ease.

"Bleak in winter," Yarrow suggested.

"You can say that again. We've been here two of them. Cut off for two months last winter. Worse the one before. You can have too much of anything."

He turned back to face us, his gaze moving from Bart's face to Yarrow's, resting finally on mine.

"You'll be the one who was enquiring about Werkley Ridge a day or two ago?"

One thing about the country, Bart had said, everybody knows everyone else's business.

"That's right," I agreed steadily.

"The chap you asked was one of our regulars. He was in the same night talking about it. He described you; it wasn't hard to figure you were the same party."

"He told me that Werkley Ridge was standing empty."

His eyes fixed on my face, he nodded slowly. Too slowly. "It is; has been for a good few years seemingly. He said you hadn't come with the idea of trying to buy."

"No." The others seemed content to leave me to do the talking. So far as Yarrow was concerned the only thing in the world that mattered were the tankard in his hand and the smell of cooking that drifted from the passage.

"We're interested in the people who used to live there."

"Oh." I think he was relieved. It was hard to tell. Certainly there was a change in his expression. "Some folk called Pulner used to have it. You'll be relatives or friends?"

"No," I told his steady gaze. Without the smile his face looked different. Saturnine, almost. "To get to the place I suppose we carry on up the road?"

There was no doubt now about his expression. Few people can disguise sudden trepidation.

"You're not thinking of going up there?"

"That was the idea," Bart put in. I noticed that Yarrow had lost interest in his tankard and was watching the various expressions that flitted across Mr. Cole's face.

"There's no reason why we shouldn't go there, is there?" I asked.

He hesitated longer than was necessary. "No. . . ." Then: "I'll go and see how dinner's coming along." He went along the passage.

"He's not happy about something," Bart diagnosed. "Wouldn't you say, Gordon? Gone to talk it over with the wife?"

Perhaps he was right. Or perhaps Mr. Cole wanted to be alone for a few minutes while he made up his own mind. He came slowly back down the passage, staring hard at the ground.

"You'll be from the town?" he asked, looking up finally.

I answered for myself and Joan. "Yes."

"Before we came here, Elsie and me, we'd neither of us been away from the city. We figured that country folk would be different. Well, it stands to reason. . . . We made up our minds once it was settled we'd take the 'Pride' that we'd lean over backwards trying to be one of them. When in Rome, you know. A good landlord's got to be like that. No use if he isn't. He's got to fit. Take an interest in the weather and crops. . . ."

I felt he had made his point.

"Give and take, as you might say; don't laugh at the things they believe in. Berries on the bushes means a hard winter coming; that sort of thing. Local stories; even maybe a ghost or two. We expected that, and we were ready to listen and then laugh at them between ourselves, Elsie and me. But we didn't expect——"

He broke off for a moment.

"You'll maybe laugh at me when I tell you," said Mr. Cole.

"We did ourselves, at first. But not now. It's something that lives up at the top of the valley, in Werkley Ridge. They call it the Black Boy."

"So you came across a ghost after all," Yarrow suggested.

"It's not like that at all. It's flesh and blood right enough. Of a sort. Me and Elsie have seen it for ourselves many a time."

He broke off again.

"If you carry straight on past the 'Pride' you come to a fork. The left-hand road leads to Maybrick's farm. He's one of those at the bar; the one without a hat. Born here in Werkley. Steady as a rock and no imagination. You've got to be like that to make a living out of this soil. Used to keep cows. One night in November, about five years ago, a knock came to his door. There was a boy there, only a youngster, just about six or seven, Maybrick says, sly-faced, filthy, dark-brown complexion, black hair, dressed in rags. A gypsy's brat if ever there was one. The kid said he wanted food. Maybrick told him to get the hell out of it. The next morning when he went out to his shippen every one of his cows was dead. Eight of them. And when he had the vet down to see what had caused it, they could find no reason at all.

"That was the start of it. The kid came banging on the door the next night, and Maybrick sent him packing again. Then he went in the parlour where he was doing his accounts. After a while something—he's not sure what—made him go into the hall. His daughter, seventeen at the time, had hung herself from the bannisters. He cut her down just in time. While they were waiting for the doctor to come the boy came back again. He told Maybrick that the next time he wouldn't get to his daughter in time to save her. So Maybrick gave him what he asked for.

"Then there's Daniel Farm just by the fork. The Nisteds live there. He lost his cattle and had a heart attack before he knuckled under. Up in the valley there's Brass Farm. Fletcher lives there. He's the one with Maybrick in the bar. The Black Boy got at him through his son. Martin was cleaning out the pigs when it happened. Fletcher saw the whole thing but couldn't get there in time to do anything. There was a tractor in the yard. It started moving of its own accord, quietly. It knocked Martin down and went over his arm."

He stopped, perhaps waiting for our disbelief. Bart cleared his throat and glanced at Yarrow who refused to meet his eyes, staring down instead at his tankard.

"Those are only some of the things that have happened,"

Cole said. "When they knew that the Black Boy had come to stay they tried to get away. Fletcher was the first one to try. His wife tried to cut her throat. And——" He shrugged. "After a while they knew they would have to stay here."

"And you?" Yarrow asked quietly.

"We came here a couple of years back. At first we took the tales with a grain of salt, even though we saw the Black Boy for ourselves. The first winter we were here was a real hard one. We were snowed up for three months. That was why we planned on packing it in. You've not seen Elsie yet. She'll limp badly for the rest of her life. She fell down the stairs. She says there was no one there, but somebody pushed her. The Black Boy came to tell me that it would happen again, only worse, if we didn't change our minds."

His wife came down the passage to stand at his side, smiling. I tried not to look at her limp. It was painful and grotesque.

"I've set a table in the parlour," she told us, "I thought you'd prefer not to go in the kitchen with the others."

A thin, colourless woman, she put one hand on her husband's arm, asking, "Well, Albert?"

"They were thinking of going up to the Ridge," was all he replied, but she understood, nodding, not losing her gentle smile.

And that was all. Whether we believed what we had been told was up to us. Take it or leave it; sneer or be horrified. It was all the same. They had done their part.

13

When there are other things to think about eating becomes a habit, a series of automatic actions. The room had bright pictures on white walls; a cool stone-flagged floor with rush mats. We saw nothing of our fellow-diners, only heard their leaving, the sudden clamour of heavy boots in the passage.

And then back to the garden again, a casual drifting out into the sun, to the shade of the benches under the trees. Bart, his hands folded, eyes closed, made pretence of dozing. At his side Yarrow brooded over his refilled tankard. Joan and I were silent on the other bench. One of us would have to break the silence. It seemed nobody was willing to be that one.

"It started about five years ago," Yarrow said suddenly after a while. He looked at Bart, who kept his eyes closed, and then at me. "He must have made his way straight here after the fire." No argument now, only acceptance.

"Yes," I said.

"The last one of the four. And the others?"

"I think they're all up there," I said.

"In a house that's falling to pieces, living on food blackmailed from the locals. God. . . ."

"We can't go up there after them," Bart said, opening his eyes.

"Nothing was further from my mind." That was complete acceptance now of everything we had told him. "A reign of terror. And nobody has done a thing to stop it."

"And if you were one of them?" wondered Bart; "the one who almost lost his daughter. What would you do? Bring in the police? Or would you try to take the law into your own hands?"

I left them to argue it out between them. And I had no doubts at all that he—or they—knew what was going on. They could read thoughts, but how far could their minds reach out? And I wondered too, almost disinterestedly, if any effort would be made to prevent our leaving when the time came.

Yarrow's demand for immediate action was set against Bart's reluctance.

"We've got what we came for," he said. "We" now, not "You." "We have the four of them. And all the proof needed to convince authority. What more do you want? Written statements from the landlord and the farmers? They'll talk their heads off if they thought there was anyone who would listen and believe and help."

"You're taking a great deal for granted," Bart said. "They might not be all that willing to talk. And before we take the thing any further we've got to have all the facts. We're still waiting to learn something about Pulner."

"Pulner?" Yarrow cried incredulously. "Good God, man! What difference can he make now? That's only waste of time. This has got to be stopped as soon as possible. Don't you understand? They're only children. They're going to grow up, marry. . . . Have children of their own. Or hadn't you thought about that?"

"I had considered that," Bart replied evenly. "That's why we have to find out what kind of man their father was. As a doctor I thought that would be something you would understand. We're supposed to be civilised people. If we can find out why the children are like this we might be able to find some way of. . . ." He paused. "Of changing them."

"That's a problem for someone cleverer than you or I."

"Then surely it's up to us to be able to supply him with all the information he needs before he tries to tackle it," Bart retorted a little desperately.

I tried to come to his rescue. "I think we ought to wait and see if any information about their father is forthcoming."

Yarrow turned his anger on me. "I'd have thought you'd have had more sense, Seacombe! You more than anyone else must know how dangerous they are. They've killed and maimed already. While we're hanging around, twiddling our thumbs, they might kill again."

I was saved from being drawn into the argument by Mr. Cole coming along the passage and blinking out into the sunshine. He was wiping his hands on a towel and telling us: "I'll be closing the bar in a few minutes, but you're welcome to stay out here as long as you like."

"That's very kind of you," Joan replied.

He seemed to sense the atmosphere. His puzzled eyes rested on Yarrow's thunderous face. And while he hesitated I heard the sound of a car drawing up outside, taking note of it simply because it was the first traffic sound I had heard since arriving. It was rare enough apparently to make the landlord glance back along the passage and then hasten away to see who had stopped outside his inn.

Seconds later he returned, more puzzled than ever, followed by a peak-capped, uniformed policeman.

"Would any of you gentlemen happen to be a Mr. Seacombe?" Mr. Cole asked generally.

I came quickly to my feet. "Is something wrong?"

The policeman shook his head, smiling. "Nothing like that, sir. Would you be kind enough to accompany us back to Banford? The superintendent would like a word with you."

"What about?"

He shook his head again. "I've no idea at all, sir. All I do know is that it seems to be a matter of some urgency. We've been trying to locate you since eleven this morning. All we had to go on was an address—Lowton Villa, Kendly—and the number of your car. It was only by luck that the constable on point duty at Korfe spotted you going through."

I looked down at Bart. "The only person who knew where I was staying was Brother Harold."

He came eagerly to his feet. "I'd better go with you." Joan

128

was at my side too. The policeman was doubtful. "We were only told to find Mr. Seacombe. . . ."

"I'll stay here," Yarrow decided. "You'll be coming back of course." It wasn't a question but Bart elected to regard it as such. "That all depends."

"You'll be back," the other declared significantly, "whether or not you do find out——" He stopped at Bart's look. "I'll try and have a word with some of the farmers."

We followed the constable back along the passage. The bar, still open, was empty save for one young man wearing corduroys who leaned against the counter over a half-empty glass. One arm was held awkwardly to his side and I wondered if this was Fletcher's son and the arm the heritage of the tractor.

At the waiting police car: "You'll be driving your own vehicle, sir?"

"That would be best," I agreed.

Bart spoke only the once during the whole of the journey. "We shouldn't have left him there. He still doesn't know what we're up against." And meeting my eyes in the mirror: "It's different when you know from personal experience. . . ."

Forced to keep pace with the police car I made better time than I had on the outward run. We nosed through the market square traffic as the town hall clock was striking half past four. I had an idea that Brother Harold would be waiting in one of the hotels. Instead we played follow-my-leader through a maze of narrow side streets to the police station.

The superintendent was waiting by the desk. Confronted with three people when he had been expecting one he was as doubtful as his constable had been, recognising Bart, addressing him by name, leaving us then with an apology, returning almost immediately.

"Only Mr. Seacombe." I was reminded of some stupid party game. He opened another door for Joan and Bart. "Perhaps you would care to wait in here. I'll see that refreshment is brought." Firm; but V.I.P. treatment. "This way please, Mr. Seacombe. . . ."

It must have been all of five years since I had seen Brother Harold. He hadn't changed at all; still as pinkly-plump, as sleekly self-satisfied as ever. The same ghost reek of operating room ether that had always clung to his clothes. Once, I had suspected him of deliberately spraying it over his person. His greeting was effusive; my hand lost in his flabby, ivory-white pillow. How could a hand like that even hold a scalpel? His bulk, his massive shoulders, topped by the full-moon of his face, hid the room and its contents from sight.

I didn't see the man who sat at the desk until he stepped aside to deal with the matter of an introduction.

"Gordon; this is Mr. Chillon. He has flown from the States especially to meet you. . . ." Big brother to little brother; you'll never guess who has come specially to see you. . . .

Mr. Chillon was the kind of person who can lose himself in a crowd or even blend into the wallpaper. Thinning grey hair, greyish face, even a grey shirt and tie with the dull grey suit. The epitome of self-effacement. The kind of face one can never quite bring to mind. Only the eyes alive, cold and brilliant behind rimless glasses. A throaty voice, almost a monotone; little or no American accent. A man who had no time to waste on apologies, or thanks. Or any other of the niceties of life.

"You made enquiries about a Stanley Pulner, Mr. Seacombe. Those enquiries were passed on to my department in Washington." He didn't say what that department was. "What can you tell me about him?"

This was Bart's authority on my very doorstep.

"Only what I have already told my brother."

"What prompted you to make the enquiries?"

I didn't like Brother Harold breathing down my neck. I didn't like Mr. Chillon's abrupt way of asking questions. And most of all I didn't like his eyes.

"I'm afraid it was only to satisfy my own curiosity."

"Tell me what made you curious, Mr. Seacombe."

Brother Harold urged: "Tell him everything you know, Gordon. It might be important." Which suggested that Mr. Chillon had already taken him into his confidence. If Brother Harold, why not me?

When I hesitated Mr. Chillon opened a folder on the desk.

"We have managed to trace your movements during the past few days. We know that you visited the local hospital and spoke with a Mrs. Biddle who has since died. We have also been in touch with a Mrs. Fox at Breston. . . ."

"Stanley Pulner died twelve years ago," I said.

He lifted his eyes slowly from the folder. "We know that."

"Then you know as much as I do."

"I see." His gaze shifted a fraction, looking now over my shoulder.

"I can vouch for him," Brother Harold said solemnly.

"Yes. Of course." The flint eyes came back to my face. "And why did you go to Werkley, Mr. Seacombe?"

"You might say a trip to the country," I told him, which was true enough. But I wasn't to be allowed to get away with it.

"It wouldn't have anything to do with Pulner's son?"

Son! not sons. So he hadn't found out everything. Of course; if he had spoken to Mrs. Fox she would simply have repeated the same story she told Bart. Only one child had been born to Mrs. Pulner. And Mrs. Biddle was dead.

I was a while thinking out a suitable reply. So long that it seemed he took my silence for refusal.

"There are reasons for my questions, Mr. Seacombe. I already have your brother's word that he will respect my confidence. Have I yours?"

I thought about Joan and Bart. They would understand.

"You have it," I said.

He bent his head over the folder again. "I will be as concise as possible. If there is any point that you don't understand, please stop me.

"Stanislav Pulcheknic was born in Warsaw in 1923. His father was a shopkeeper. In 1940, when he was seventeen, he was taken by the Germans and used as forced labour until 1942. Then, for some reason that our records don't show, he was sent to Belsen concentration camp. In 1945 he was liberated by an American unit, subsequently becoming officially attached to that unit as an interpreter. In 1948 he was admitted into the States and became an American citizen the following year, changing his name to Stanley Pulner. He enlisted in a semi-military organisation that provides security guards for research establishments. He was sent to the atomic research centre at Fort Kindly.

"The same year there was a minor explosion at the centre, with some escape of radio-activity. Hospitalisation of those concerned showed that nobody had suffered permanent damage. There was, however, the routine suspicion of sabotage. Pulner, along with the others concerned, was duly cleared. But it seemed that a stigma of sorts still clung to him. Perhaps because of his accent and Slavonic appearance. In 1950 he resigned from the organisation, and dropped completely out of sight."

Mr. Chillon glanced up.

"A straightforward enough story so far, Mr. Seacombe. Not an unusual one. And so it would have remained but for a second explosion at Fort Kindly." He looked down again. "In the following year. As before, sabotage was suspected, more acutely for it being the second time. More stringent investigations were made, both regarding present and past security staff. And certain interesting facts came to light. Trying to trace Pulner's whereabouts at the time of the second explosion we questioned one of his associates, a Gregor Stubits.

Stubits, we learned, had been in Belsen at the same time as Pulner. He told us that in March of 1945 Pulner was removed to the camp hospital, remaining there in the hands of Dr. Heimut Fechter until the camp was liberated. Pulner later told Stubits that he had no idea what had been done to him. There had been several operations—Stubits was unable to tell us where the scars were—and a series of injections. Does the name 'Fechter' mean anything to you Mr. Seacombe?"

I thought. "No."

"A bio-physicist," inserted Brother Harold; "a genetic expert with revolutionary ideas. Genes, chromosomes; hereditary factors. He was one of the pioneers of the system now known as the D.N.A. Chain. A brilliant scientist." He sounded enthusiastic.

"He was an ardent Nazi and a personal friend of Hitler's," Mr. Chillon supplied unemotionally. "At his trial at Nuremberg it was shown that over two hundred people had died on his operating table. He was subsequently executed. There was little trouble proving his guilt; he was methodical enough to keep records, and foolish enough to allow them to be captured intact. In point of fact he was actually burning them when captured. I have photostats here of two pages from his journal. The first: '9 March 1945. Have selected a healthy male of Polish extraction for the final experiment. Name: Stanislav Pulcheknic. Age: 22. Number: 7518922.'

"And the second: '17 April 1945. Pulcheknic. Operations successful. Reactions normal. Injections almost completed. Supremely confident of outcome. I have made the fulcrum. Pulcheknic himself will ultimately and inevitably supply the lever. Our enemies will have little enough time in which to enjoy the fruits of victory'."

Closing his folder Mr. Chillon leaned back.

"A sweeping and perhaps over-dramatic statement, that last one. But because of the man who wrote it, one that must be regarded seriously. If you are as perceptive as I hope, Mr. Seacombe, you will have realised many of the implications of what you have just heard."

"Yes," I agreed steadily.

"And why it is essential we find Pulner's son."

"The experiment—Fechter's—could have been a failure."

He smiled for the first time, but without any trace of humour. "You must give us credit for having considered every possibility."

"Disease," observed Brother Harold in his diagnostic voice. "Something designed to reach uncontrollable epidemic proportions. That's the obvious answer. But something new? Or a variation on an old?"

"We have our own ideas about that," replied Mr. Chillon gently. He looked at me, still using his deceptively gentle tone. "Well, Mr. Seacombe?"

More than anything, just at that moment, I needed time to think. The important part, the threat contained in the photostats of Fechter's journal, would have to wait. Now I had a decision to make. In my own mind I felt positive that Mr. Chillon, with his department of anonymous-featured men and the power they represented—for that was how I envisaged his background—was not the man to tackle the job. And neither was Brother Harold and his world of laboratories and operating theatres. Fighting fire with fire is not always the answer. And perhaps I was swayed by thoughts of Bart and his fears for Simon. I made my decision.

All right. So they had already covered some of the ground in our wake. I would have to assume they had covered it all. And I would have to take my own conscience into account.

I took a deep breath. "We started off by trying to trace the parentage of one of my pupils, an adopted boy——"

"Who is 'we'?"

"Miss Grey, another teacher, and myself."

"Go on," said Mr. Chillon.

"We traced him back to a nursing home here in Banford. The place had closed down and is now an hotel, but we found records that told us my pupil was one of a set of twins. . . ."

"Which explains your first enquiry," observed Brother Harold with some satisfaction.

"We found that the brother had been adopted by a Mr. Brereton who lives out at Kendly."

"The address you gave me," inserted Brother Harold. Even as a child I had never been allowed to tell an uninterrupted story when he was around.

"We didn't meet the man himself, only his father, the adopted boy's grandfather. While we were sorting out facts at the hotel we came across the name of a Dr. Todmarsh——"

Mr. Chillon made a note.

"—and later, talking to Mr. Brereton at Kendly, I happened to mention this, and he rang up a Dr. Yarrow." This time I paused deliberately. Mr. Chillon nodded curtly. "We know about him. Go on, Mr. Seacombe." His voice told me nothing.

"Apparently Dr. Todmarsh was an unqualified man, a quack; and a friend of Yarrow's, a Dr. Pringle, was anxious to get something on him so that a stop could be put to his

133

tricks." Was I making sense? It seemed so. Mr. Chillon nodded again.

"We traced Todmarsh to Breston but found out that he was dead. But he had had a housekeeper, a Mrs. Biddle, and she had a daughter. So we spoke to the daugher."

"Mrs. Fox," said Mr. Chillon. "And——"

"That was when we heard about the baby that Todmarsh had delivered for Mrs. Pulner. When we later spoke to Mrs. Biddle she told us how she had taken it a year later to Stapley, and left it in a promenade shelter. The police at Stapley supplied us with the address of people called Gregory who lived at Haydon and who had adopted the child. But when we went to Haydon we found that the Gregorys were both dead, and the child presumed burned to death in a fire."

"But apparently his body was never found," commented Mr. Chillon. "And why did you go to Werkley?"

"There was always a chance that some of the local people might know something of what had happened at Werkley Ridge. Mrs. Pulner had a sister. We thought that if we could trace her we might find out why the child had been dumped in the shelter."

"You went to a great deal of trouble over a child that you knew nothing about."

I shrugged: "I suppose we did. Maybe I fancied myself as a detective. And we were on holiday with all the time in the world at our disposal. You know how it is."

"Yes," said Mr. Chillon. "I think I do." He considered for a moment. "Thank you for your trouble, Mr. Seacombe. You will have appreciated by now why this interview must remain confidential."

"Gordon," said Brother Harold pontifically, big brotherly hand on my shoulders, "understands."

"Is that all?" I asked.

"For the time being," replied Mr. Chillon.

Brother Harold opened the door for me but thankfully came no further. He called me "old son" and said how nice it was for us to meet again. And how were things in the world of teaching? All right, I told him briefly.

The desk sergeant collected Joan and Bart and we went out to the car.

"Back to Werkley?" Bart wondered, watching my face.

It was five-fifteen according to the dashboard clock.

"Tea first, I think; then back to pick up the doctor." Reaching for the starter I nodded back to the police station. "I had to give my word not to repeat anything."

"So it was like that," he said woodenly.

134

"I don't think they know enough to do anything. Not yet, anyway. They don't know about Simon." This wasn't a breach of confidence. "So far as they're concerned Pulner only had the one child."

"The Black Boy," he supplied.

"And they think he's dead. Or at least, that's the impression I got."

I pointed the bonnet in the direction of the square. In a way I had burned my boats behind me, for there could be no altering or adding to the story I had told Chillon. Neither Joan nor Bart could be taken into my confidence. Which meant that to a certain extent I was on my own. Not a very pleasant feeling.

I thought about the extracts from Fechter's journal. His mention of fulcrum and lever was puzzling. According to Brother Harold he was a brilliant scientist, not likely to be the kind of man who would use words lightly or out of context. So there had to be a deeper meaning, a significance to them.

He had done something to Pulner in the concentration camp, and the four children were the outcome. That was patently obvious. And they had been brought into being to serve some special purpose. So that "our enemies wouldn't have long to enjoy the fruits of victory."

And: "I have made the fulcrum. Pulcheknic will supply the lever." Not "levers"; only the one. So, not four boys, but only the one. Was that how he had meant it to be? Then had something come unstuck somewhere along the line?

The first explosion at the atomic centre. An escape of radio-activity. Not sufficient, so they had said, to have caused any harm. But there all the same. Pulner had been one of those involved. And that was the factor that Fechter couldn't possibly have taken into account.

All right. He had intended that Pulner should father one child. The child who was to be the lever. . . .

Instead he had finished up with four different children, who were still, for all that, a single entity. At least, that was how I saw them.

But why in heaven's name had he used the analogy of lever and fulcrum? What had he had in mind when he wrote those words? For there had to be some reason. . . .

And then, just as we were approaching a café, with Bart leaning forward saying: "This looks all right, Gordon," I suddenly remembered something from my schoolboy days, and incredible, horrifying understanding exploded in my mind with an almost physical impact.

135

Dazed, my foot found the accelerator instead of the brake. I fought the wheel frantically to avoid an oncoming lorry. The front wheels bounced over the kerb, the car coming to a halt with the bonnet inches from plate glass. It was a few moments before I was able to pull myself together sufficiently to back on to the road. Thankfully there was no policeman in sight. The small crowd soon dispersed.

Bart took a deep breath. "That could have been nasty. . . ."

"Sorry," I said.

And my mind in a turmoil, still incapable of thinking rationally, I asked myself: Ice or fire? And: How long would it take? And, with steadily mounting panic: How can they know what it is they have to do, and why they have to do it?

Later, sitting at a table with a green-tiled top and a vase of wilting flowers, with the unimaginable magnitude of the thing before me, I tried to tell myself that it was impossible, that even they would be incapable of such a thing.

And after a while, when I had time to think, I was able to find the flaw, and was unbelievably thankful and relieved at finding it, in my reasoning.

14

While the waitress was busy at the table, making half-a-dozen trips when it seemed that one and a tray would have sufficed, Bart tried to make conversation.

"A not unpleasant interlude, although police station tea leaves much to be desired. One imagines that it is prepared in bulk at certain specified times and then drawn upon as occasion demands, maturing, in the meantime, in the urn. This imparts to it something of the colour, consistency and taste of brown windsor soup."

"The superintendent"—Joan was busy with her handbag— "has three daughters and he grows carnations for a hobby." She seemed faintly surprised that a ranking police officer should be ordinary enough to have a family like anyone else, and human enough to spend his time pottering in a green-house.

Bart inspected his nails. "An accident?" he asked them.

I knew what he meant. "An accident. I'm sorry about it. No outside influences."

"The thought had crossed my mind," he said.

The waitress completed her loading of the table. I helped myself to a tea-cake.

I knew a little about heredity factors and something of the manner in which genes are arranged in lines of chromosomes. Brother Harold had added to the knowledge; common-sense filled in the gaps. It wasn't too difficult to understand the accepted theory of how character comes to be transmitted from parent to child. I imagined that character as being composed of a series of instincts.

Basic instincts tell the child to copy the adults of its little world. Finer instincts would transmit natural talents. The child of parents who were gifted landscape painters would probably inherit the talent and become a landscape artist itself. But supposing they confined themselves to painting only the one scene, over and over again, and supposing they both died leaving the child to fend for itself. It was reasonable to assume that it would still become a landscape artist, but it wouldn't confine itself to that one scene, because that would require knowledge, not instinct, and knowledge cannot be inherited.

When I had worked that out in my mind I turned back to Fechter. In some way he had tampered with Pulner's chromosome set-up, altering, adding, strengthening. He had set in motion a completely new series of natural talents. But it was inconceivable that he could have inserted a built-in message, telling the inheritors of those talents just how they were to be employed. And that was the flaw in my earlier reasoning, my interpretation of the riddle of the fulcrum and lever. The children might be the lever, but there was no way in which they could know the fact, or where and when it was to be applied.

All Fechter could have done was to adjust Pulner's potential so that any children he sired would have mental faculties developed well beyond the normal. And that development was something I could understand. In each one of us is the dormant sixth sense, a way of using the mind; a combination of extrasensory perception, of the ability to transmit and receive thought, even of the ability to move inanimate objects solely by the power of thought. Mind over matter. Telekinesis. The four children were abnormal but not supernatural. It might even be that collectively they had the power to do the thing I had imagined. But they could have no way of

137

knowing what that thing was. Instinct might tell them to destroy, but it couldn't point out one particular object for destruction.

There was an alternative, though. . . .

Their power lay entirely in their minds. But it might have come accidentally, caused by the action of radio-activity on an artificial delicately-balanced chromosome arrangement. Brother Harold could be right. They could contain the seeds of an epidemic. But could a virus remain inactive for so long, being transmitted from father to son, and then manifesting itself at some later date? I didn't see how that could be possible.

One thing I felt certain about: Fechter had never intended that there should be four children.

"So we go back to collect the doctor," Bart observed, spreading liberal jam on a butter-dripping muffin. "And then what?"

"I'm not sure," I said.

He cut the muffin carefully and neatly into four quarters. "Another dead-end, then."

"Not exactly. The picture's complete now." There were some things I could tell him without betraying confidences. "They know all about Pulner's background."

He arranged the segments round the rim of his plate. "They?"

"Brother Harold and a man called Chillon. An American. He's flown over from the States."

"Some kind of policeman?"

I shook my head. "I don't know. I don't think so. Something more important I would say."

"I would have liked to have met your brother," he said a little wistfully.

"We'll get round to it one day."

"And this Mr. Chillon came over simply to talk to you about Pulner?"

"That's the impression I got."

"So it must be something important." Now he was deliberately fishing. I couldn't find it in my heart to blame him.

"He's checked off all our movements. He seems to have covered most of the same ground. Including a talk with Mrs. Fox."

He smiled faintly. "I hope he found the experience enlightening. I wonder if he paid off in dollars?" Then: "So that's why he thinks Pulner only had one child. And if he's been to the trouble of checking off with Dr. Pringle he'll have had her story confirmed."

I nodded. "Chillon wanted to know why we'd been making

138

the enquiries. I told him only part of the truth. Enough to satisfy him. . . ."

Bart glanced up quickly at my tone. "But he's not a man to be easily satisfied."

"He'd make a good school-teacher," I said.

"So the picture is complete. You had authority there in front of you, ready to accept anything you told them. But you only gave them part of the story."

"I don't think the picture is complete yet. The background, yes. And I'm not sure that they would have accepted everything I might have told them. But it would have been taken out of our hands. We'd have been told to go back home and leave things to them. And I feel a responsibility towards Rodney Blake."

"And Simon happens to be my grandson."

"It could be that they weren't responsible for the things that have happened. Not directly, that is. That's why I said I don't think we have the complete picture yet. But it would be complete so far as Chillon is concerned."

He nodded understandingly. "Root out the menace and destroy it regardless. Or try to destroy it. They might find they'd bitten off more than they could chew. But still, with proper resources. . . . They do regard it as some kind of menace?"

"They do," I agreed.

"Chillon will find out the truth sooner or later," Bart said grimly. "He'll be a professional. We are only amateurs but we almost got to the bottom of it. He'll rake through everything that's happened."

"We've still got a little time in hand."

He pushed muffin segments about his plate. "And how do you propose we spend that time?"

"I want to have a talk with Rodney Blake," I told him, and created a silence into which the sounds of the café filtered. I was thankful for Joan's part of that silence. It told me that she understood, perhaps in part, what I was going to try to do.

"We can't be certain they're up at Werkley Ridge," Bart said after a while.

"We can't be certain."

"Unless you know a lot more about this than I do. Unless they told you something. . . ." He answered himself. "But if they don't know of the existence of the other three, they couldn't have done. I'll go up to the Ridge with you."

"I think we should all go," Joan inserted quietly.

I shook my head to that. "Not you, Joan; we can't risk that. So far as we know Rodney has only concerned himself

139

about my safety. It's that concern I'm banking on." I looked at Bart. "And if things don't work out, then someone will have to tell Chillon the full story."

He wasn't convinced. "We'll see. . . ." Then he caught the waitress's eye so that he could ask for the bill for a table-full of almost untouched food.

We drove back through the square and out on to the Chari-don road. The idea of talking to Rodney had come more or less on the spur of the moment. But thinking about it now, it seemed the only thing possible. And there couldn't be all that much time. Mr. Chillon might already be checking my story. I glanced in the mirror; the road was clear behind. But he wouldn't be that obvious. And if he intended going to Werkley then he might already be there. I wondered if he knew about Thorne's death. And how long would it take him to associate us with a hotel and a handyman who had been killed in an inexplicable car crash?

There was a great deal to think about. Rodney, for in-stance, and his apparent concern for my safety. But would he feel the same way about his parents, the Blakes? And the others. . . . Simon would surely feel some kind of affection for his grandfather. How did Peter Latham feel about his people?

I might find the answer if I knew why Rodney had gone out of his way to try to protect me from the Tony-part. Be-cause I was his teacher? Certainly we'd got on well enough together in the twelve months he'd been in my form. And I had gone out of my way, as any teacher would, to encour-age his talent for writing. It had been through me that his stories had found their way into the school magazine. A little enough thing, and he had shown no gratitude at the time, but it could have been there all the same and now he was trying to repay me. That was something to go on; he couldn't be completely devoid of normal feelings.

Nearing Charidon, the Three Sisters there above the trees, I said: "There's one thing we haven't taken into account yet; the boys' parents. They have a right to know what's happening if things come to a head. We ought to know where we can contact them."

"We can forget Harris," Bart said. "He's somewhere in Spain, address unknown. Not that it would make any differ-ence. I can't imagine any emergency connected with Simon bringing him back." He sounded bitter.

"I know Blake's address," I said. "It might be tricky try-ing to locate the Lathams."

"Somewhere in Wales," Joan supplied. "Llanberis according to the last post card."

"They might still be there. Or Mrs. Foster may have heard from them again."

"You know what Mrs. Foster's like," she said. "She'll want to know all the whys and wherefores. And time's getting on."

"Leave it to me," said Bart.

I stopped the car some distance past the cottage. Bart walked back. He was away only a few minutes.

"An old friend of the family's," he informed us, "anxious to contact them for old time's sake. I flatter myself I did it rather well. The last Mrs. Foster heard the Lathams were staying at the Bryn Mawr Hotel in Llanberis. That was three days ago, but she thinks they may still be there. Apparently they make the same trip each year and usually stay a few days at Llanberis."

We swept by the church.

"I assume," he added pensively, "that your idea is to contact them if Mr. Chillon shows up and looks like taking matters into his own hands?"

"Something like that," I replied.

We passed through Korfe a few minutes after seven. Then came the empty road, the slow steady climb with the low hills, the bleak patches of scrub and stunted trees spreading out on either side. There was the hidden valley again, and a little further along on the opposite side of the road, the small hotel that I had missed before but which Joan had remarked upon to Yarrow. And I would have missed it again now but for having to slow to avoid a tractor and trailer that was parked half-way across the road.

The building itself was set well back off the road, almost hidden by trees; a low white-fronted structure with a semi-thatched roof and a sign—"The Grey Goose," it read—that defeated its purpose by an over-elaboration of metal scrollwork. And on the long, narrow forecourt was a tight mass of vehicles, cars, farm-lorries, another tractor. And people too, their heads turning to watch our passing. A busy place in the evening, it seemed, for all its comparative isolation and proximity to a competitor.

Too busy, perhaps; and there seemed something odd in the frozen postures of the people. . . .

I knew that something had happened, even before the car became filled with the acrid tang of burning, and before Joan saw and drew our attention to the smoke haze that hung against the sky, drifting from behind the trees ahead.

There was a solitary cottage, people standing in the tiny

front garden, and then the last corner, and rounding it cautiously, the way blocked by a lorry that had been slewed broadside on across the road, bonnet pointing towards the grassy bank, tailboard resting against the privet of another garden.

An accident, it could have been, but that wouldn't explain the now strong smell of smouldering timber or the fact that the lorry was undamaged. As I climbed from the car so a man came from the bushes to meet me. I recognised Mr. Fletcher's battered felt hat, his blue eyes in their mesh of fine wrinkles.

He said roughly: "You'll 'ave to go back, mister; there's no way through 'ere."

"What's happened?" I asked in a voice sharpened by anxiety.

Another man edged his way between lorry bonnet and bank; a lanky, loose-boned individual with a lean face and shaggy brows. He wore a brown overall and a filthy cap pulled well down over his forehead. And across the crook of his elbow, the butt resting in his armpit, he carried a double-barrelled shotgun.

Fletcher's eyes shifted across my shoulder to the car, with Joan and Bart climbing out to join me. "You're the folks that was 'ere earlier . . ." he discovered. And to the newcomer: "These are the ones that came before; the ones he came with. . . ."

We all knew who "he" was. Bart's hand clamped down on Fletcher's arm. "What happened to him?" he cried harshly.

"Take it easy," Fletcher said unemotionally; "carrying on don't do no good. You'd better come an' see for yourself." He led the way round the front of the lorry. A few paces took us past the screen of trees. "The Farmer's Pride" was a roofless smoking ruin; a desolation of blackened walls and gaping windows; an empty shell. Glass crunched under my feet and I remembered the shelves and their neat rows of bottles, Mr. Cole shirt-sleeved and smiling in front of them.

The man with the gun kicked at the charred timber of what had once been a white-painted fence.

"A mess," he observed in a voice of dispassionate calm. This was his world and this one of the things that happened in it. We were foreigners—intruders—and couldn't be expected to understand. Joan was clutching my arm tightly. Fletcher, hands at his side, stared at the ruin.

"It'll be a while afore we can get to sort them out," he said.

"I saw it all," said the man with the gun. He shifted the

142

weapon to his other arm. "I was in the lane. My name's Nisted; Daniel Farm. It was over an' done with in ten minutes. Went up like a blast furnace. I couldn't get anywhere near. They didn't stand a chance. None of them. . . ."

"My son was in there," Fletcher said. "Nisted saw him at the window. Talkin' to your friend. He saw them. . . ."

"Set on fire all over at the same time," Nisted added. "Just like someone 'ad soaked the place in petrol." He glanced sideways at us. "No rain in weeks; timber like matchwood."

"We should have known that something like this would happen," Bart said in a voice I didn't recognise. Turning, he made his way back round the lorry, stumbling, feeling his way blindly.

Nisted watched him go. "Taken it badly," he commented. "You can't blame him. His son?"

"A friend," I said.

"Ar." He nodded, straightening. "You've seen what happened; you can't do anythin' more for the time being, mister. We'll take them—what's left—down to Korfe as soon as we can get to them."

He was ready to escort us back to the car but there were things that needed explaining. Not the fire—that was obvious enough—but the road-block and his gun and his obvious anxiety to see us on our way.

"The Black Boy," I said, and he looked surprised. "You know about him?"

"We know all about him," I said.

He grounded his gun. "Is that why you came here?"

Fletcher spoke before I could reply. "He's never killed before. He's not goin' to get the chance again. We should've done this years ago."

"He's up there at the Ridge," Nisted told me. "This is the only way he can get out. Either down the lane or across the fields. He can't get over the hills. There's eleven of us, strung out across the fields, mostly with guns. An' more coming. We've got all the folk out of the valley, an' we've stripped the houses of food an' cut off the water. He's got to eat an' drink. Sooner or later he's got to come down." He laid his hand on the barrel of his gun. "We don't care how long we has to wait."

"We should've done this afore," Fletcher said again.

"You want to keep out of it, mister," Nisted said bleakly. "If you want to stay somewheres 'andy you'd best go to the 'Goose'. All the folks are there."

Eleven men strung across the mouth of the valley, most of them armed, their intentions obvious—to shoot on sight. And they couldn't know that there were almost certainly four children up there and not just the one. Four boys of identical appearance with only dress to tell them apart. Desperate men—as these must be—wouldn't bother about dress. They would shoot at the first sign of movement.

"The police?" I asked, and he spat in the dust. "We'll take care of this ourselves. What the hell's the use of bringing them in? They don't know anythin' about it."

"You can't take the law into your own hands," I said desperately.

"That's what you think." He brought the gun to waist level. "You may've lost someone in there but that don't give you the right to tell us 'ow to 'andle it. We're goin' to 'ave no interfering. You'd best get back to your car."

I remembered Chillon. "Has anyone else been up here—any strangers?"

"No." He swung the barrel with growing impatience.

Taking Joan's arm, I led her back round the front of the lorry, Nisted close at our heels. A tow-headed youth, single-barrelled gun in his hand, stood by the car. Bart was sitting on the bank, his face buried in his hands. Joan left me to crouch at his side, her arm about his shoulders. Nisted watched the tableau.

"These folks will be goin' to the 'Goose'," he said to the youth. "Tell Mr. Chandler why they're here, an' to look after them."

I helped Bart to his feet, and with Joan at his other side, supported him back to the car. All the use seemed to have gone out of his body. I said in a low voice with as much conviction as I could muster: "Simon had nothing to do with the fire. I'm sure of that."

But for the moment he wasn't so much concerned about his grandson. "I shouldn't have left him here," he said brokenly. "I should have known that something like this would happen."

"He'd made up his mind to stay. We couldn't have talked him into coming with us if we'd tried." Which I felt was true enough; Yarrow had been that kind of man.

The youth, his thin freckled face filled with the importance of the occasion, sat at my side, the gun poking up clumsily from between his boney knees. It took me some time to reverse in the narrow confines of lane and road-block. With some idea of giving Bart time in which to recover I drove very slowly back to "The Grey Goose." There was just enough room to back the car between the hedge and a tractor. Our escort left us to talk to a bulky-shouldered, heavy-jowled man wearing thick-rimmed spectacles, clearly, from his earnest, head-on-one-side attitude, the landlord.

He came over to meet us, introducing himself—"Chandler," and telling us that he could find a couple of rooms. . . .

"Only small and at the top of the house, but comfortable enough." He seemed to take it for granted we would be staying at least overnight. Perhaps Nisted had had something to do with that assumption. "We're almost full; the people from the valley. Seemingly you know what's going on. I'm sorry to hear about your friend. And the Coles; friends of mine."

Still talking, he led the way towards the door.

15

There was the same curiously detached atmosphere about "The Grey Goose" as there had been by the smouldering ruin of "The Farmer's Pride"; the same feeling of this being a private world with no place for outsiders. Losing a friend to the common enemy had created no bond. We were there for necessity's sake, tolerated simply because we could not be allowed to leave.

We stood, the three of us, in the deep recess of the lounge window, overlooking the forecourt. Behind us two women talked in private undertones, an old man nodded in a corner and a child in rompers played with a wooden horse. The rest of the people—mostly women—were outside, gathered in intimate, serious-faced groups. The youth who had escorted us was down at the entrance to the forecourt, talking to a girl, their seriousness unnatural—the gravity of age instead of the light-hearted banter of youth. There was an irritation about his movements, the impatient way he swung the gun against his legs, the sunlight gleaming dully on the barrel, that perhaps indicated his annoyance at having to be here when he would rather have been with the men.

"Mob rule," Bart said tonelessly. "The law into their own hands. . . . How long do they think they can keep it up?"

I had brought brandy from the bar, and drinking it had taken some of the greyness, smoothed a little of the grimness from his face.

"A self-contained community," I said. "I don't suppose they're used to seeing strangers up here."

"A kind of organisation to it. Almost as if they had been planning for some time; waiting for the inevitable to happen." He nodded to himself. "No rushing aimlessly about; no panic. Cold organisation. The way they brought the women here. A cordon of men across the valley." He looked at me. "And they've stripped the houses of food and even turned off the water."

"That's what they told me."

"There's bound to be some water up there; ponds, at least. But they'll have to come down for food. And that will mean showing themselves, whether they come down the lane or across the fields. Even if they wait for nightfall; with a clear sky and a full moon it will be like daylight."

I emptied my glass without replying. Discussing the future could serve no useful purpose; it was filled with so many unknown factors.

Instead I nodded to his glass. "No," he said. I looked at Joan who shook her head silently. I went back to the bar. The long, narrow room was empty save for Chandler, leaning on the counter reading a paper as if this were just an ordinary evening in his life. He straightened at my approach.

"Same again, sir?"

"Please." I set down my glass. "Have you a phone I might use?"

"We have a phone, sir," he replied smoothly, tilting a bottle, "but under the circumstances we are keeping it free. For emergencies, you understand."

I understood well enough.

"If I were to write out a couple of telegrams would you be kind enough to send them for me?"

He fingered the flabby folds of one cheek while he regarded me warily.

"I'm not sure that would be possible. . . ."

There was a small notepad on the counter, probably used for totting sales, and I pulled it towards me, pausing with pencil poised while I considered. The messages would have to be worded in a way to pass Chandler's inspection but at the same time convey an impression of urgency to the recipients. The Blakes would surely recognise my name as the sender. Under their address I wrote: "Your son here. Suggest you come immediately. Urgent." Then I added my name and that of the hotel. Chandler completed the address at my request.

I worded that to the Lathams in much the same way. "Peter here. Suggest you come immediately. Urgent." Ripping out the sheets I set a pound note on top and pushed them across the counter. "I think you'll understand what they're all about."

He read them carefully.

"They're about your friend that died in the fire, of course."

"His people will have to be told," I said. "And if there is any delay in contacting them now they might start asking questions later."

He nodded wisely. "That's true enough, Mr. Seacombe. All right; I'll send them for you." He reached for the phone and I listened while he relayed the messages. It was almost half past eight. I wondered how long it would take the Blakes and the Lathams to reach Werkley if they decided to act upon the telegrams. It had taken Joan and me over three hours to come from Cookley to Charidon. Add another half hour for the journey from Charidon to. . . .

When Chandler replaced the receiver I asked: "Where is the nearest railway station?"

"Korfe. They'll have to take taxis from there."

"Do you have a railway guide or happen to know the times of the trains?"

He shook his head. "I'm afraid not, Mr. Seacombe."

Thanking him, I picked up my refilled glass, started back to the lounge, changed my mind, set the glass back on the counter and went through the front door to stand on the step. The youth, more observant than I had given him credit for, broke off his conversation with the girl to eye me charily. My original intention had been to collect the road-map from the car so that I could get some idea of the lay-out of the valley. Now it struck me that I might at the same time confirm a notion of mine and perhaps add to my store of knowledge. It always pays to learn as much about the enemy as possible. I knew quite a lot about the weapon at the boy's disposal but I had the feeling that horrifying and lethal as it was there were still limitations to its use.

When I set off quickly in the direction of the car, the youth, as I had guessed, came obliquely to meet me, weaving an urgent way through the parked vehicles, the girl at his heels.

I called reassuringly: "Just a few things I need from the car," and that slowed him up sufficiently to give me time to slip the map unnoticed in my pocket. By the time he had come to glare suspicion over my shoulder I was taking an unnecessary packet of cigarettes and slab of chocolate from the glove compartment.

I offered him a cigarette which he accepted after a moment's reluctance.

"This is a nasty business altogether," I observed equably, flicking my lighter.

"Yes," he agreed ungraciously.

"You'll know of course that a friend of mine lost his life in the fire."

"I know."

The girl had come to stand at his side. She was pretty in a gypsyish fashion; dark hair and eyes, swarthy complexion. She seemed a little ashamed of her companion's boorishness. "It was terrible," she offered breathlessly. "We're ever so sorry."

"I know all about the Black Boy. By all accounts you seem to have had a rough time in Werkley." I watched their faces. "I can't say I blame you for taking matters into your own hands. I feel much the same way."

He relaxed a little at that. "It's been bad right enough. I live 'ere; in one of they cottages up t'wards Maybrick. That's where I work, at Maybrick."

"The man who almost lost his daughter. Were you there at the time?"

"I were workin' for 'im then, but I weren't there when it 'appened."

"Can you remember what day of the week it was?"

"What day?" He screwed up his face in thought. The girl answered while he was still pondering.

"It were a Saturday, Joe, the first time 'e came. Sunday when Eileen all but killed 'erself. I remember it were a Sunday because I'd been with 'er to church in the morning."

"And Mr. Nisted's heart-attack; can you recall when that was?"

The youth answered this time, without having to stop and think.

"It were about a month after. Almost on Christmas."

"And then there was Martin Fletcher. Can you remember now when it was he had his accident with the tractor?"

"You're askin' a devil of a lot of questions, mister," he grunted suspiciously. The girl laid her hand on his arm. "He seems to know most of it anyway, Joe. Talking to him can't do no harm." And to me: "It were quite a while later when Martin lost the use of his arm; in the next summer. Just about this time of the year."

Unconvinced and glowering, perhaps at her usurping of

his authority, the youth stepped aside. "You'd best be getting back inside agen, mister."

They had confirmed what I had suspected. A week-end, a Christmas holiday and a summer holiday. It was too much to suppose that it was purely coincidental that the Black Boy had chosen those particular times on which to launch his attacks. Week-ends and school holidays were the times the other three chose to wander away from home. Tony might be the focal point, the originator of the thought-weapons, but everything pointed to his having to rely upon one of the other three for use as a kind of launching-pad or relay-station.

"You had quite a chat with our guard and his lady-friend," Bart observed when I rejoined them at the lounge window.

I patted my pocket. "I went to the car to collect the map. I thought it might give us some idea of the lay-out of the valley."

"So you're still thinking of going up to the Ridge? Even after what's happened?"

Joan shook her head. "They won't let you through, Gordon."

"There's bound to be a way across the fields," I told her. "And they'll have their pop-guns pointed in the opposite direction. There'll be no trouble getting through the picket-lines."

I spoke lightly and confidently, smiling, trying to make as little of the thing as possible. But she didn't return the smile, and Bart, watching me over her shoulder, lifted his shoulders in a gesture that could have meant acceptance or denial of my assessment.

"I've sent wires to the Blakes and the Lathams," I added. "If they take notice of them they should get here in the early hours of the morning. I'd like them to be here before I start out."

This time he raised his eyebrows. "So you decided not to wait for Chillon after all. God knows what you'll find to say to them if and when they show up. Apart from anything else we still can't be certain all four boys are up there."

"I'm more certain than ever now," I told him.

"The outcome of your chat with our spotty-faced guard?"

"Yes."

"You mean they know there's more than one Black Boy?"

"No," I replied. "They think there's only the one."

"So you've been reading between the lines, as it were. All right; so you know they're all up there, and you're going up after them. What good can that possibly do?"

I couldn't explain to him what I believed; that the four

children were only parts of a single entity. That was something that in his present condition he would never be able to understand. I would have to explain my motives in the simplest terms and hope that he would be able to make sense out of them.

"We know that they're closely linked. So closely that they share each other's feelings, both mentally and physically. The links are so solid that we can almost think of the four as being parts of a single child.

"Each of us has a nature made up of basically good and bad characteristics. The same applies to them, only in their case the goodness is divided between Rodney, Peter and Simon, while the evil has confined itself to Tony. That's why I told you I was certain Simon wasn't responsible for the fire."

"I'd give my right arm to believe that," he said flatly.

"You've got to believe it. It's more important than you realise. You've got to convince yourself."

It was difficult putting abstract ideas into words. To make him understand I had to risk sounding affected and pedantic.

"I'm not a good school-teacher, but it's the only work I've ever done. I have my own ideas about it. In class there are two ways of dealing with naughtiness. With a child who is generally well-behaved but has occasional lapses, punishment is generally the answer. But from time to time I come across a boy who is inherently bad. Punishment in a case of that sort becomes a negative process. The only way to deal with it is by trying to appeal to the latent, better side of his nature."

Bart smiled sideways. "You've been reading Harris' book."

"I've read it, but only because I had to. This is something I worked out for myself. Sometimes it works. When it fails I set it down to my own inefficiency. But I'm sure it's the only thing that will stand a chance of working now. Whatever else the four boys might be they're still basically twelve-year old school-boys. Or at least three of them are. I've got to make those three see things my way.

"I want to be able to tell Rodney and Peter that their parents think enough about them to come dashing across the country if they think their sons are in trouble. And I want to be able to tell Simon that his grandfather can't bring himself to believe that his grandson was responsible for anything that has happened. And it will be no use lying to these children. Everything I tell them will have to be the truth."

"Because they can read thoughts," Joan said.

I nodded. "Because of that. Somehow or other we've got

to separate them from Tony. In every sense of the word. The mental ties have got to be broken and we've got to get them down from the Ridge, unobserved, before the balloon goes up."

"I can't see that talking to them will do any good," Bart said wearily. "All this is above my head. I need time to think. . . ." He looked at his empty glass. "I think I'll have another after all." He went slowly across the lounge and out to the bar.

"When you go up there," Joan said in a small but firm voice, "I'm coming with you."

"No," I said.

She turned to look out of the window. Chandler was talking to the youth with the gun, the girl standing to one side. He seemed to be giving him instructions.

"I know Rodney Blake well enough to feel sure he wouldn't try to harm either of us," Joan said. "I want him to read my mind as well as yours. You'll need all the help you can get."

I had to admit the wisdom of that. "Hoist with my own petard," I said a little wryly, and she turned, smiling. "I don't intend to let you out of my sight more than I can help. At least until all this has been cleared up."

Then she became serious again. "If we can manage to persuade them to leave Tony, that means he will be up there on his own. Won't they kill him, Gordon?"

Would he be completely defenceless without the other three? I didn't know. I thought it hardly likely.

"I don't think so, Joan. Bart was probably right when he said that if Chillon did take over he'd probably find he'd bitten off more than he could chew."

"But supposing he does get killed," she persisted; "what will happen to the others? We know how closely they're linked together."

That was something we'd discussed before. Cut off one of the fingers of a hand, I'd told her, and the other three would be unharmed. But it mightn't be like that at all. I couldn't see that Tony's death would mean death for the rest, but there would be some kind of repercussion. The four links of a chain. . . . I had a sudden picture of a conjurer on a stage; four metal rings entwined; firmly linked together. . . . Take away one ring, a quick flick of the wrist and the rest fall clattering to the ground. Separated. Was that how it might be?

It was some time before Bart returned to lower himself to the window seat and continue a conversation he seemed to have been having with himself.

"The times when we were able to get together we always

seemed to hit it off. I was the only one he seemed to have time for. We used to write to each other regularly. I told him once that I was feeling a little off-colour. I forget now what the trouble was; something very trivial. But in his reply he seemed concerned. There are other things, too. . . ."

He drew a deep breath. "I'm positive now that he would never intentionally do anything that might harm me. I must have known that all the time, but I had to work it out for myself through the confusion of what has been happening. I'm certain now. That's part of it. . . ." He looked up at us. "And the rest. . . . You must have realised by now that I feel more than a little affection for him. And not only because my own son wasn't all he might have been. For his own sake alone. . . . That might be important."

"Yes," I agreed. "That might be important."

"Well, then," he smiled, rubbed his hands and regarded us almost benevolently. "The landlord informs me that sandwiches are being prepared. It appears that a running buffet is his only way of coping with the multitude." He made an elaborate gesture of consulting his watch. "Almost nine. When is dead-line for the early-morning sortie?"

"Not later than four o'clock," I told him.

He shuddered. "The hour when the spirit is reputedly at its lowest ebb. I intend coming with you, of course. Now that I know my thoughts are pure." He cocked an eyebrow at Joan who smiled and nodded back. "Mine too. . . ."

"I thought you wouldn't let him go up there alone," he said, and then started to tell us about a mind-reading act he had once witnessed in a night-club. "Clever," he said; "but a fake. All the same, it puts one in the frame of mind to accept such things."

I had the uncomfortable feeling that he was taking the matter far too lightly. But with Bart you could never tell. He used flamboyant verbosity as a shield when other men might have taken refuge in silence.

Some time later Mr. Chandler brought a plate of sandwiches.

"I've asked Joe to keep his eyes open for the relatives when they arrive, Mr. Seacombe," he told me, perhaps a tactful way of letting us know the guard would be on duty all night. "I've told him to send them directly to you. I assume you'll wait up for them?"

"Yes," I said.

"Relatives?" Bart puzzled when the landlord had gone. I explained how I had managed to have the wires accepted.

"Yarrow wasn't married," he said quietly. "I've never

heard him mention relatives. I suppose sorting that out will be a job for the police."

We were still by the window an hour later, dusk now, the moon silver-tipping the tops of the trees and the cottage roofs —when the lights of a car came sweeping along the lane without stopping. It was too early for either the Blakes or the Lathams. Bart had his idea at the same time as me.

"He'll come here sooner or later," he said. "I'd expected him before now."

"If it is Chillon," I said, "we'd best keep out of his way. He'll want to know what's going on, and we can't risk telling him the truth. Not yet, at least."

Chandler had also seen the car. He came to the lounge door.

"Will this be one of the parties, Mr. Seacombe?"

"No," I said. "It's too early. But we think we know who it might be. Someone who will want to ask questions. Under the circumstances it might be just as well if he doesn't know we are here."

He looked alarmed. "The police, you mean?"

"Something like that. He may recognise my car. If he does you could tell him that it was left here earlier and now you have no idea where its passengers are."

He came to join us in the window just as the car returned, this time to pull up outside the forecourt. I recognised Chillon the moment he stepped into the glow of the lamp hanging below the inn-sign.

I nodded to Chandler and he said: "There's a small conservatory at the back. You'll be out of the way there."

Leading the way he said worriedly: "I don't like this, Mr. Seacombe. What am I to say to him?"

"We're only getting out of the way to help you," I said callously. "This is your own private war. We just don't want any part of it." Bart grinned briefly. I think he was enjoying the brief cloak-and-dagger episode.

The conservatory was a small place with shelves of despondent potted ferns, a bench, a pile of deck-chairs, a dim roof light and an electric fire. The outer door—I tried the handle as soon as we were alone—was unlocked. Evasive action to avoid Chillon's question had served a double purpose; we were over the first hurdle of finding some way of leaving the hotel unobserved.

Bart set his fingers on the bench, grimaced at the dirt they had collected, and set up three of the chairs. The place smelled earthy and disused but it still retained the warmth of the day. We were cut off completely by white-washed brick walls and a solid door from the rest of the hotel, no sounds at all filtering through.

Chandler returned some ten minutes later.

"They simply asked if I had any rooms vacant," he reported, sounding somewhat relieved, "and when I told them I was full they wanted to know if they could stay in the lounge. They were very insistent."

"More than one?" I queried.

"Two gents. If I hadn't known different I'd've said they were commercials. I had them sign the register. A Mr. Chillon and a Mr. Paxton."

"And they didn't try to question you at all?"

"They simply wanted somewhere to stay the night." He hesitated at the door. "I don't suppose you've any idea at all what times the others will be arriving?"

"I don't even know they'll be coming." A thought struck me. "They won't know each other; I mean the two parties I sent the telegrams to. It might be best if you were to keep them apart."

He looked worried again, now perhaps regretting ever having sent the wires, not anticipating complications. Under the circumstances I had little enough sympathy to spare for him.

"If it will help you can use our two rooms. We can stay the night in here. Will that make things easier?"

It did, and his relief showed again. "That should be all right, Mr. Seacombe. You'll have a word with them when they get here?"

"Whichever party gets here first, settle them in one of the rooms and then let me know. I'll go and talk to them. And if it's any consolation to you I don't intend to mention the Black Boy or anything about your local carryings-on. They'll have enough to cope with without having to listen to a story like that."

If I had been expecting him to react in some way to my near-sneer—introduced purposely to reassure him of my intention to keep my mouth shut—I was disappointed. He said dispassionately: "I'll let you know as soon as they show up," and closed the door gently behind him.

When he had gone I settled myself in one of the deck-chairs. Bart, his hands folded, seemed to be already dozing. Joan sat upright, uncomfortably on the very edge of her chair, her hands clasped in her lap. In the dim light, she looked fragile, her skin almost transparent. Meeting my eyes she smiled, then looked at Bart whose mouth had fallen open.

"It's funny," she mused softly, "but ever since we first

154

found out that there were four of them I've had the feeling that sooner or later we'd meet them face to face; you know—all at the same time. It's almost as if it had been intended that way. Do you know the feeling, Gordon?"

"I know it," I told her. "I suppose I've had it myself. Everything that has happened seems to have slotted into place like pieces of a jigsaw. One thing leading to another. A dead-end comes, and something new shows itself. Like the treasure-hunts we used to have at parties when we were kids."

"Notes tucked in a crack in the sundial." She smiled, nodding at memories. "A bag of sweets as the prize. Do you think they intended that one day we would come here? I'm thinking of the time Rodney came to see you alone. You said you thought it was simply because he wanted to show off. Remember? But he might have had another reason."

Another reason? For a moment I was puzzled. Then I saw what she was hinting at. If he hadn't come to talk to me we would have been at a dead-end. It could be that the purpose behind his visit was not, after all, a childish urge to show off, but so that I could work out for myself where their retreat was.

But why?

There was only the one answer to that: So that, filled with my own cleverness, I would find my way to a ruined farmhouse and come face to face with all four children for the first time.

I leaned back in the chair, hands clasped at the back of my head. Bart was breathing slowly and stertorously, an oddly comforting sound. I closed my eyes. Something nagged persistently at the back of my mind with the irritating sensation of a remembered face, but a forgotten name, there on the tip of the tongue, refusing to take shape.

Somewhere in the past was the significant piece of the puzzle, the missing step. I went back to the start; not to Thorne's death, because that was only the side-door through which I had entered the corridor, but to a hospital in a concentration camp. To a man called Heimut Fechter. The soft, soothing roar of Bart's breathing became waves breaking on a gravel beach. Breaking, creaming, receding. . . .

I woke with a jerk. My hands had slipped so that my head lolled stiffly on one shoulder. It was a few moments before I was able to pull myself together sufficiently to realise where I was and to look at my watch. It was ten past one.

Joan was smiling at me. "I hadn't the heart to wake you, even though you looked so uncomfortable. Who is 'Fletcher',

Gordon? A friend of yours you haven't told me about? You sounded very concerned about him."

"Who?" I stared at her. The name sounded familiar.

"You were talking in your sleep. Mumbling, rather. . . ."

"Not 'Fletcher'," Bart said without opening his eyes. " 'Fechter'. At least that's how it sounded to me. Gordon must have been browsing through Harris' private reference library."

"I can't remember what I was dreaming about," I said warily.

"You must have been back at Kendly, pottering in the library. It's odd how things sometimes stick in your mind. You must have come across Heimut Fechter's name and remembered it without knowing. Fechter is Harris' little tin god. All his books are there; some in the original German."

"I can't read German," I said inanely.

He opened his eyes. "You haven't missed anything. And if you've read Harris' book then you've read Fechter."

Which was food for thought. I was mulling over it when the door opened and Chandler, still fully-dressed, came in.

"I've just taken Mr. and Mrs. Blake up to one of the rooms," he told me.

Still not fully awake I followed him up the stairs to where Mr. Blake turned anxious eyes on me from the window, and his wife rose from sitting on the side of the bed to ask what had happened to Rodney. . . .

I told them. . . . What did I tell them? Something about there being some trouble about a fire; that the local people were blaming a boy for it—a gypsy boy—and that Rodney might know this boy, might even be with him now, although he had nothing to do with the fire. But the people didn't know about Rodney and I was going to try to get him away before any trouble started. A wandering, indefinite story; if I had been more myself I could have thought of a better one. But they accepted it.

"Gypsies," Blake commented heavily; "so that's where 'e used to get to. I thought it'd be somethin' like that. . . ."

"He always was one fer wandering," sighed Mrs. Blake. "It was real decent of you to have taken all this trouble, Mr. Seacombe."

Blake lowered his bulk to a creaking, flimsy chair. "I borrered a van from where I work. We came soon as we got your wire."

"Try and get some rest," I urged. "I'll let you know as soon as I hear anything. And it might be just as well if you were to stay in this room."

"Ar." Blake nodded wisely. "No point in askin' fer trouble. I knows what country folk are. . . ."

Mrs. Blake's face was alive with questions, but I escaped before she could put them into words. Chandler was waiting in the passage. "So far so good," I told him. It was something that the Blakes had shown up.

At ten minutes past three Chandler came to the conservatory again, this time to tell me he had shown the Lathams up to their room. I gave them almost the same story, word for word. It had worked once; there was no reason why it shouldn't again. Mrs. Latham, fluttering anxiously, was a tall, willowy woman with a pink-and-white porcelain complexion, vague gestures and a harrassed expression. Her husband was compensatingly stolid; a large man with an over-square brown face.

He grunted: "Gypsies, eh?" and regarded me intently. "More to this than meets the eye. What?"

"You know how it is, sir," I replied feebly. "This isn't the town."

"No." Then: "Decent of you to take the trouble of letting us know what's going on. How did you come to be mixed up in it?"

Which was a poser. But there was an answer of sorts.

"Through a Mrs. Foster at Charidon."

He raised his brows. "So that's it. You've been talking to our local gossip."

"Henry," his wife reproved mildly.

"I'll see you later," I told them hastily, and went back down the stairs, through the bar—Chandler divested of jacket and tie, making himself comfortable in an easy chair that looked out of place in the carpetless room—and to the conservatory.

"We'll give the landlord a few minutes to settle down," I told Joan and Bart, "and then we can start out."

16

It wasn't the easiest thing in the world trying to make sense of the small scale road-map in the dim light of the conservatory.

"An inch to the mile Ordnance Survey would have been better," Bart complained over my shoulder. The map had been of his choosing but I let the remark pass without comment.

The valley seemed to be about a quarter of a mile across at its widest point, and about a mile long, ending in a spur of hill that must be the Ridge. No buildings were marked, not even the village of Werkley, only the dotted line that was an extension of the Breston road and which twisted its way upwards.

Bart, a commander surveying enemy territory, traced a route with a delicate, tapering finger.

"This will be about where we are now. This fork must lead to Maybrick Farm. The cordon will be somewhere across here; we won't have any trouble getting through." He sounded confident. "We'll cut across this way, meeting the road here. . . ."

Joan said in a tense sort of voice: "It's funny; I've never been able to look at a map and visualise what the places really look like."

"With this one," Bart commented, straightening, "not many people could. Fortunately Mr. Cole gave us some idea of the layout." He moved to the door, clearly anxious to be away. Folding the map I slipped it back into my pocket and then glanced at my watch. It was quarter past three.

"A clear night as we expected," Bart informed us generally, the door open, his face turned to the sky. We followed him along a gravel path bounded on one side by a tall hedge. I was content for him to take the lead, relying upon his map-reading ability and lay-of-the-land assessment being better than mine. There was a fence to be climbed, and we were on the verge of an open moonlit space. He cut directly towards the shadows of a line of stumpy trees. There was the more difficult problem of a briar hedge to be coped with. I held back branches while Joan slipped through. Hills, previously hidden by the trees, were dark, thunderous masses to the left and ahead. More open country stretched ahead, but now Bart shook his head at it, turning instead to cut towards the right, keeping close in the shadow of the hedge, treading with exaggerated care. On a night like this sound would travel far.

I was conscious of no particular emotion, not even satisfaction in knowing that both my telegrams had produced results. There was no sense of purpose behind this moonlight walk across strange country. Only a numbed feeling of inevitability. What lay ahead was something we would discover when we reached our destination. Until then it was pointless even to think about it.

The hedge we followed swung until we were going in our original direction. Another fence where the shadows ended; another exposed stretch of gorse bushes and wiry grass, with hills suddenly revealed on our right. Bart, climbing the fence, paused while he surveyed what lay ahead, a silhouette statue against the blue-black sky. There was another line of trees to follow, and now we were obviously well into the valley—for the hills were close on either hand—and so probably through the cordon.

The trees ended abruptly. A bank sloped down to a silver line of road. To the left I could make out the shapes of buildings.

"Maybrick," Bart mouthed, and I nodded. Some distance ahead was another dark cluster of buildings, and they—from what Cole had told us—would be Daniel Farm. An odd, biblical-sounding name. Now there was the exposed road to be crossed. I looked up at the inverted bowl of the sky, pin-pricked with an infinity of stars. There was not even the merest whisp of cloud that might hide the moon for a moment.

His mouth by my ear Bart whispered: "Wait," and was hurrying, stoop-shouldered, down the bank to become lost in the shadows of a clump of tall bushes. A ludicrous game of cowboys and Indians. . . . Adults behaving like children. Even though I was almost sure we had slipped unobserved through the string of waiting men I still tensed, ready to flinch at the crash of a shot. A shadow rose to beckon urgently. We followed down the bank. Bart was smiling, his teeth gleaming white. Was it Yarrow who had once hinted at his taste for adventure?

We crossed the lane; followed another hedge; turned in at a gate and were walking on the cobbles of a farmyard, the smell of the place pungent and strong. I wondered what had become of the livestock. Had that been brought out of the valley too? It seemed so; stable doors were open; cow-sheds patently deserted; a pig-sty empty. A silent, deserted world.

Now we were treading the rough, broken surface of the lane. With how far to go? Half a mile? Three quarters? More huddled shapes loomed to the right. "Up in the valley," Cole had said, "Brass Farm. . . ." Whose place was that? Then I remembered. Fletcher. That was why the name had sounded familiar when I had woke to Joan's wanting to know who "Fletcher" was.

Had I been dreaming about Fechter? I must have been to have spoken his name in my sleep. I had dozed off thinking about the concentration camp, trying to drag to the surface the something that lurked so irritatingly at the back of my mind. That was still there. . . .

That came shockingly to the surface now, without any effort at all. The last piece of the picture fell into place, making a whole that was beyond conception, but had to be accepted in the way one accepts the unimaginable infinity of the universe.

Earlier, outside, the café, there had been my sudden understanding of the riddle of the lever and fulcrum. But then I had discarded it, not because it was so incredibly impossible, but simply because a vital step had been missing from the staircase of reasoning.

Now I had found that missing step. I knew what Fechter's purpose was, and how it was to be brought to accomplishment.

A brilliant scientist, Brother Harold had called him. So obviously a clever man in other ways. . . . And yet, even though he must have known how close his enemies were, he had delayed burning his records until it was too late. Purposely delayed, I felt certain, so that the entries relating to his experiment should be taken intact. And he had noted Pulcheknic's name on each entry so that there should be no mistake.

His experiment had worked out the way he figured. Pulcheknic, now Stanley Pulner, had fathered four sons. That there were four instead of just the one might be accidental; radio-activity could be blamed for that. But the purpose behind them remained unchanged. And they had been brought into being for a special purpose.

They were possessed of abnormal faculties that sooner or later would be remarked upon by a worried authority. And authority investigating, would duly trace back their parentage to the two entries in Fechter's journal. And there they would also come across the reference to the lever and fulcrum. And as I had done, they would find the answer to it from their schooldays. That Chillon—or anyone else, for that matter—hadn't come up with the answer was simply because he didn't know of their ability to move inanimate objects by power of thought alone.

Faith, the saying goes, can move mountains. Figuratively in the accepted sense. But literally where the four children were concerned.

I had seen a window open without being touched. An invisible hand had pushed a woman down a flight of stairs. A tractor had rumbled across the farmyard without anyone being at the controls. All done by the power of thought. The lever large enough to move a world.

How did that schoolboy tag go?

"Give me a lever and fulcrum large enough," Archimedes is supposed to have said, "and I will move the world."

A tremble, at first; barely perceptible. Just an earth tremor. Then a shuddering, a slow moving out of course; a widening of the precarious orbit, or else a narrowing. And then the unimaginable cold of space or a plunging towards the sun. I didn't know much about that sort of thing, but I fancied that the end would be fire.

I had asked that question, ice or fire, once before. But then there had been no need to find the answer because a step had been missing. Fechter might have given the children the unbelievable power to nudge the earth out of orbit, but there was no way in which he could pass on to them the message of what they had to do. There was the lever but no fulcrum.

But now I was on my way to the Ridge, to the four boys, with that message there in my mind for them to read. It was as simple as that. The lever and fulcrum were coming together. For all I knew they had already read my thoughts.

I walked automatically, in a daze, barely aware of Joan's arm through mine, of Bart a few paces ahead, his step almost jaunty, perhaps confident in the knowledge that Simon would let no harm come to him, that Rodney would try to protect Joan and me, that Peter would be equally harmless, and that there was only the unknown quantity of Tony to be considered, and he would be one against three.

Trees came crowding in on either side, the menacing vanguard of the black, flattened hills. The road, such as it was, climbed steadily, petering out until it was little more than a grassy track. Another bend, with the branches all but meeting overhead, with the melancholy rotting timbers of a broken gate almost hidden by tall grass, and we came suddenly to an open space.

Ahead of us, a stone's throw away, its outlines silvered against the sombre, overpowering backcloth of tall trees and taller hills, was a house. A gaunt ugly structure with what seemed to be a corrugated-iron roof, broken away at one side, the skeletons of beams showing through the gap. Ragged bushes had invaded what must once have been the front garden, crowding thickly round the walls. Some kind of creeper —ivy, perhaps—had engulfed one wall, swallowing some of the windows—the remainder left to gape emptily—even finding its way to the roof to send tendrils across the exposed rafters. A little way to one side the blackened wooden ribs of what once must have been a fairly large greenhouse thrust desperately upwards from a patch of tall weeds.

No path led to the porchless front door. There was nothing save the almost circular space of coarse grass and scrub, surrounded by densely-massed bushes, backed by dank trees and towering hill-shapes. It was almost unbelievable that this could be the place where the children chose to meet. But then this was where the Black Boy had made his home. I had been expecting to find a ruined house on an isolated ridge, but not this wilderness and decay. I don't know how long we stood in that narrow entrance. . . .

I didn't see or hear them come, for I had been watching the door, expecting them to be in the house. But they must have been waiting for us amongst the trees. One moment the space was empty; the next, they were there, standing in a silent row to one side. Three of them; Rodney with his white shirt; Simon, recognisable by his school uniform; and the third—the same black hair, the same narrow features—wearing a dark-coloured high-necked pullover and white shorts. Not the ragged dress of a child that had run wild, and so he had to be Peter Latham. Three boys in a row; three of the paper dolls. One still to come. . . .

They watched us, disinterestedly almost, yet with a kind of arrogance. If there had been expressions on their silent faces it would have been difficult to read them in the moonlight. They were waiting, it seemed, for us—the intruders—to be the ones to break that weird silence.

Bart was the first to find his voice. He spoke steadily and earnestly.

"You know why I've come, Simon. I've come to take you away."

I wondered without any particular interest if he too was

162

experiencing the uncomfortable sensation of mental fingers probing into his mind. Perhaps I was imagining it. . . . But then Joan's grip suddenly tightened on my arm and I guessed the same thing was happening to her.

The children stayed silent and watchful.

"You must leave this place," Bart said, and now there was a tremor to his voice. "All three of you. There are people waiting down there——"

He broke off, perhaps realising the futility of words. Even though I knew speech was unnecessary, habit made me voice my thoughts, add my persuasions to his.

"They don't know you three are up here, but they're waiting to kill Tony. They will shoot the moment they see any one of you. Your parents have come for you, Rodney. And for you too, Peter. If you come with us now we'll find some way of getting you safely out of the valley."

And that was that. There was nothing more I could say, and certainly nothing I could do. I looked beyond them to the house, to the door. I think I knew that Tony was somewhere inside and that he would only show himself in his own good time, secure in the knowledge that the others would make no move without him: the dominant part of an entity with four bodies.

Where the warped timbers of the door had been was an oblong of blackness. A shape moved into the moonlight. It came silently across the grass to join the others, standing a little apart and to one side.

The Black Boy wore some kind of sleeveless shirt, filthy and torn, tucked into ragged trousers that were tied about his waist with string. His arms and legs were bare and streaked with dirt; his hair matted and long. But there was no mistaking his features. Identical, at first glance, to the other three, but then a difference becoming noticeable, even in that half-light. There was a sharpening to the slant of cheekbone and brow, a narrowing to the corners of the eyes. Subtle differences that made his face an evil caricature, like a reflection seen in an imperfect mirror.

So there they were, the four of them; the first time—and I felt sure of that—that they had allowed themselves to be seen all together. The outcome of Fechter's unholy experiment; his threat to the future of mankind. Four twelve-year-old boys. The four fingers of the hand that was to press the lever. . . .

The ground beneath my feet shuddered, a slight tremor of movement that could have been my imagination. I heard Joan's sharp intake of breath. The ground rocked again, not imagination now, as if something was trying to force its way

163

upwards. When it came a third time, accompanied by a distant rumbling, I found myself staggering backwards, almost losing my balance, the feeling of insecurity strong enough to set my head spinning sickeningly.

Another tremor—the ground heaving as if shaken by giant hands, and my back was hard against a tree trunk and I was looking up at a sky where the moon and stars moved slowly, revolving like the dome of a planetarium. I knew what was happening. This was how I had imagined it would be. The message in my mind had been read and was being acted upon.

Clinging to the trunk I forced my gaze down from the fascination of the moving sky. The clearing in front of the house was empty; the children had gone. Bart was on his knees, hands in front of his face, palms outwards, as if warding something away. I was looking for Joan when the moon sank behind the trees and a velvet blackness came swooping down, blotting out everything.

Overhead, the stars still marched. Night lasted only a few more minutes. A brightness came to tip the crests of the hills ahead, bathing them in a wild scarlet beauty. The blood-red of dawn became streaked with orange, changing quickly to a fierce yellow-white. Even before the sun rose the world was filled with vivid light. The stars faded away. I watched the sun come up for the last time.

But not the sun as I knew it. This was a fiery shapeless glow in the eastern sky, ringed with shafts of flame, spreading rapidly in size and brilliance, fully three times as large as the old one and still growing, pouring out an intolerable light that lanced blinding agony into my eyes. Turning, my hands over my face, a furnace heat beating on my shoulders, I pushed my way into the bushes, branches raking and tearing, until I could go no further. Panting, I leaned against a tree, shading my eyes as best I could while I peered upwards. Flames were already leaping amongst the topmost branches. Blazing masses came floating down. A pile of dried leaves burst into instantaneous flame. A bush became a flaming, roaring torch.

I tried frantically to force a way in another direction but the flames pursued, now with choking billows of smoke in their wake. Through a flickering scarlet frame I had a momentary glimpse of the burning pyre of the house and the holocaust of the dying world beyond.

A blazing branch came crashing down, sending up a shower of sparks. Some of them clung to my jacket, setting it smouldering before I could brush them away with hands that were cushions of blisters. I knew that there was no escape from the ring of flame, that I would be burned to death, but the blind instinct of self-preservation drove me on, each breath searing agony.

I took one last step forward, stumbling, dropping to my knees, my arms outstretched, flames licking from the material of my jacket, then I was face downwards on the ground. There was one final moment of supreme agony and then the merciful oblivion of death.

17

Someone was calling my name, the sound echoing, seeming to come from a long way away. I opened my eyes with an effort to find I was lying on the ground looking up through a tracery of branches to a sky filled with a soft grey light. It was a few moments before I was able to remember what had happened and how I came to be here. Holding up my hands, filthy and scratched but free of burns, I marvelled at them, remembering them as they had been a short while ago. How long ago. . . ? There was no way of telling, except that dawn seemed to be breaking and all around the world was green and fresh.

The voice called again, nearer, Joan's voice, and filled with such urgency and fear that it brought me to my feet. I found my way back by following the path I had smashed through the undergrowth in my frantic efforts to escape the holocaust that had been the last and most vividly horrifying of all the hallucinations.

When I broke out into the clearing she came flying to meet me, and I gathered her into my arms, holding her tightly while she sobbed out her relief and I comforted her as best I could —as I had done the other times—telling her that everything was all right. . . .

And while I soothed her I looked over her shoulder, searching the clearing, afraid of what I might find.

Mist rising and drifting made it difficult to see clearly in the pearl light, but two statues standing together under the trees became two of the children; Rodney in his white shirt;

Peter in his dark pullover. The mist lifted and another tableau appeared, some distance away. Bart lay on the ground, Simon at his side, crouching on his heels.

I asked urgently: "Bart?" and made to set her gently aside.

"He's all right," she replied shakily. "I must have woken up about ten minutes ago, and I thought it was you lying there. But it was Bart and he was sleeping, so then I tried to find you."

She turned a tear-streaked face up to me. "Did you have your abyss again, Gordon?" When I nodded without replying—there would be time enough to tell her how I had seen the end of the world—she managed a faint smile. "And I had my spider again. Only this time it was much worse and lasted longer and——" She broke off, losing her smile in a fit of uncontrollable trembling, and I drew her back into my arms while she relived her memory.

When it was all over I said gently: "I can only see three of them, Joan."

She knew what I meant. "The other one—Tony—is over there in front of the house. He's lying on the ground. I didn't go to him—I was afraid—but I think he's dead."

She followed me across the clearing. Tony lay face downwards, almost hidden by the tall grass. Kneeling at his side, fighting down a wave of revulsion, I turned him over.

"He's dead right enough. . . ." I glanced up as a shadow fell across his face, expecting it to be Joan's, but it was Rodney who stood there.

"What happened?" I asked him.

He seemed dazed, stupefied almost, his self-possession gone. "I don't know. I tried——" He broke off, frowning, shaking his head, correcting himself: "He tried to do something, I think. I can't remember properly."

Then his face puckered suddenly so that he seemed on the point of tears. Joan was at his side, her arm about his narrow shoulders, his face pressed tightly to her breast. I came slowly to my feet. It seemed that one link taken from the chain the other three links had fallen apart. But only time would tell that. At this moment Rodney was just an ordinary schoolboy, and a frightened and puzzled child at that.

And Peter Latham, standing alone, looked forlorn and lost. I went over to him. "Are you all right, Peter?" Now I came to think it was the first time I had spoken to him. And I remembered too that we had never heard Tony speak at all.

He made a vague gesture. "I'm all right," and added, oddly incongruously: "Thank you."

"We'll soon have you back with your parents again. You'd like that, wouldn't you?"

He nodded, his face brightening. "Yes. I want to go home." He put his hand to the side of his head. "I feel sort of— empty."

"You've had a rough time," I said. "We all have, come to that."

Then I went over to where Bart was sitting up and staring about him in a kind of stupefaction, Simon watching him anxiously.

"Feeling better, Bart?" I asked lightly.

"You might say that," he grunted, flexing his knees and grimacing distaste at the shreds of grass and twigs that clung to his trousers. He looked at Simon.

"And what about you, old son?"

"I'm all right, Grandpops."

Bart smiled. "That's the ticket." He looked up at me and I lent him my hand while he grunted himself to his feet to immediately become busy dusting himself down, breaking off suddenly to look round the clearing and discover Joan talking with Peter and Rodney.

"Are they all right, Gordon?"

"They're fine."

"That's something." He resumed dusting. "But Tony's dead," I added steadily, watching Simon's face.

Bart stopped again. "Dead? How did it happen?"

"I don't know yet," I told him. "There aren't any marks on his body."

Still squatting on his heels, balancing himself by clutching a tuft of grass, Simon groped for words, talking to himself more than to us.

"I tried to——" he started and then broke off, perplexed, as Rodney had done. "I think he tried to do something that was too big. I went away because Grandpops was frightened. Rodney-me. . . ." Again the hesitation while he seemed to be adjusting himself to a new way of thinking. "Rodney left him as well to go to you"—looking up at me—"because you were with what Tony was trying to do. It came with you, and ——" He used Peter's gesture of putting one hand to his forehead. "I can't think properly."

The picture seemed clear enough to me. Tony had tried to act upon the message in my mind. He had needed the help of the others, but that help hadn't been forthcoming. So he tried to go it on his own.

"I can't remember," Simon said, his face a small unhappy mask.

"You'll be all right once we get you home," I said quickly.

"Home," Bart echoed, and looked round the clearing again. The sun, the old gentle sun, had risen, and the mists were starting to clear. It was going to be another fine day. Joan, the two boys at her side, came over to us. Bart smiled at her. "Gordon told me you were all right. We can exchange experiences later." He turned back to me. "Now we've got to find some way of getting away from here without the local gentry filling us with buckshot."

"The local gentry will go back to their homes as soon as they know the Black Boy is dead," I told him. "So I'll take the body down for them to see. When the way is clear I'll come back again with——"

This was going to take a deal of sorting out. I wanted to arrange things so that I wouldn't be faced with the problem of explanations. And so that the farmers wouldn't discover that there had been four boys up at the Ridge and not just the one.

"I'll come back with the Lathams in their car," I said slowly, thinking it out as I went along. "We'll take Peter with us, and I'll get them to drop me off at 'The Grey Goose'. Then I can come back again with the Blakes in their van. The Blakes know that Rodney has a twin brother, so it won't make much difference if they meet Simon. But it would be best if you were to keep Rodney and Simon out of sight while the Lathams are here."

"The three card trick," said Bart. "Now you see the lady; now you don't." He seemed to be almost enjoying himself again. "I'll have Peter waiting alone down by that broken gate. That'll save them coming up to the clearing. But how do you propose getting the body down to the village?"

"It'll mean carrying it," I said, not looking forward to the prospect but knowing there was no alternative. "I'll keep to the lane so they'll be able to see me coming."

And that was how it was. Carrying the Black Boy's body in my arms I set off back down a lane that was strange by daylight, hating every moment of it, keeping my gaze fixed ahead so that I shouldn't see the inverted face that hung over my arm.

At Brass Farm I had to stop to rest, laying my burden on the verge for a while. Then I started off again. Nearing the road junction two men, both carrying guns, came from the bushes to meet me. They looked at the body in silence, and still in silence turned away to make their way along the road that led to Maybrick, leaving me with still a quarter

168

of a mile to go before I came in sight of the road block and the empty blackened shell of "The Farmer's Pride."

But it seemed they had passed the message on in some way, for Fletcher and Nisted were waiting for me, standing on the crown of the road, guns cradled across their arms and looking almost like pioneers of the old West.

Nisted stared at the body without speaking, spat in the dust, tucked his gun under his arm and turned away to climb into the driving seat of the lorry, starting the engine, manoeuvering it expertly before driving off in the direction of "The Grey Goose". It seemed that so far as he—and the other two—were concerned, the only important thing was that the Black Boy was dead. How he had died was of no consequence.

Fletcher, his hat at the back of his head, his face of meshed lines expressionless, did ask briefly: "How did it 'appen?"

I gave him the truth so far as it went. "He was like this when I found him."

He jerked his head in the direction of the nearest cottage. "You'd best take it in there." I followed him up a narrow path, along the side of the building to a washhouse of sorts. There I deposited the body on a low bench and stepped back, massaging feeling back into cramped arms. Tony hadn't weighed all that much but it had been a long walk.

Fletcher stooped over the bench without speaking. I supposed that he was remembering some of the things that had happened in the valley during the past five years. And perhaps he was thinking of his son.

"The police will have to be told," I said after a while, when it seemed he was content to do nothing but stand there, reliving the past. Outside I could hear the sound of traffic passing along the lane.

He still didn't speak. Straightening, he turned to walk out into the sunlight, ignoring me as if I wasn't there. I followed him back down the path to the lane. A decrepit car chugged past, followed by a farm lorry and a clattering tractor. The farmers and their families were returning home.

And Fletcher, without a word, without a backward glance, set off in the same direction, a stocky, slow-plodding figure, the gun hanging loosely at his side. It seemed that he had washed his hands of the whole affair. I was still at the gate, wondering what next to do, when a black saloon slowed and pulled up. Chillon climbed out, followed by a man wearing a black Homburg and a beltless black raincoat.

"Good morning, Seacombe," Chillon greeted me placidly. "I rather fancied we would meet up with you again. I recognised your car back at the hotel."

169

He turned to watch another lorry rumble by. "Some kind of exodus seems to be in progress. Would you care to put us in the picture?" The sun glinted on his rimless spectacles as he swung back to regard me with steady eyes.

"Come and see for yourselves," I invited, and took them to the washhouse. "Stanley Pulner's son."

I half-expected him to show surprise, perhaps ask how I was able to identify the body. But he did neither of those things. Instead the two of them moved without any hurry to inspect with calmly assessing eyes. It was the other man who spoke, not lifting his gaze, asking the inevitable question, "How did it happen?"

"Your guess is as good as mine. He was like that when I found him, lying up on the Ridge."

"Well?" Chillon asked shortly, looking at his companion.

"Like father, like son," retorted the other laconically. "There's no doubt in my mind."

Chillon received the verdict without manifesting any particular satisfaction.

"Nor in mine either, Paxton. So this is Fechter's evil genius that was to have set the world in flames again. He looks harmless enough now."

He seemed to have forgotten my presence. Or perhaps it made no difference now my overhearing their confidences.

"The outcome of pressure on a lever," contributed Paxton, and by the way he said it, mouthing the phrase deliberately, obviously quoting someone else's words.

The word "lever" brought my head round with an involuntary jerk. Chillon, catching the movement, smiled thinly.

"Double-Dutch to you, Seacombe; you did tell me that the name 'Fechter' meant nothing to you. Otherwise you would probably be aware of the reference quoted by my colleague."

His mood had become one of ponderous joviality. "I feel that there is a deficiency in your education that as a schoolteacher you ought to remedy. Heimut Fechter may have been dead for a great many years but his books are still regarded as standard works of reference. I am certain that you would find many of his theories invaluable in your work."

"I'll bear that in mind," I retorted, and he turned back to Paxton, asking: "Well?"

The two seemed to be accustomed to working together. Paxton, working on the body, shook his head. "Impossible to tell without an autopsy. There's fluid in both ears indicating cranial pressure. . . ." He launched into technical details and I moved towards the door.

"We'll take charge of the details," Chillon called after me.

170

"I assume you will be staying at Kendly for a few days?"

"So far as I know," I replied curtly, and walked along the path, into the lane, and then in the direction of "The Grey Goose". The traffic had ceased. When I reached the hotel the forecourt held only two cars—one of them mine—and a small green van.

Chandler, bleary-eyed, told me that the Blakes and the Lathams were still in their respective rooms and that he served them breakfast there. I went to speak with the Lathams, telling them that the trouble was cleared up and that Peter was safe and waiting to be collected and taken home. Mrs. Latham fluttered through a volubility of relief and gratitude. Her husband eyed me with open curiosity, made to speak, looked at his wife who was still talking as she collected her things together, shrugged and was silent. I drove back with them in their car to where Peter waited alone by the broken gate.

When Mrs. Latham climbed out he ran to meet her and she gathered him into her arms. By the wonderment on Mr. Latham's face I gathered that the exuberance of the meeting was something new. On the way back I sat at the front with Mr. Latham while Peter and his mother exchanged low-voiced confidences in the back.

At "The Grey Goose" I left them, looking about to make sure no one was watching who might comment on Peter's likeness to the Black Boy. The forecourt and hotel seemed deserted. Mr. Latham offered his hand.

"I want to thank you, Mr. Seacombe." He smiled suddenly. "I'm not quite sure for what. But no doubt we will have an opportunity some time in the future of discussing the episode. Perhaps you will let me have an address where I may contact you."

I gave him my Cookley address. In her turn Mrs. Latham shook my hand, adding incoherent gratitude to that of her husband, while Peter watched with what might have been the beginnings of a smile on his dark, peaked face.

When they had gone I went back inside the hotel, this time to collect the Blakes, riding back with them in their van to the Ridge, this time having to walk the last part of the way to the clearing in front of the house where Joan and Bart and the two boys waited.

There was another meeting, another small confusion of greetings and explanations that were only half-truths.

Mrs. Blake, her arm about Rodney's shoulder, marvelled at Simon's appearance.

"As like as two peas," she discovered; "you can't tell one from the other. . . ."

"My grandson," Bart said with a certain pride.

"An' what sort of trouble 'ave you bin gettin' yourself into?" Blake asked gruffly of his son, perhaps because he felt something like that was expected of him.

"Everything is sorted out now," I said quickly. "No harm has been done."

"Takin' up with gypsies," he snorted in disgust, but then he grinned. "I used to fancy that sort of life when I were a kid. I reckon most of us 'ave at one time or another. . . ."

Joan smiled. "I don't think Rodney will run away again," she said.

On the way back to the village Joan sat at the front with Mr. Blake while the rest of us crowded uncomfortably into the back, Mrs. Blake sitting on an upturned orange box, her arms still about Rodney's shoulder. Meeting my eye, he flushed and squirmed uncomfortably as any ordinary schoolboy might under the same circumstances.

An ordinary schoolboy. . . . The three links of the chain had fallen apart. Three boys would have to start the long process of building up separate characters. It was an odd thought. . . . I wondered how long it would take. Through the small grimy window in the door I watched the lane ribbon away, the trees and the hills slide back. Smoke rose from the chimneys of Brass Farm; a man in shirt-sleeves herded cows across the yard of Daniel Farm.

At "The Grey Goose" Blake stopped the van while I climbed out to stretch my legs and then go to collect my own car. I followed the van then for a few miles. When I judged it safe I sounded the horn and the van drew into the verge. There was a small delay while Bart and Blake exchanged addresses and promised to visit each other. Then Joan took her usual place in my car while Bart and Simon sat together at the back. I waited until the green van was out of sight before pressing the starter.

We reached Kendly a few minutes after twelve. Bart and Simon, hand-in-hand, went up the drive to the front door. Joan and I, my arm about her waist, followed more slowly.

"Gordon," she mused, "when did it all start? I mean, how long ago was it when we left Cookley?"

She laughed when I had to tell her that I didn't know.

"Then what day is it today?"

And I couldn't tell her that, either. Not offhand; not until I had had time to think.

The first thing I did when I had a moment to myself was

172

to go to the library. It wasn't difficult to find the collection of Fechter's books, nine of them, large, bound in green with gold lettering, six in the original German, the rest translated into English. I took out the one entitled *A Study of the Balance of Mind,* opening it at the first page. "By Dr. Heimut Fechter", followed by three lines of qualifications and appointments. An impressive display. I turned the leaf; a foreword there, in the form of an extract.

"In its simplest form the mind of the sentient child may be regarded as a collection of characteristics, divided into the two main groups of evil and good, evenly and precariously balanced on the fulcrum of inheritance. It is of prime importance that this balance be maintained under all circumstances. If undue pressure is brought to bear on either side then the balance, in effect, will become a lever. And if the pressure be increased still further then one of the groups will invariably become dominant. A saint, or an evil genius. . . ."

There was no need to read further. This was the answer to the riddle. The real solution, and not the one I had so laboriously dreamed up. . . .

I found some small consolation in the knowledge that things had worked out despite myself, and that Brother Harold with his theory of a latent epidemic, couldn't after all be as familiar with Fechter's work as he would have had us believe.

Then I went through to the kitchen where Joan was getting lunch ready, and Simon was helping her by laying the table, and Bart was bemoaning a suit spoiled with grass stains.

18

It rained on the first day of the new term, a steady dispiriting downpour that brought a stale dampness into the school to neutralise the after-holiday strangeness of antiseptic and floor polish. In the common-room Philby was in his element, heavily significant about another collection he would shortly have to organise. One to which, he pointed out generally, neither I nor Miss Grey would be invited to subscribe to. Then came the expected flood of congratulations, followed by the usual banter, all of which Joan took coolly in her stride.

I spent the first period with a new Form 4B, compiling the register, giving them details of the revised time-tables, then setting the thirty-odd boys an essay while I organised my own routine. My old form had moved to the adjoining classroom, becoming 5B, with Philby as their form-master. But I would still be taking them in English and History.

When the bell went I collected my papers and books and made my way to the next room where Philby, who invariably ignored the bell and overran his time, was still holding forth, arms folded in his habitual gesture. He bustled officiously away and I took my place behind the desk and surveyed the rows of faces. Rodney Blake, seated in the centre, met my eyes with an unwinking gaze. Next to him little Tomkin, his ginger hair tousled, grinned, and when I didn't return the smile—not because I didn't want to, but it would be bad policy to show favouritism—wiped the grin away and became serious.

There was a certain amount of ice-breaking to be done before we could get into the swing of things. Usually I gave them a short talk about how I expected better results from them now that they were a senior form. But today I let that pass.

"All right. The holidays are over and we're back at work. Take out your Shakespeares." And when the desk lids had stopped clattering: "Now can anyone remember where we were up to?"

Tomkin's hand was up, waving urgently. "*Midsummer Night's Dream,* sir."

"I'm pleased to see you've managed to remember that much." Rodney's hand was up as well. "Yes, Blake?"

"Act three, scene two, sir. A clearing in the woods."

Oddly, I found my gaze faltering under his steady eyes. A little annoyed with myself I said shortly: "All right. Find the place; page 262. Now let's try to bring it to life." I chose a boy at random. "Paget, you take Lysander. The next boy, Tomkin, you take Oberon. Blake, Puck. Who else have we got? Demetrius; you can take that part, Johnson. Start from the top of the page with Oberon's speech. All right, Tomkin; now try to give the words some kind of meaning."

The same old routine. How many times had I done it before? I went over to the window, to my usual place, resting one foot on the radiator pipe, my elbow on the sill. It was still raining. Slater was trudging across the playground with a roll of netting under one arm followed by half-a-dozen senior boys, raincoats over their heads, laughing and jostling, carrying goal posts.

Blake was reading, declaiming, rather; his voice forced attention.

> " 'Up and down, up and down,
> I will lead them up and down:
> I am fear'd in field and town:
> Goblin, lead them up and down.' "

Then Paget took up the tale and the spell was broken. I looked out of the window again. One day Rodney Blake would become a famous writer. Or even an actor. Perhaps both. With his talents he would go right to the top. And Peter Latham too. His name would become a household word. The greatest artist of our time. . . .

Simon Brereton. A physicist, growing up into a world where science would be dominant. A world where mankind would be venturing out into space. Perhaps he was destined for the greatest future of all. . . .

The droning voices stopped. I turned enquiry into the silence.

"Sir"—that was Tomkin—"we've got to Helena an' there's no one for 'er."

I chose Oliver for the part because his was the first face my wandering gaze fell on. He came to his feet, one hand on his hip. Schoolboys are never original. The same things that I found amusing when I was a boy still brought giggles now. I cut into their amusement.

"There's nothing to laugh at. In Shakespeare's day all the female parts were taken by men. Oliver is only carrying on with tradition."

And how many times had I made that little speech before? The same old routine. . . . Oliver finished his speech in an affected voice. Blake took over.

> " 'Yet but three? Come one more;
> Two of both kinds makes up four——' "

Makes up four. Four boys standing in a silent row in a clearing in the trees. I looked out again over the now deserted playground. Down by the gates the tarmac was broken, water lying in dismal pools in the hollows. Rain streaming down the window made the scene hazy. The gates, the shelter, the wall with the row of trees beyond, misted, wavered, became transparent. Shadows took shape out of nothing, crowding in.

Hazy outlines solidified, filling with soft colours. As with the other times I knew what was happening. But now there was no sense of fear to it. I was in a woodland glade, a place of cool green shadows and leafy branches, my nostrils filled with a cloying familiar sweetness—"I know a bank where the wild thyme blows. . . ." And I was wrapped in a silken weave of peace and utter contentment.

The colours faded, the scents evaporated, the trees, the flowery bank and the winding path dissolved into nothing. The rainswept playground was back again. And behind me the class was silent. I turned to face them. The five actors were on their feet, waiting. . . .

"We've come to the end of the scene, sir," said Rodney Blake, smiling.

Was it the end? I didn't know.